BEAR IN MIND

A Bear Jacobs Mystery

Linda B. Myers

About This Book

Bear in Mind is a work of fiction. Names, characters, places and happenings are from the author's imagination. Any resemblance to actual persons – living or dead – events or locales is entirely coincidental.

Edited and published 2017 by Mycomm One

ISBN: 978-0-9838158-9-1

For updates, news, blog and chatter:

www.LindaBMyers.com

Facebook.com/lindabmyers.author

www.amazon.com/author/lindabmyers

myerslindab@gmail.com

Dedication

For my sister, Donna Whichello.

Bear doesn't have a clue without her help.

CHAPTER ONE

Case Notes
March 14, 11 a.m.
Bear Jacobs let his Private Investigator's license expire about the time he nearly did the same thing himself. A crash team shocked his heart out of the Arrhythmic Boogie and back to its natural shuffle. Afterwards, Bear growled and moaned from hospital to nursing home, his attitude damn near getting him booted out to the streets. Now denned up at Latin's Ranch Adult Family Care, he has recovered a fair amount of his strength and a little bit of good humor. He thinks he's a real sweetheart now. Yeah. Sure.
Anyhoo, his big old brain doesn't have enough to think about now that his physical worries have eased up. Simple boredom has him chewing on any mysterious bone that comes his way. Bear in mind that when the big man gets involved, he needs a strong-willed sidekick to stick like a burr and keep him on point.
Who better than a one-legged tough customer like me?

- Lily Gilbert, Lovely Assistant to PI Bear Jacobs

Lily powered down, closed the lid on her laptop and stretched her back. At seventy-seven, she figured she could call herself lovely if she damn well felt like it. And, in fact, she was. Her daughter had clipped her dove gray hair into a fluffy cloud, and her skin was rosy with health, never mind the wrinkles that crosshatched her cheeks like the fine grain of old suede.

It was a mistake to think of her as a sweet little granny. Lily was opinionated, feeling she had a right to be. She'd done a hell of a lot in her years on this earth. Seen a lot, too. As she once said to Bear, "I was a multitasker long before the word was invented."

Lily liked to write down her adventures with Bear, calling them her case notes. Of course, she'd never seen actual case notes, didn't know what they were for and didn't care. She did it for the fun of it. She was proud to have mastered the little Toshiba so late in life and loved the opening riff, the touch of the keys, the gentle clicking sound. She felt like an eWatson.

Lily set the laptop on her nightstand then swung herself to the side of the bed. She eyed her wheelchair but decided on the walker instead. She'd been practicing with it, building up the arm strength to get around without wheels. It wasn't easy, what with having only one leg, but she'd learned to balance herself and hop along. Bear said her arms were as buff as a lowland gorilla.

All and all, Lily was content. She'd gotten over shaking her fist at the sky long ago, resigned to the physical outrages of old age. She'd rather be young and in charge of her life and raising hell, of course. But she had all those times tucked away in her memory bank. She could take out each deposit to study, enjoying the memory almost as much as the experience. Mentally, she hadn't lost a step. As long as that was true, she could make do with some loss of mobility.

Of course, it was always possible Bear would get her killed, and she wasn't crazy about that.

CHAPTER TWO

Case Notes

March 14, 3 p.m.

The whole thing started with the bookkeeper's call. Eunice Taylor and Charlie Barker were in the living room watching All My Great Great Grandchildren. *Bear and I were there, too, and I was whipping his sorry ass at Scrabble with a triple word score that included a q.*

Jessica Winslow – she's the owner of Latin's Ranch – came in and asked Charlie if she could speak with him. "A personal matter," she called it. Her voice is naturally soft, but I noticed she lowered it even more.

"Hell, Jessica," Charlie answered. His voice is high, often rat-a-tat-ting in staccato bursts like a triple-tongued trumpet. "Everyone here knows I got sores on my nuts. Not much left that's too personal for them to hear."

That was true enough. We all knew a nurse came in special to medicate the backside of Charlie's scrotum. He was troubled with sores from sitting all day. Not an uncommon complaint for wheelchair jocks.

"Well, Charlie, the bookkeeper called to say you have some unclaimed PNA funds," Jessica said.

"PNA?"

"Personal Needs Allowance. For things like tooth paste, shaving cream, deodorant – "

"- and a hooker?"

"I don't think that's what the State has in mind. But I've noticed you could use a few new clothes." Jessica cocked her head, causing her natural curls (and not so natural blonde streaks) to bounce as she eyed him up and down. He was wearing a Hawaiian shirt so old it looked like the fronds would drop right off the palms. It was way too big for him, too. He'd lost weight trying to put less pressure on the aforementioned unmentionable bits of his anatomy. "If you like, I'll call your wife. She could use the money to buy you some new things."

Bear and I went dead quiet. Eunice tried, but the tinkling of her jewelry always rivals a wind chime. We all knew Charlie's wife never called him or visited any more. She'd flat out abandoned him. Jessica knew it, too, but Louise Barker must still be listed as his emergency contact. I'll bet she's listed somewhere as a heart breaking bitch, too, pardon my damn French.

Charlie gave Jessica a winsome smile. "Sure, go ahead. If you reach Louise, let her know I miss her."

- Lily Gilbert, Judgmental Assistant to PI Bear Jacobs

Jessica Winslow was aggravated which was rare. She was by nature even tempered, and that served her well in all of her businesses. She boarded horses, gave riding lessons, and raised Paso Finos. Her stallion, Latin Lover, had sired a line of champions, his stud fees supplementing her income.

She'd been widowed one winter night when her husband jackknifed his truck on an icy mountain pass in the Cascades east of Seattle. He'd left her with a shattered heart and a backlog of expenses. No matter how hard Jessica worked to shoulder the burden, she'd been failing financially, bit by bit.

To stave off selling her horses, she'd taken on her most demanding job of all. By remodeling her house, passing the state-required courses, and hiring a staff, she'd opened an adult family home called Latin's Ranch in honor of her stallion. She gave her two-legged residents as much fine care as she gave her four-legged.

That's why she was so aggravated with Charlie's wife, Louise Barker. If the woman didn't want to buy new clothes for Charlie, Jessica would help him pick a few things out of a catalog. No big deal, no reason to make Charlie feel like a bother. Jessica just needed the approval, that's all. She'd left three messages on Louise's voice mail in as many days. No answer. That settled it. Jessica trounced out to her old Camry and drove toward Louise's house to make a demand or two. A knock on the door would be harder to ignore than a ringing phone.

Jessica made two wrong turns looking for the Barker house, which did little to sweeten her mood. She caught a look at herself in the rearview mirror and saw the frown line puckering her forehead. "Great," she muttered to no one in particular. "Wrinkles instead of laugh lines." She took a deep breath and relaxed her face muscles. Soon all signs of irritation left her fair skin free of anything but freckles.

The Barker place was hidden in a hilly neighborhood between Everett and Seattle, not far from the Puget Sound coastline. Some roads were only a couple blocks long but twisted and looped so the little cottages weren't side by side in tidy rows. Even though the area was congested, overgrown rhododendrons and photinia blocked the houses' sightlines. Neighbors wouldn't easily keep an eye on each other.

Still, when she parked in the Barker drive and approached the front door, Jessica wondered if anyone else had noticed the rank odor in the yard. Had a raccoon or rat died in the bushes? No, the stench seemed to be coming from the neat bungalow itself. A window near the door was open just a crack.

What on earth can this god-awful odor be?

The closer she got, the worse it reeked of decay. Meat gone bad. Jessica's eyes began to water as she reached the front door. She fought back nausea.

I don't want to be here. I want to leave now!

Jessica battled the impulse to take flight. She rang the bell. And rang it again. No answer.

Finally, she dug in her purse for Kleenex. Holding a wad up to her nose with her left hand, she tried the door knob with her right. It turned. With a loud shout out for Mrs. Barker, Jessica pushed the door open.

A swarm of blowflies blasted out of the house, riding the fetid airwave.

Jessica shrieked as the filthy, buzzing cloud flew into her face. She turned and ran back to her car, flailing a hand in front of her eyes all the way. Once inside her dependable old Camry, doors and windows closed tight, she waited for the shivering chill of repulsion to pass. With great gulps of air, she finally got fear under control. Then she called 911.

"She's dead! I mean, I think."

✦ ✦ ✦

Jessica got out of her Camry when she saw the first patrol car pull up to the front curb. It was a county sheriff Crown Vic. Before she had a word with the uniformed deputies who emerged, an unmarked Charger pulled into the Barker driveway and parked behind her. It was a color that Dodge probably called White Gold Pearl or Sunlit Desert Sand.

Or Boring Beige.

Jessica was having a hard time focusing as she watched two people in plain clothes get out.

Maybe I'm in shock?

The cops glanced at her, and one flashed the briefest of smiles before saying, "Please wait here for us, Ma'am." Jessica nodded, and they both walked past her. The guy took a quick look back at her then went on with his female partner into the house.

Plain clothes.

The guy's sure were. A white shirt and jeans. Wolverine lace-ups that might have been new around the turn of the century. But that butt was anything but plain. Jessica figured he was a few years her junior, enough to make her feel like a cougar, and she was only thirty-something.

Probably girl hearts break with audible pops whenever he passes by. OMG. My mind's flitting around like all those flies.

Jessica shook her head and concentrated on reclaiming her composure while she waiting for the authorities to deal with it. The uniforms had followed the plain clothes inside so she was alone.

A dead body. Has to be.

Finally, the detectives came out of the little house and walked toward her. Neither looked upset or sickened or angry. They didn't look anything at all, like finding a body was business as usual.

What must it be like for death to be commonplace in your daily life? Not that it isn't a worry for me with my old tenants. But still ...

The female officer spoke first. "Ms. Winslow, I'm Deputy Detective Josephine Keegan of the Major Crimes unit. This is my partner, Clay Galligan. You reported the body, yes?"

Galligan. That explains the blue eyes and dark curls of the Irish.

"Ah, yes. No. I mean, I reported smelling a body."

Keegan cocked her head, frowning slightly. "You didn't see it?"

Jessica thought the investigator was pretty in a tough sort of way. Like Ripley in those Alien movies or –

Stop it.

"Well, no. I didn't actually go inside. An odor like that ... it was nothing living. I couldn't help her."

"Her?"

"Yes. Mrs. Barker. Louise Barker. It's her house."

"You think she's dead?"

Jessica was confused. "Well, we haven't heard from her, you see. Her husband or me. For a long time."

"You spend a lot of time with her husband?"

Jessica felt the heat of indignity. "He lives in my adult family home. Latin's Ranch. Neither Charlie – that's Charles Barker – nor I have heard from his wife for several weeks. That's not unusual, but I need some instructions on his care. She didn't return calls so I thought I'd come see her. Am I wrong? Isn't there a body? All those flies and the odor." Jessica wound to a stop.

"There is a body but not what you think," Keegan said. "It's a dog. Poor thing was locked in the foyer."

"What? A dog was locked in there long enough to smell like that? That's ... that's awful." The wellbeing of animals was as sensitive a subject as the wellbeing of her pack of humans.

"Died of thirst most likely. It tore up the entry pretty well trying to get out. But the rest of the house looks untouched. And Mrs. Barker isn't there."

"You mean to tell me she just locked her dog in there and LEFT IT TO DIE? How could anybody do that?"

"Don't know, Ma'am," Deputy Detective Clay Galligan finally spoke. "Either she didn't intend to come back ... or she couldn't come back."

"Whichever, it's a missing persons case for now. Let's go have a chat with this husband of hers. We'll follow you to, what was it?" Keegan looked at her notes. "Oh yeah. Latin's Ranch."

CHAPTER THREE

Case Notes
March 15, 8 p.m.
Before coming to Latin's Ranch, we lived in a nursing home called Soundside Rehab and Health Care. The place wasn't evil or anything. There were some first rate people working there. But even good nursing homes have a bad rep for a reason. They can't avoid the smell of overcooked greens and medicines and bodily functions, no matter how much lemon disinfectant they use. Or the sight of diseased bodies and the deepest despair. For me, it was the noise that was worst. The blaring televisions, alarms, and shrieks from broken human beings.
Bad as it was, we found each other there, Bear, Eunice, Charlie and me. We were the lucky ones with minds still intact even though our bodies were on the decline. If we stuck together we could just make it through each day. But then, Soundside began to kick out its Medicaid patients. Lots of nursing homes are handling the budget crunch that way. It would have left us with no place to go but the streets. We were in some seriously scary shit until the cavalry arrived.
Jessica's heart – and my daughter Sylvia's know-how – got Latin's Ranch up and running in the proverbial nick of time. It's not a nursing home; it's an Adult Family Home. It's much smaller and, as the name implies, feels like family.
Four of us moved here from Soundside. Eunice and I are roomies as are Bear and Charlie. There's a fifth resident here, too, a guy named

Frankie Sapienza. We think he's mob, but we don't ask a lot of questions about his past. Good looking dude. Suave. Still has his hair and teeth. He also has Eunice Taylor's old heart pitter patting in a way a whole bottle of nitro tablets wouldn't help.

Some of the staff from Soundside took jobs here at Latin's Ranch. Our aides Chrissie, Rick and Alita have stories damn near as important to us as their ability to keep us healthy. Our critters made the move, too. Furball the cat and our cage of canaries are trying to get along with Jessica's dog Folly and, of course, the horses. The jury is still out on whether Furball and Folly can live on the same planet much less the same ranch.

The saddest cases can't be cared for here; we know that. They still exist in miserable rooms away from public view. None of us will ever forget we're just one fall or one brain freeze away from going back.

Anyhoo. That's a snapshot of how we got here, but back to Charlie's missing wife. We all knew Jessica had gone to see Louise Barker so we gathered together to wait for her return. Damned if she didn't beat feet through the front door right along with two detectives.

And might I say this about that young stud cop. He shouldn't be sprung on LOLs – my anagram for little old ladies – without warning. Mercy.

- Lily Gilbert, Hot and Bothered Assistant to PI Bear Jacobs

Lily and the rest were gathered around the door in a wheelchair, walker, and quad cane traffic jam when Jessica got back to Latin's Ranch with the two detectives.

"We look like the street gang that lost the rumble," Bear muttered. He was in the thick of things with everyone else to hear Jessica tell Charlie that the authorities wanted to speak with him.

"Detectives? No!" Eunice said with a theatrical hand to forehead. "They'll take him down to headquarters and get out the waterboards!"

Lily was pretty sure Eunice had been watching too much television.

"Actually, we can talk right here, Mr. Barker. No need for torture devices," said the woman dick while the dick with the dick smiled at Eunice. The cop introduced herself and her partner to everyone then asked Charlie, "You have a private place where we can go?"

"We can use my room, I guess," Charlie said, looking glum. Of course, with his cheeks wrinkled in velvety pleats like a basset hound, he always looked pretty glum.

"Think I'll come along, too," said Bear. He used his low growly voice in counterpoint to Charlie's high squeaky one. Lily knew that meant he expected to get his way. He leaned hard on his quad cane and shoved out his chin in a display of aggression.

Detective Keegan said, "But we – "

Bear interrupted her. "Hiya, Cupcake."

At the use of that endearment, Keegan squinted hard into those small obsidian eyes. They were nearly buried behind the fringe of silver hair and beard that surrounds Bear's huge round head. After a slight intake of breath, she asked, "Al? Al Jacobs?"

"At your service." Bear doffed an imaginary hat at her.

"Al! I thought you were dea ... uh, Clay, this big galoot used to be a PI for the classiest law offices around. Worked with law enforcement more often than against us. Helped solve some tough cases. We met when I was just a rookie."

"You can call me Bear," the big man said, shaking hands with Keegan's partner.

In case any of the Latin's Ranch residents or staff had doubts about Bear's bona fides, they were cleared up right then. Keegan invited him to sit in on the questioning of Charlie. After the delegation left for Charlie's room, Lily and Eunice sat in the living room. A startling realization smacked Lily in the face for the first time. "Charlie is the hubby. That makes him Suspect Numero Uno in a case of foul play!"

"Cheese it," Eunice replied. "Here comes the heat."

As Jessica came into the room, Lily was hoping Eunice would soon give up on the hard boiled shtick. "Come on, ladies," Jessica said failing to quite stifle a yawn. "I'll help you get ready to hit the hay."

"But what if something really juicy happens?" Eunice protested.

Lily saw the yawn even though Jess tried to conceal it with her hand. Those pretty eyes were marred tonight with dark smudges on the delicate skin beneath them.

"We'll find out first thing in the morning, Eunice. Let's go." Lily used her walker to lift herself from the living room chair. She knew Jessica had too much to do, what with all those hayburners and all these people. She never wanted the caregiver to choose between the two, because the horses might just win out. Even with compliance from Eunice and herself, it would take Jess an hour to get them in and out of the bathroom, given their meds, dressed in their nightgowns and provided an evening snack for late night TV.

✦ ✦ ✦

The next morning at breakfast, Bear and Charlie told the rest of the household about their interview with Keegan and Galligan. Chrissie, Lily's favorite aide, was serving the green chili burritos made by Aurora who ran the kitchen as pleasantly as a pit bull patrols her yard. The little Latina was a tyrant, but her cooking was worth her fractious moods.

"Okay, you guys. Fess up. Who committed the crime?" Eunice chirped. Her hoop earrings were braided strands of white, rose and yellow gold. Lily waited for her each morning to accessorize with gems and scarves. The octogenarian would never consider appearing in public any other way.

"So far there is no crime," Bear said. He took a grizzly-sized bite from the burrito and chewed for a moment. "Charlie's wife is a missing person, not a victim. She might have just done a runner."

"I can't believe that, Bear. Why would she leave without a word?" Charlie shook his head, the folds in his cheeks wobbling gently. "I mean, she doesn't visit often, I know, but that's because she says it makes her feel too sad."

Eunice rolled her eyes.

"And she always tells me when she is going out of town for one of her many charity functions."

Everyone at the table rolled his or her eyes.

Lily didn't believe anybody could seriously suspect Charlie of harming Louise even if her body was found with wheelchair tread marks across its chest. He'd been in mourning ever since she'd stopped coming to see him. Besides, someone would have noticed if he left Latin's Ranch long enough to push himself miles away and back. With activity like that and sores where he got them, he'd never sit again.

"I don't know yet, Charlie. But I agree that it is suspicious," Bear said.

"Why?" Lily asked.

"Well, first the dog, of course. Charlie says his wife doted on that mutt. That she would never hurt it."

"She loved Fluffy-san," Charlie confirmed.

"Any idea how long it's been dead?" Lily asked, controlling an impulse to giggle at the name.

Bear scratched the beard on his chin. "Detective Keegan guessed three weeks, maybe more. A week to die of thirst, and the rest of the time for eggs laid in the remains to reach adult fly size. The flies that greeted Jessica."

"Eeeuuu," Eunice cringed and set down her fork.

"The lab will know for sure if they process the dog's carcass, which they won't without any more reason than they have now." Bear said. "But there's something else. Tell them, Charlie."

Charlie leaned forward in his wheelchair, placing his elbows on the table. "Louise is not the only missing person that's been reported. Other seniors have disappeared recently, too. That's what Detective Keegan said."

Everyone stared at him.

"*Dio mio*," Frankie said in his smooth Italian. "*Sono venuta per uno di noi?*"

All heads now turned toward him.

"What's that you said, my dear?" Eunice asked.

Frankie translated. "Are they coming for one of us?"

✦ ✦ ✦

Jessica walked to the barn as she did every morning, carrying a bunch of carrots. All the horses would have been fed by her barn manager Sam Hart, but each knew she'd be along with the treats.

When Jessica left the house, Chrissie Metzger was in charge of the residents. She was the most experienced aide at Latin's Ranch. She might not look competent, what with that string straight hair, weak chin and defeated posture. But Chrissie was a marvel of efficiency and a natural born nurturer, respected by all the residents.

Walking up to the barn, munching on one of the carrots herself, Jessica considered the rest of her staff. Rick Peters was a good aide, big and strong enough to handle the heaviest duties. Like, say, Bear. The only problem with Rick? He and Alita could barely keep their hands off each other until their shifts were over. Alita was the housekeeper who was learning the CNA trade. She was as drawn to Rick as a wildflower to the sun, and Jessica hoped a serious burn wasn't awaiting her. Rick could be too charming for a young woman's good.

Having a dependable staff meant Jessica could take time with the horses. She loved to help Sam with chores or give riding lessons or just pet noses and scratch behind ears. Her little dog Folly stuck close at her heels in case some of that petting and scratching came his way. He was part cocker spaniel and part dachshund, a pound puppy she called her cockadock. Almost everything and everyone living at Latin's Ranch was a rescue of some kind.

The horses she boarded ranged from ponies to one elderly workhorse. Those she owned were championship Paso Finos. Lily had once asked her if that meant they were past their best. Jessica had squawked, "Paso Fino means fine step. A Paso Fino horse is a very smooth ride." Then she'd seen the twinkle in those old eyes. "You're teasing me again, Lily Gilbert. But still, it's true they're the best horses in the world. I'll have you up and riding like the wind one of these days."

Lily had ducked down on her walker. "Did you see that pig fly by?"

This morning Jessica went box stall to stall, handing out carrots and sweet nothings. At the end of the line were the two horses owned by Ben Stassen. Gina Lola, the work horse, was her oldest resident. Now retired from a lifetime of hauling logs from the Pacific Northwest forests to waiting trucks, the enormous dappled gray spent her days in leisure. Ben would often stop by just to take the old girl for walks around the pasture.

Latin Dancer in the next stall was the son of her champion stallion, Latin Lover. The colt did not have the natural *brio* needed for the show ring. Still, he would make a wonderful trail horse. Ben had bought Dancer and hired Jessica to train him for that purpose.

Over time, Ben had also become Jessica's lover. He was patient with the young widow, smart enough to let her fall in love again at her own speed. She ran her hand over Dancer's neck, muttering to him, "I'm grateful to your owner, Dancer. But is that a basis for real love? Especially when I feel the way I do about his daughter?" The horse flicked his ears, impatient for another carrot.

Today, Ben and she had planned to take Dancer on their first real trail ride. She'd been eager to tell him all about the cops and Charlie's missing wife. But he'd called to cancel an hour ago. His daughter Rachael had been found unconscious in a Seattle alley. Again. She had a long history of drug abuse, petty theft and pan-handling.

Jessica wanted to be sympathetic. But she couldn't abide how Rachael hurt Ben again and again. He needed to protect himself. Jessica had once told him how she felt. "Rachael's in her early twenties now, Ben. It's time for her to cowgirl up and stop depending on you to bail her out. Your love is wasted until she does."

But Ben refused to give up on Rachael and always whisked her away to any rehab center that would still take her. "If her mother hadn't walked out on her when she was a child, if I'd been a wiser father, maybe she'd have a fighting chance."

It was now a sore point between them. Jessica resented it when Rachael destroyed what little time Ben and she had together. Not that her own hectic schedule helped either, as Ben was quick to point out.

"Don't give up, Dancer. We'll go another day," she said to the colt, handing over the final carrot. "Ben's losing the battle for his daughter. But maybe we can help him win one for himself."

CHAPTER FOUR

Case Notes
March 16, 10 a.m.
If you compare us to morgue patrons, we're in pretty good shape. Otherwise, we're a decrepit lot. Charlie is wheelchair bound, I lost one leg to diabetes, Eunice's ticker is touchy, and Frankie's hands tremble as if Parkinson's may be gaining ground. Bear's lost so much weight and exercised so hard, he gets around pretty well with a quad cane, one of those gizmos with the four little feet. Most of them are metal, but he had one special made from chestnut. He says it's heavier duty which it may be. But I think that handsome wood suits his ego, too.
None of us is about to run wind sprints, but our minds are still sharp. Jessica tries to see we're entertained, but time can hang pretty heavy. We do what we can to keep each other out of the dumps. Charlie stocks the birdfeeders, Bear tells stories about past cases, Frankie reads aloud in a voice smooth as chocolate, I beat everyone at board games, and Eunice has money. That last explains Sitting Bull.
Eunice wanted us all to be able to explore Latin's Ranch. It's ten lovely acres at the foot of the Cascades. There's a covered riding rink where Jessica gives lessons and a barn with stables for her Paso Finos and the boarders. Sam's mobile home is up near the barn, but of course it's off limits unless he invites us in. Two grazing pastures adjoin the barn and a large field behind them is bordered by forest. Access to riding trails is right there. The woods are a little dreary

right now because the chestnuts and oaks are just budding out and the evergreens are soaked through from a long wet winter. But it will soon be rich with wildflowers and song birds, ferns and life.

The problem was that most of us couldn't get to any of it. So Eunice bought us a golf cart. Oh, not just a golf cart. She pimped our ride with a street worthy Sitting Bull Customs job. Damn thing is candy apple red with enough bells and whistles to rival a marching band. It holds two of us in the front on cushy leather seats. The passenger seat even swings out for easy access from a walker or wheelchair. The back seat faces forward, too. A person can sit there next to a folded wheelchair, or I suppose two could squeeze in if we weren't always toting chairs and walkers and canes along.

You math whizzes will have figured that's at most four seats for five folks, but it's not been a problem. Old poops never feel good enough at the same time for everyone to be out and about. So far, we've maxed out at three.

I did mention street worthy, didn't I? Sitting Bull has the lights, belts, mirrors, reflectors and warnings to make it legal on roads with speed limits up to 35 mph. Of course, really burning rubber it couldn't go over 30. Besides, Jessica is prone to lectures if we take it out on the road.

Eunice and I were cruising along the driveway earlier today, peering into the woods for wildflowers. The only things blooming this early were a few trilliums and, in a wet patch, skunk cabbage. The breeze was too cold for our old bones so we didn't stay out too long.

On the way back, I mentioned how I always looked forward to spring. Eunice answered that at her age, she treated each one like her last. "After the Mister died, I thought I'd live out my years in some kind of suspension like a hibernating squirrel. Nice to know this squirrel can still fly." She gunned Sitting Bull up to 15 mph.

Eunice may be flighty, but she's right about life on the back nine. I learned at the nursing home that you don't spend so much time with old memories that you fail to make new ones. However much life you have left, you want to keep right on using it. You never know what surprises lay ahead.

Anyhoo, Bear growled at us when we got back. "If it ain't Lucy and Ethel."

"Nice to see you, too," I answered.

"Get in here. You need to help solve this mystery."

"Doesn't that make us Cagney and Lacey?" Eunice asked.

To help solve a mystery. Who'd have ever thought I'd be a PI's assistant? Or that Bear would be a PI again? See what I mean about the surprises ahead?

- Lily Gilbert, Philosophical Assistant to PI Bear Jacobs

The living room at Latin's Ranch was larger than most. When nobody was in it, there was enough floor space to look like somebody had pushed the oversized furniture, widescreen TV and game table out of the way for a hoedown. But Lily thought that should be no real surprise. When all the residents were assembled, they needed extra room to maneuver their mobility equipment. They were all gathered now at Bear's request and the spacious room felt almost cozy. Lily could hear Aurora banging pans out in the kitchen and singing to salsa rhythms on the radio. The canaries caged in the corner of the room sang along happily.

"I'm thinking about what the detectives said," Bear began. "About seniors disappearing. Of course, there are more seniors every year so there are more of us to get lost. But what makes a geezer walk away from his home and not come back?" He glanced from person to person, ending with Lily.

She was aware she was considered a ring leader by the others. She hoped it was that instead of just a know-it-all. "Well, I'd like to think he was off being happy, attending to his bucket list." She pulled a tissue from her cardigan pocket and blew her nose which was still reacting to the nippy ride in Sitting Bull. "But it's more likely he's suffering some type of dementia and can't find his way home. You hear about that happening to Alzheimer victims. Thousands every year."

"Could be an accident," Eunice piped up. "Or he's been set upon by thugs who conked him on the head, and he's in shock or a coma or, no, has amnesia with no idea who or where he is. And the hospital has to release him so he ends up in the woods, living rough where wolves take care of him."

Bear just nodded then asked, "Frankie? What do you think?"

"Maybe he sleeps with the fishes."

Lily wasn't the only one who shuddered.

Bear tried again. "Anything to add, Charlie?"

He'd been pouting, not without reason since it was his wife who was among the missing."You guys just think Louise went off to Vegas to find a new lover and spend all my money or some other goddamn thing. But what about the dog?" Charlie's jowls quivered with frustration.

"We're talking in general here, Charlie, not just about Louise," Bear said. "Like maybe this missing senior has something left undone that he has to go do. Make a face-to-face apology or visit an old war buddy on the other side of the Rockies."

Lily said, "I read about a grandparent running off with an abused grandchild that he was trying to save. Or a missing person could be escaping from a son who is abusing him."

Bear said, "He could have received devastating news about his health and wants to save his loved ones from that pain, so he's gone where they can't find him. Maybe to commit suicide."

"I know, I know!" said Eunice, perky as the canaries. "Maybe he was a real snappy hoofer in his day so he runs off with Holland America to be a paid dance partner for all the old gals on a cruise ship, and he gets to see the world while having lots of sex."

Lily had never before realized how many reasons a senior might have to run away from home. "It's so sad," she said as much to herself as the rest of the room.

Eventually, Eunice and Frankie lost interest in the topic and turned on Jeopardy. Charlie rolled to the game table and shuffled a deck for another hand of solitaire. Lily leaned close to Bear in order to speak softly. "You're really getting involved with this thing aren't you?"

"Yeah, I guess I am. Charlie's a good guy. He needs some answers about this. Jo Keegan is a dedicated cop, but with no real clues that the missing seniors are connected with each other somehow, this won't hit her priority list."

"What will you do first?"

"Make a few calls, renew some contacts, do some research. See if Keegan will let me peek at those recent files on missing adults. I'll have to stay out of her way, though. Don't want her to think I'm just a pest."

Old people are used to being treated like pests. Lily understood that.

Hell, we do repeat stories and bitch about modern methods and think young people today are chuckleheads.

Lily squinted at Bear, trying to assess him from a young cop's point of view. Alvin Jacobs could have been a retired lumberjack based on his size. His eyes were so dark they were nearly black which made them abnormally shiny, like two jet beads. He was in his seventies, still big with muscles that had lost tone when he'd let himself run to fat. With silvertip hair and beard, Bear got his nickname from his looks, of course. But it described his attitudes, too. He could fool you into thinking he was a big ambling dope, slow and easy to underestimate.

Lily knew it was a mistake for a cop – or anybody – to think of Bear as slow. Since coming to Latin's Ranch from the nursing home, his mental health had improved right along with his physical. Lily had no doubt he could be a dangerous opponent. If Jo Keegan was as bright as Bear seemed to think, she would look at him as a genuine asset.

Lily said, "I think Detective Keegan will take all the help she can get."

"Are you in, too?"

She felt a shiver of delight to be asked. Bear must think she was up to it or he'd never have asked for her help. "Where do I start?"

"Good. Get Charlie to give you the name of his wife's best friend. See if you can find her. Make her like you. She'll maybe give you some dope on Louise Barker that will help get us started. Something that Charlie doesn't know or isn't sharing."

As a rule, Lily didn't care whether people liked her or not, but she knew how to work it so they would. When Charlie gave her the name of Candice Kenilworth, he added, "Never got along with the woman myself."

"Yes, but I can be as captivating as a snake charmer," Lily answered.

"Well be careful. Cobras can strike."

CHAPTER FIVE

Case Notes
March 17, 3 p.m.
I know who Candice Kenilworth is, or at least I thought I did from my old garden club days. I Googled her just to be sure. Rick Peters, our only male aide, showed me how to do it. BTW, he's also our only member of the Alutiiq tribe from up in the Kodiak area. He says work is easier to find here than in Alaska. I know Alita is certainly glad he's here.
Anyhoo, about Candice Kenilworth. She calls herself Candi's Climbers. Well, that's what she calls her vines. She raises all kinds of rarified clematis. Even perfected a double white hybrid as hardy as a basic species. Candi's Climbers turn up at every garden show, always taking the category prize and often the grand prize. Back when I used to garden we all recognized her as the one to beat. Nobody had much good to say about her. But then, if you're familiar with garden club members, you'll agree ... a person with a green thumb often has a green-eyed monster, too. It could just be envy talking.
I figured I could lie to Candi, claim I was with the Department of Social and Health Services and in need of information. I don't believe that honesty is necessarily the best policy, but it is usually the easiest one. Less chance of getting woven up in that tangled web of deceit. When I got her on the phone, I just told the truth. With a little extra sugar. "Mrs. Kenilworth, I've been a gardener for years. And let me tell you that I am amazed by the quality of your clematis

year after year. Such variety! Such vigor! You are a miracle worker, I must say."

"Why thank you so much! It's not every day I get such a glowing compliment from a fellow enthusiast. Please, call me Candi."

After that, she blossomed like one of her vines. By the time we were done with our little chat, I had told her only that I lived in the same care facility as Charlie, and that we were concerned with the whereabouts of his wife. In return, Candi had told me that Louise was twenty years younger than her husband, still had a lot of life left in her and wanted to kick up her heels a little. Charlie had not always been such a loyal hubby, having left his first wife for Louise. Louise knew he'd had his little bit on the side during their marriage, too. No wonder she'd abandoned him now and selected the cheapest burial package for him from the Chesterton Funeral Parlor and good enough for him if you wanted Candi Kenilworth's opinion.

Let me interrupt myself right here to say, Charlie, you old ass wipe. Still waters and all. Maybe you're not such an innocent after all. Maybe you deserve those sore balls.

Candi gave me the names of a couple more of Louise's friends, then said they planned to take a Single Seniors color tour of New England together next fall. No, Candi hadn't seen Louise since they'd had dinner, let's see, in mid-February to celebrate the first new leaf on her clematis vines. And wow, didn't time pass quickly? Now Candi figured she should be worried about Louise, too, and would try to reach her friend.

While I was talking to Candi, Detective Keegan called Bear. Charlie had let her check their post office box. She said mail hadn't been picked up since the last week of February.

So. Four weeks ago, dinner with a friend. Three weeks ago, the last mail pick up. Nothing more about Louise Barker since then.

Wow. This detective stuff is spine-tingling.

- Lily Gilbert, Enthused Assistant to PI Bear Jacobss

Will Haverstock stood back and cocked his head at the corpse on the gleaming table in front of him. He'd already disinfected the body and covered the old woman's privates with a modesty cloth. After gently placing her head on a block, he'd tilted it fifteen degrees to the right so mourners could more easily see her when she was on display in the visitation room.

At the moment she was a hag with caved in cheeks, sagging jowls, and splotchy skin. "When we're done, your face will be as lovely as it ever was in life," Will said to her. It was his way to speak with the bodies, as if his mellow voice might ease their long journeys.

Will honored old people. Experience had taught him they were the ones to trust. His slender nose was a bit crooked and he had a slight limp from beatings his father had given him years ago. His mother had chosen the man over the boy and dumped Will on his grandparents. Gram and Gramp raised Will with affection and concern, providing the first love he'd ever known. They and their friends, also old people, played cards or board games with him, told him stories and taught him to read the wonderful books of their youth. Now in his twenties, Will still lived with his grandparents.

"But more and more, I take care of them instead of the other way around," he said to the corpse. He knew people thought that embalming was a fucked up choice in careers. But to him, it was a payback factor. He helped people to rest with dignity and respect. In that, Will was an artist.

It was when he began to set the woman's features that he ran into the problem. He started with the eyes, which had sunk back into their sockets. He was about to insert an eye cap over an eyeball when he saw them, those purple pinprick sized spots.

"What has happened to you?" he asked, receiving no reply. The tiny spots would have been nearly invisible without the bright lights of an embalming room.

In, say, the subdued lighting of an old folks home.

"What to do now?" Will asked the body and himself. He liked his job. But with the economy the way it was, fewer people were choosing funerals with all the fringes. Cremations didn't require embalmers. Will worried that there would not be enough work to keep him employed. So he tried to be a particularly excellent employee, helping his coworkers with other chores, never complaining or bringing attention to himself. That meant avoiding problems for Orlo Chesterton, owner and mortician of the Chesterton Funeral Parlor.

But this is too much.

Will removed the latex gloves and went to the phone. He was told the boss was with a bereaved family but would be given his message when possible. "Please ask him to come to the embalming room," Will said to the voice in the phone, his own voice tentative in the request. He hated to be a bother. "When it's convenient. When he can."

Will mustn't waste time while he waited. He put on fresh gloves and continued setting the rest of the features, leaving the eyes for now. He sutured the lower jaw to the upper, skillfully threading from gums into the right nostril, through the septum, into the left and back into the mouth. He was tying the two ends of suture together when the boss strolled in.

Orlo Chesterton must have come down the stairs from the subdued, thick carpeted viewing rooms above. Will didn't hear him so he nearly yelped when he looked up and the boss was right there, hands clasped behind his back while assessing Will's work. At least he hadn't been there for long. His eyes were still squinting from the intense light in the only area of his funeral home that was as bright as an operating theatre.

The bereaved family must have gone, because Mr. Chesterton always replaced his dark suit jacket with the gray cardigan when not on public view himself. The funeral director did not have the sallow and spooky mortician's countenance as seen on TV. Instead, he was a mild Mr. Rogers type, one who would surely offer calm and comfort when needed most. Will supposed that was exactly why Chesterton Funeral Parlor was so popular, by far the largest operation in the entire Snohomish valley.

Behind closed doors, however, Mr. Chesterton had a strict 'time is money' policy. Will knew better than to dawdle so he began to speak even without a greeting. He tucked his head down on his chest, delivering his words more to the dead body than to the boss. "I'd finished the checklist to be sure the deceased was, ah, deceased. Pulse, lividity, rigor, you know."

"Yes?" Orlo asked, frowning at a tiny speck of lint on his sweater. He unclasped his hands long enough to flick it away.

"I'd moved on to setting the features. That's when I saw them. Petechial hemorrhages." The spots in or around the eyes were caused by bleeding under the skin. It was a strong indication of asphyxia by strangulation.

"Ah, petechial hemorrhages," Orlo nodded sagely and peered closely as Will lifted an eyelid on the corpse. Orlo did not touch the body himself. He stood back up straight and said, "I wouldn't concern myself if I were you. This body was picked up at Driscoll Manor Assisted Living. Often in the death throes, an elderly person will deplete his oxygen and struggle for breath. I am sure the doctor would have noticed if anything was ... suspicious."

"So this is normal?" Will asked, feeling relief roll through his body. "On an old corpse? I mean on the corpse of an older person?"

"Unusual but normal, yes. I suppose you were worried that a family member might have put a pillow over the lady's face. Such things happen, of course. Sometimes families are a little too eager for an inheritance. More often, though, they just want to help a loved one end her misery."

"But ... but that's illegal." Will tensed again.

"Yes. Even in those cases where it could be considered the kindest act. But we depend on families to pay for our services. And care facilities like Driscoll Manor depend on our discretion."

"I know, but –"

"- and doctors don't wish to be accused of missing a symptom. We simply don't know as much as they do, do we?"

"No, I suppose not."

"Nobody really wants any questions to be asked that might be awkward to answer. Understand?"

Will understood that he'd just been told to keep his thoughts to himself.

Chesterton flashed an over-whitened smile at him. "I'm so pleased you're conscientious enough to have noticed." He patted Will on the shoulder then turned back toward the archway that would lead him back upstairs. "I'll follow up with Driscoll Manor just to be on the safe side. In the meantime, continue your excellent work. We're very glad to have you here."

Will returned to the corpse. He often felt more competent with the dead. He inserted a mouth form before applying stay crème to hold the lips in place. "There now," he assured the body. "We got an expert opinion. I'll finish your eyelids, and no one will know I had to ask for help. It'll be our secret."

The boss hadn't really told him to mind his own business. In fact, Mr. Chesterton had complimented him on his observation.

Maybe my job is safe. But why do I still feel worried? Is Mr. Chesterton really sure about that oxygen depletion stuff? I never heard that before.

But then, Will wasn't the expert in death that Orlo Chesterton was.

✦ ✦ ✦

"How goes the investigation?" Ben asked while holding Jessica, naked chest to naked chest.

She could feel both their hearts calming after their mattress aerobics. She was cozy, safe in his beefy arms, in her private rooms above the rest of Latin's Ranch. "You mean for Sherlock Bear and the Latin's Ranch Irregulars? It's giving them something to do together. They're enjoying themselves."

"I suppose solving puzzles keeps their minds agile."

"That must explain why Lily is so involved. She's taking orders, keeping notes and making calls. Freeing Bear up to talk with the deputies and whatever he's doing online. Hacking into government records probably."

"Have the cops been back?"

"Oh yes, a couple times. With more questions for Charlie and to give Bear some files on other missing persons. All the womenfolk here have the hots for the boy detective, Clay Galligan. Even Aurora. She gives him baked treats each time they're here. It's kind of scary to see her actually smile. Sort of like a gargoyle."

"*All* the womenfolk have the hots for Galligan?"

"Well, all but one." She looked up and batted her lashes. She knew he found her eyes to be killer. "I wouldn't lust after a mere boy when I have a real man right here up close and personal."

"I'm more worried about the mere boy lusting after you."

They nestled in comfortable silence, Jessica pleased to know that Ben wasn't above a touch of jealousy. But she didn't feel so cozy after he asked, "Not getting themselves in any danger are they?"

"Gosh, I don't think so. The cops don't seem concerned." Now he'd gone and made her worry. She rolled over on her back and retrieved her glass of wine from the nightstand. "I'm sure they'll be fine. But speaking of danger, is your daughter okay for now?"

Ben sighed and rolled away as well. "We're never really alone for very long, are we?"

CHAPTER SIX

Case Notes
March 18, 11 a.m.
Bennett Stassen spent the night with Jessica and stayed for breakfast this morning before leaving for work. We all like Ben. He helped remodel Jessica's house for us. They added rooms and handicap bathrooms and a big smooth patio where we can plug in Sitting Bull and also pot garden, although Jessica tells me I should call it container gardening. Sometimes it's fun to make her squawk.
Ben remodeled Jessica's love life, too, after her husband died. He's older and, from the sound of things, a damn site steadier. We have a pool going on when the two of them might tie the knot. Seemed like a sure thing a few months back. But lately, I don't know. There's a sadness in Jessica that I can't quite put my finger on. Right now she's got her mouth shut tighter than a trap door, but I'll get her to open up sooner or later.
Not that all this has anything to do with the case of Charlie's missing wife, so I'll get back to business.
Bear's spent hours on his computer. He hums old standards while he thinks, so I've been hearing gravelly bits of "One For My Baby" and "I'll Be Seeing You," and of course I can't get them out of my head now. He's been on the phone a lot, too, reacquainting himself with contacts. Police, sheriffs and staties. A few old buddies are still working toward their pensions ... must have been young hot shots when they worked with Bear. Others have just heard legends about

him. Whatever, he's not short on resources with the good guys. With the bad guys either, would be my guess.
He's been gathering the 411 on missing persons. 411. That's an old phrase they used on TV for information. I'm nowhere near as up on cop-speak as Eunice, though. She's always been fascinated with Bear's background even though he says all it takes to be a PI in Washington is a clean record, fingerprints, a surety bond, a few hundred bucks and a hard head. You ace a test and bingo, you're Magnum, P.I. Now that Bear's back in the game, Eunice is reading Mickey Spillane and Raymond Chandler from his collection of paperbacks. It's not easy for a woman as big as a minute to sound hardboiled, but she's trying. In fact, Bear found her very trying earlier today.

- Lily Gilbert, Moll with Moxie Assistant to PI Bear Jacobs

"Tip your mitt, gumshoe," Eunice-as-Bogart demanded. All the residents were gathered in the sunny living room while Alita cleaned their rooms.

"Pardon?" Bear answered.

"I believe she means, 'Tell us what you've found out, Bear,'" Lily said. She'd been peppered by Eunice's new vocabulary all morning as they got ready for the day. Eunice had also tried for the look of the 40s. She couldn't quite get her orange spiky hair into finger waves or tight curls, but she had arched her brows and applied fire engine red lipstick in a curvy cupid's bow.

Bear began. "First, you have to understand how many missing persons there are. Over one hundred thousand a year. Among the seniors who disappear, most have some type of dementia."

"Not Louise," Charlie said with a stubborn jut of his chin. "She has every marble she was born with, along with a handful of mine."

"The Barker dame is a hot tomato hitting on all eight," Eunice said in a monotone, hands on her hips.

Bear glanced at her with his head slightly cocked, but he continued. "Several services track missing persons and unidentified bodies. Keep photos, dental records, DNA data. Keegan will send a report on Louise to the state patrol's Missing and Unidentified Persons Unit. But I have to warn you, Charlie. There's no real evidence that her disappearance is what the law calls endangered or involuntary. Until it is, it's not going to be a priority for anyone."

"Christ, Bear. She disappeared, vamoosed, flew the coop, took a powder," Charlie squeaked, flailing his arms as if he, too, might take flight. Even his comb-over flapped in the breeze he created.

"Maybe that's just what she wanted to do," Bear replied.

"But the dog! I keep telling everyone that she would never have hurt Fluffy-san. Something's happened to Louise, something bad."

Eunice said, "He sunk so low he was blinded by the curb." Lily frowned at her and gave Charlie's hand a pat. She felt bad for him even though Candi Kenilworth had trounced all over his reputation. It was damn hard to accept that a beloved spouse just didn't want your sorry ass any more. And, of course, Charlie's ass was sorrier than most.

Bear said, "I believe you, Charlie. So I made some calls and dug out details on older adults who've disappeared this spring within a five mile radius of us. There are eight who were born before 1955. That makes them fifty-five or older. Three are men. Two of them were lost hiking in the woods, and they've been found. The other one was known to have Alzheimer's. His body was discovered last week."

"Poor old soul," Lily said soft as a prayer.

"That leaves five women. The oldest of them is seventy-eight and has some form of dementia, too, so let's exclude her for now. One was found as soon as she returned from an AARP bus tour to Branson. She'd neglected to tell her son she was going. That leaves three, including Louise, between the ages of fifty-five and sixty-seven. That's way too many for an area this size."

"So what does that mean?" Charlie asked, squeezing his arthritic hands into fists that had to be protesting the gesture with pain.

Lily drew a sharp breath as she got what Bear meant. "The only people unaccounted for are *women*. Does Detective Keegan know that? We have to tell her!"

"The angel face copper with a body for --"

"Eunice," Bear snapped. "Are you going to keep this up much longer?"

"Why I oughta punch you in the beezer, you two-bit shamus!"

"Yeah? Well, Angel Face Keegan might find you with a load of lead in your lungs."

"Oh, okay then." Eunice's smile replaced her mock scowl, and her eyes twinkled with humor.

"My little dove," Frankie crooned, viewing Eunice fondly.

"But what's happening to old women?" Charlie asked.

Frankie had given Lily an idea. "Maybe one of those Casanova types is working the area. You know, those men who hit on single women to steal their money." But as she said it, it didn't really sound right. "I guess not. Casanovas don't make women disappear ... they just disappear with women's money."

Bear said, "True enough, Lily. So I'm afraid this could be darker than that. Someone may be attacking them. Like the Boston Strangler did."

"His victims were *old*?" Eunice gasped, her eyes round as Cheerios.

"Many were. Oldest was eighty. They were sexually molested and each strangled with their own clothing."

"Oh, dear God," Charlie said with a groan.

"Speculation at the time was that the Strangler hated his mother. But I think it's more likely that old women were easier targets." Bear shook his head. "This may be something different. But it's definitely aimed at mature women."

"This is worse ... the not knowing. This can't be happening to Louise." Charlie put his hands over his eyes.

"Oh, it can be happening," Eunice said, her voice trembling. "It happens."

Lily saw that the joy had drained from her old friend's face. Eunice knew exactly what could happen to a defenseless old woman. She'd shared a room with one who was sexually violated by an aide back at Soundside nursing home. Eunice hadn't been able to stop it. She'd gone through many dark days because of it.

Bear said as gently as his big voice would allow, "I promise, Eunice. I'll find out what's going on and put a stop to it."

Frankie spoke in a voice used to giving commands. "Don't worry, my little dove. Frankie is here to watch over you."

Lily hoped that would be enough to make Eunice twinkle again soon.

✦ ✦ ✦

Keegan and Galligan sat in their cruiser at the Burgermaster. Clay was downing a bacon cheeseburger while Jo picked through a salad, resenting Clay's inability to gain weight.

"So what is it with this old cocker?" Clay asked just before crunching into a fat Walla Walla onion ring.

"You mean Al Jacobs? Bear?"

"Yeah, seems like a buttinski to me."

"Well, I guess he is. But as long as he's butting into Louise Barker's disappearance that means we don't have to put it anywhere near a front burner. She's probably just run off with another man."

"I don't like turning work over to a civilian."

"Normally, I agree. But Bear's good, Clay. I say let's give him a little leeway and see what he comes up with."

"What if it's a homicide?"

"Then we'll throw more resources at it. In the meantime, it isn't like we need more to do." As if to make her point, their radio burped to life with another call. Jo detached the window tray, set it on the ground where the carhop would find it, and wheeled the big car out of the lot at warp speed, not really minding that it caused Clay to dribble chocolate shake down the front of his shirt.

✦ ✦ ✦

Candi Kenilworth read the copy on the chamomile tea tin while she waited for the brew to steep. It promised to reduce stress, promote relaxation and restful sleep. "God knows I could use all of the above," she said aloud. "Too bad it tastes like piss."

She gave some thought to that nice woman – Lily was her name, wasn't it? – who had called about her friend, Louise. Candi determined to call Louise herself once she could sit down and put her feet up. That's when her doorbell rang.

She was so tired she wanted to ignore it, which she would have if it was just one of those Jehovah's again. But she'd told that Larry, no Lewis, no – oh hell what was his name? – that he could call. So she shuffled down the hall in her fleece lined slippers, patting her hair into place as she bent to peer through her peep hole. "Who is it?"

"It's Luke Carmichael, Mrs. Kenilworth, from Carefree Occasions. We have an appointment?"

Candi assessed the bland faced young man on her doorstep, holding up an ID card with his photo next to a colorful corporate logo. Standing there in his dark pin-striped suit and short cropped hair, he had that mild cookie-cutter look the FBI would hire.

"Come in," she said, opening the door and offering a weary smile. "I'm just making a hot cup of tea. Would you care for one?"

"Yes, ma'am, I surely would," Luke said as he followed her to the kitchen. "March may go out like a lamb, but it's still feeling a lot like a lion."

She wasn't great with chitchat but she tried. "Yes, this much wind makes the rain seem even more – "

Her last thought as her head exploded was that the chamomile probably wouldn't be able to handle this much stress.

CHAPTER SEVEN

Case Notes
March 20, 7 p.m.
Bear and I were on the phone a lot today. Not with each other but with relatives of the missing women. I came to bed early tonight – sure hope Eunice stays up chatting with the others for a while. I want some quiet to get my thoughts straight. And time to mourn a little for these poor people. Imagine not knowing where your mother or grandfather has gone.
Detective Keegan gave Bear the names of the people who had reported the missing persons. She told him that he could investigate as long as he contacted her with any serious developments. Bear says what she means by that is any proof that these disappearances are homicides.
It's peculiar when you think of it. If your loved one is missing, she's not a priority. If she's dead as a damn door nail then they'll get right on it. Seems sort of ass backwards to me.
Bear had asked me to sit in on the calls with him because our two old brains equal one fresh new one. Before we started, I said, "Bear, let's assume that one person, place or thing is behind all these missing women."
"Okay. Got to draw a line in the sand somewhere."
"How would he, she or it know the women live alone? Or that they're all old people?"
"County records, real estate transfers, census data. Lots of ways on-

line, especially if you are willing to pay for it."
"Scary," I felt a mental shiver. Nothing from your income to your bra size is private anymore.
Bear nodded. "Scary, indeed. And if they didn't find them online, then somebody knows all these women from a book club or a sewing circle or a church group. Something strings them together. We have to find out what."
We used the speaker phone, although Bear insisted on calling it the squawk box. While dialing the first relative he said, "But don't you do any squawking. Just take notes."
"Why would you think I'd squawk?"
"You're squawking now."

- Lily Gilbert, Muzzled Assistant to PI Bear Jacobs

Lily was about to give Bear a piece of her mind when someone answered the phone. "Hello?" said a voice made thin by the speaker, sounding like it was inside a fruit juice can.

"Is Sheila Blakely there?" Bear asked.

"Speaking."

"Ms. Blakely, my name is Al Jacobs. I'm a private investigator working along with the sheriff's office on missing person cases."

Lily looked up from her note pad and rolled her eyes at Bear. He'd played a little loose with the truth, of course. Good thing Sheila Blakely couldn't ask to see his PI license over the phone.

"Oh, yes? Have you found my mother? Where has she been?" She sounded excited, even relieved.

"No, ma'am, I'm sorry. We're still looking, and I have a few more questions. I know you've given deputies the basic facts, but can you tell me more about your mother? What she's like, where she goes, what she enjoys doing"

There was a pause. When she answered, Sheila Blakely sounded dubious. "You mean like she makes double wedding ring quilts? She's a Baptist? Stuff like that?"

"Yes, ma'am, exactly like that."

"Why?"

"To help me picture her better. I need to understand what she might have in common with other missing seniors in the area."

"You mean to tell me there are more?" Lily could hear skepticism as well as dread in the woman's voice, and wondered if it was a form of denial. Maybe Sheila Blakely had believed her mother would simply return home one day, like Little Bo Peep's sheep.

"We're looking into that possibility," Bear answered.

"Like maybe they've all been abducted by aliens or something?"

"Yes, ma'am, although that particular occurrence seems unlikely to me."

Slowly, Bear worked with Sheila to develop a profile of her mother. He didn't rush her, allowing her time to accept the harrowing thought that her mother might not just reappear unharmed. Lily figured the next emotion to take its toll on this daughter would be guilt. She hadn't heard from her mother in several weeks before reporting her missing.

Bear gently gathered the information that Catherine Blakely was sixty-four, athletic and outgoing. She loved living near the Cascades, was a birder who hiked with other members of her club. She volunteered at the library, very occasionally dated, played pickle ball on the local senior's team. Catherine's own mother lived with her until she died six months ago of heart failure.

The next call was with a son. His mother, Karen Oostrom, was a quiet woman who kept a neat-as-a-pin house and did all her own yard work. She was a Midwesterner who had moved to Washington two decades ago when her husband retired from his security job at O'Hare Airport. Her son called her shy and habitual, not inclined to vary her routine. He hoped that might change a bit, now that his father was deceased. Dad had been ill for a long time so Karen performed heavy-duty home nursing for years until the man was finally placed in hospice care. Karen Oostrom was 67. Her son hadn't seen her for over a month before she disappeared. He was in tears when the call ended.

The third and youngest of the missing group was Charlie's wife. Still in her late 50s. Bear and Lily believed she had grown weary of him. Once he went to the nursing home, she was free to pursue her primary interests of Nordstrom and tanning beds and attending dog shows with Fluffy-san, her pure bred Japanese Sheba. Now a dead pure bred.

✦ ✦ ✦

Bear stayed up late thinking about what the hell he was doing. He was involved with these disappearances because he'd wanted to help his buddy, Charlie. And, if he were honest with himself, because being an investigator was in his blood. But now that the case had grown to include three women, was he really up to it? Was his brain as spry as it used to be? Certainly his body wasn't the dependable engine it once was. There'd be no bar fights with broken bottles in his future, not if he hoped to survive them.

When Bear looked at each missing person case on its own, there was no reason to assume the worst. Each was just a missing woman who was likely to reappear one day, embarrassed she'd caused a fuss. The problem for law enforcement was that a deputy or officer talked with a relative, then wrote and filed a report. It was unlikely that the same cop talked to other relatives about other missing persons. Probably didn't even read all the other reports. Only when you took them together did the three women smell like foul play. And only Bear was nosing around with that.

I damn well better be up to it.

He read through the descriptions of the houses from files that Keegan gave him. All were single-family dwellings. Different officers had gone through them, but in their reports the homes all appeared lived-in with a normal amount of clutter. The occupant of each could have just gone out for a stroll and not come back. Nothing looked searched or vandalized or burgled. No dangerous appliances had been left burning or water running. Some lights were on, and a TV was playing in each house.

Walking with the help of his quad cane, Bear went out to the patio and clambered into Sitting Bull. He drove the short distance up the gravel drive to see Sam Hart. The taciturn barn manager's mobile home was parked half way to the barn, close enough to the horses to hear trouble in the night. Sam kept a loaded Winchester rifle just inside the trailer's door. Bear had seen it, but he doubted that Sam ever mentioned it to Jessica.

It turned out Sam was only taciturn around women. When Jessica opened Latin's Ranch to people as well as horses, Bear and Sam had formed a friendship that involved poker in the old Airstream. Now and again, those poker evenings involved a little alcohol, maybe a cigar. Bear considered it no one's business although Lily gave him hell one night. He'd thought she was mad because he'd been drinking. Turned out it was because he didn't sneak a couple of brews for Eunice and her.

"Got a six pack if you'd like a little refreshment for the ladies," Sam said when he opened the trailer door. His eyes were shadowed by the battered straw cowboy hat that everyone assumed was welded to his head. He was tall and willowy, no spring chicken but still more than a decade younger than Bear. Bear figured he kept in shape with all the chores he did around the ranch.

"Not why I'm here tonight, Sam. We need to do some drive-bys."

✦ ✦ ✦

When Candi Kenilworth came to, she wasn't sure whether she was blind or not. It was pitch black. Her head pulsated when she moved even the slightest bit so she opted to stay still and try to gather her scattered wits.

I was in the kitchen, making dinner. No, tea. And the phone rang. No, the door bell. I opened the door, but who was there? I don't remember. Oh yes. Something about carefree living. No, carefree times. Carefree Occasions, that was it. And the nondescript young man. Luke.

Try as she might, she could remember no more. She felt around her. It was not her bed. At least not her blanket. A nubby woolen roughness that smelled of moth balls was touching her skin. Candi made an effort to sit up but collapsed back on the bed as her head began to beat like a tom-tom. She touched a sore spot tenderly and felt a goose egg of epic proportions. She couldn't help but whimper.

"Are you all right?" a voice whispered.

"Shit!" Candi yipped. "You scared the crap out of me!"

"Close your eyes. I will turn on a light."

She squeezed her eyes shut but felt like the room was suddenly as flood-lit as a Walmart grand opening. Once she adjusted and could bear to open her eyes a sliver, she saw it was just a table lamp between two narrow beds. Eventually she could see she was in a small barren room with no more than the beds, the nightstand and a wooden straight backed chair. And an elderly man sitting on the other bed staring at her.

"Who the hell are you?" she asked, hoping her blood pressure med was working overtime.

"My name is Bronek Pokorski."

"Where the hell is this, and why the hell am I here?"

His answer sounded absurdly formal to her. "Dear lady, I wish I had those answers for myself as well as for you."

✦ ✦ ✦

Bear had enough height to swing his leg up and haul his frame into Sam's Silverado. He was riding shotgun as the cowboy drove them away from Latin's Ranch.

"You know, Jessica will have my hide if anything happens to you," Sam said.

Bear looked at him. Sam was, of course, wearing the hat. He might have been okay looking but for a missing front tooth and the broken veins in his nose that bespoke some hard living in his past.

"Why the hell would she want a tough old hide like yours?" Bear asked.

"Why the hell would she want an ornery old buzzard like you?"

It was a good point. Jessica did seem devoted to her oldsters. It had started with her love for Lily and had spread like locoweed to cover Frankie, Charlie, Eunice and himself. It still amazed him to have landed in a place he actually liked. "Maybe we shouldn't ask too many questions about her taste in friends."

"Agreed. Waste of time trying to understand a woman anyway," Sam said. "Safer to avoid talking with them altogether."

"They're a mystery all right." Bear gave a brief thought to the fractious relationship he'd had with his own wife so many years ago. He quickly returned to the subject at hand. "Our farthest destination is just outside Everett, then we'll work our way back." On the way, he told Sam about the missing women. He wanted to see each of their houses for himself, if only to look at them from the outside.

"Why? What'll that tell you?"

"Won't know until I know."

The three homes didn't look much alike. One was a rambler, the other two more what he'd call simply cottages, not being an architect by trade. They were nothing fancy, but all appeared to be in good shape. One lawn was out of control from lack of mowing. The other two must have lawn services. Each house had a vehicle in the drive or carport and a porch light on at the front door. Lights could be seen in upstairs rooms, some of them flashing the way television screens would. He knew from the files that a handful of lights had been left on in each house.

"Looks like people are living here now," Sam said. "Like they're up in their bedrooms."

"I think that's the point."

"What do you mean?"

"Somebody wanted the homes to look occupied at night."

"So neighbors wouldn't get curious?"

"Be my guess. It worked, too. Nobody reported them gone. Somebody staged these houses to look lived in. To buy themselves time before discovery."

"What kind of jerk wads snatch old women?"

"*Old* seems to be relative here, Sam. So far nobody seventies or up. The missing three are late fifties to late sixties. Just sort of medium old."

"My age."

Bear's cell phone rang. He frisked himself until he discovered the little Samsung in his shirt pocket. "Speak," he growled.

"Bear? It's Keegan."

"What's up, Cupcake?"

"We have another one."

"A missing woman?"

"Yep. She lives outside Marysville. She was supposed to go to a movie with her niece but didn't show up. The niece went over to the house."

"Same type of thing? Like she just walked away?"

"But not long ago. Her cat is still alive. Pissed off, though. It deposited kitty fudgies in the bedroom."

"How old is she?"

"Um ... um ... here it is. Candi Kenilworth is 62."

"Holy shit! Lily talked with the Kenilworth woman three days ago and ..."

"Lily?" Keegan interrupted. "You mean that sweet old lady that Galligan and I met at Latin's Ranch?"

"She'd cut you off at the knees for that sweet old lady crap, but yes. She found out that Candi Kenilworth is a friend of Louise Barker."

"Finally a connection. Can I stop by?"

"Ah ... tomorrow. It's late. I'm not home. And I imagine Lily is in bed." He wanted time alone to think about this. These women weren't just off gallivanting. That much was obvious. There were too many of them. He felt every orifice tighten as images worthy of a horror movie flickered through his brain.

They're in a world of trouble.

"All right, but Bear?"

"Yeah?"

"Don't call me Cupcake."

✦ ✦ ✦

While the Latin's Ranch humans were going about their business, Folly the cockadock had his own agenda.

Jessica was his special favorite of all the two-leggers. She was his very own companion human, and if she was out doing chores Folly was never very far away. When Jessica had brought the old people home, Folly had been a little skeptical at first. He hadn't understood the strange conveyances they favored, the metal wheels and carts and canes. But he soon realized they weren't a danger, that they asked nothing of him but to be a clown. He could wiggle and lick and smile with the best of them. He considered entertaining the old people to be an important part of his job at Latin's Ranch.

As to the horses, he was particularly fond of Gina Lola. She was Ben's retired work horse, a wise old girl who was massive compared to the other horses. Folly liked to snuggle down in the trough that held her hay. While she chewed, they communicated as animals do. She'd pulled many a heavy load in her day and was now allowed to munch away with nothing more strenuous to do than take walks with Ben around the pastures. Folly usually joined them, especially when Ben took along the injured Latin Dancer. Gina Lola soothed the anxiety of the suffering youngster, and Folly proved that not all dogs would rip his flesh apart.

But that cat. Folly had been told he could not bite or chase the ugly smelly villain. Furball was given the run of the ranch that used to be his alone. The fat bastard took his favorite spot in the late morning sun and appropriated his beloved doggy basket.

Since Folly knew very little English, he would never understand the expression *every dog has his day.* But the day came when he discovered the truth of it. He was snuggled in Gina Lola's manger when Furball had leapt to the top of the stall gate and peered right at him. The ratter made that low rumbling sound deep in his throat. Gina Lola turned her massive head in Furball's direction.

The cat gathered its enormous self together, poised on the gate post to pounce.

Folly hunkered down, rolling his golden brown eyes. He'd never admit to cowering.

Gina Lola looked at the cat.

Furball's full attention was on the dog.

Gina Lola tiptoed forward.

Furball launched just as Gina Lola smacked him with the enormous cheek on the side of her long head. The cat flew like a pop-up baseball. He landed upright on the barn floor, hissed, and high tailed it for the house.

Folly was assured a cat-free spot in the barn to dream dog dreams.

CHAPTER EIGHT

Case Notes
March 21, 2 p.m.
Holy crap! A fourth missing woman and it's none other than Candi Kenilworth, the Clematis Queen. Bear told me to hurry this morning because we needed to do some work before Keegan showed up. I was at the computer before I had a chance to do justice to Aurora's huevos rancheros.
I put together all my notes from the interviews with the missing women's relatives. After I showed them to Bear, he said he needed to know how the three women were alike, not how they were different. I told him he should have said so in the first place. I mean I'm not the fancy schmancy private dick. I can't even find matching earrings half the time.
Anyhoo, I went back at it. And here's the list of similarities:
- All of them live in unincorporated parts of the county.
- All of them are gardeners.
- All of them like to walk, although it varies from rounds of golf to trail hikes to bird watching.
- All of them visit the Tulalip Casino now and again.
- All of them have library cards.
- All of them are patients of the same doctor.
I heard a rumbling from Bear which usually means he's about to laugh. This time, it was sort of a surprised snort. "Now that last one is a remarkable coincidence. Nice piece of work, Lily."

Can you imagine? A compliment from the big man. Yowza.

When Keegan showed up Bear gave her my list. He said we'd find out more about Candi Kenilworth, too. Keegan told us to do nothing more until she had a chance to find out what's what. I believe the lecture included something about no way in hell are the two of us to get into trouble or we'll be in plenty trouble with her.

The minute she left, Bear grabbed an address from his computer.

"Keegan said to back off," I protested.

"Hell, she can't keep a little old lady from visiting a doctor when she needs to." His beady black eyes shot a challenge in my direction.

And that's how this LOL found myself going to see Dr. Peter Flannery at the It's Swell to Be Well health clinic.

- Lily Gilbert, Malingering Assistant to PI Bear Jacobs

Lily hated to lie to Jessica. They'd been too close for too long.

They'd met when Lily was still in her own house, just after her amputation. Jessica had applied as an in-home caregiver. Lily was still in pain then and furious that her body was out of control. She hated the idea of strangers in her house, but her daughter had said it was that or assisted care.

Almost the first words Lily had said to Jessica were, "I am older than God and less predictable. I am not cute. I hate cute so do not confuse me with The Golden Girls. I would prefer never to be given anything with kittens or teddy bears printed on it. I like junk food when I can get it, but I don't smoke and rarely drink, although that doesn't make me holier than any thou. I have been a waitress, a florist, a picture framer, and a hundred other things. I did them all well, else why do them at all? People often don't like me, and I just as often don't care. If you want to work for a pushover, please leave. If you're willing to stand up for yourself and not pity me, stick around."

Jessica had taken the job, and together they'd bullied each other into a long abiding and respectful friendship. When Lily had finally gone into Soundside, Jessica had visited all the time. Together they'd hatched the plan to open Latin's Ranch.

That was all history. But it was still why Lily hated to lie to Jessica.

Nonetheless, she told her that Bear and Sam were going to Man Land, and she was riding along. It was sort of true, since Sam was actually making a stop there.

"Man Land?" Jessica asked absently while nibbling on a cuticle and wrinkling her brow. She was going through a stack of bills, and all the residents knew that's when she was the most distracted.

"Yeah. The Home Depot. The aroma of all that raw lumber calls to men like catnip to Furball."

"Emm-hmm. Okay. Have fun."

Sam dropped them off and went on to the store. Bear and Lily entered It's Swell to Be Well. The clinic specialized in geriatrics. Only the receptionist looked young and, as it happened, only from the distance of the doorway. When Bear pushed Lily's wheelchair up to the front counter, Lily detected the woman had received more than a few nips and tucks. A little brass sign on the desk indicated her name was Suzie.

"I'm Detective Al Jacobs, here to see Dr. Flannery." Bear was dressed in a sports coat and tie instead of his usual suspenders and flannel shirt. Lily figured if Jessica hadn't been super distracted she'd have questioned his fancy attire. Maybe she'd thought Man Land was holding a formal.

"Do you have an appointment, Officer Jacobs?" Receptionist Suzie asked. Bear didn't clear up the officer thing.

And he lied. "Yes."

Lily began to wheel herself away, taking a look around the lobby. Several people were flipping through office copies of the AARP magazine and *Senior Living* and brochures on things like arthritis and cataracts.

"I don't see you here on my list." Receptionist Suzie frowned at her computer screen while tapping a syncopated rhythm on the keyboard.

"No, I'm here in your lobby."

"But if you're not on my list then you don't have an appointment." The tap tap tap got a little more frantic.

"If I didn't have an appointment, why would I be here in your lobby?"

"Well, Officer, you're the detective. Not me."

Bear turned to face the people awaiting their appointments. Lily could see they were beginning to perk up at the drama unfolding at reception. Louder than necessary, Bear boomed, "Dr. Flannery's patients are disappearing, Receptionist Suzie. They are dropping like flies. Someone may be slitting their throats or performing unspeakable acts on them. Someone who may see them here. In this office."

People stopped pretending to read and openly gaped. Lily thought it was time to give Bear a hand so she wheeled toward one fragile old man and began to whimper, "My sister Betty Jean came to see Dr. Flannery and never returned home." She pulled a Kleenex from her pocket, dabbed at her eyes and trumpeted toward the exam rooms, "ARE YOU IN THERE BETTY JEAN?" Then she added a dramatic aside to the old man. "I wouldn't stay here another second if I were you."

Patients cast jittery looks back and forth. The old man slowly rose to his feet, then tottered toward the door and away. A couple cast wary glances at each other, gathered up their jackets and beat a retreat.

Bear watched the exodus then turned back to a gaping Suzie. "It appears that Dr. Flannery may have an opening now."

As Bear spoke, a stressed looking man in a white coat appeared in the archway to the inner sanctum. If his male pattern baldness were any more pronounced he would have looked like a slender Friar Tuck. "What on earth is going on out here, Suzie?"

"This ... this ... *officer* insists on seeing you," the receptionist huffed then pointed at Lily. "And *she's* frightened poor Mr. Vesuvi away."

"*You're* a cop?" the doctor asked, eying Bear up and down no doubt thinking the old fart looked well past his use-by date.

"I'm working on a missing person case involving several women who are your patients."

Dr. Flannery paled. "My patients? Missing? You better come into my office."

Bear turned, winked at Lily, and followed the doctor. Lily shot a sweet smile at Receptionist Suzie who glowered before beginning a double time tap dance on the long suffering keyboard. Lily wondered if surgery had given her those puffy lips or if she had really been stung by bees.

While she waited for Bear, Lily rolled over to the brochure rack and looked at the selection. Somewhat to her surprise, she actually found a flyer among the clutter that intrigued her. It was about prosthetic devises suitable for seniors.

Back when her leg had been amputated, a prosthetic had not been an option. She was too weak then, too prone to infection. But she was doing better now. Might a prosthetic work for her? Was it possible she could walk again? She took the brochure and folded it into the tote bag that hung from the handle of her wheelchair, a bag that was imprinted *Senior: Give me my damn discount.*

✦ ✦ ✦

Bear shushed Lily while he pushed her out of the office and through the building's front entrance. Sam was waiting for them. As soon as the cowboy loaded them into the cab of his truck, with their wheelchair and quad cane in its bed, he and Lily asked in unison, "How'd it go?"

"As you'd expect, the good doctor claimed all sorts of client-doctor privilege."

"Didn't he ask for your ID?" Sam asked.

"Not at first." His eyes had that mischievous sparkle that meant he was pretty pleased with himself.

"Probably he thought Receptionist Suzie had already checked it," Lily said. She was sandwiched between the two men as the truck bounced along. It felt kind of safe sitting between two big guys even if they were both over the hill and coming down fast.

"Or he was too upset about his missing patients to think about it. He seemed really concerned when I told him what was happening." Bear cracked open the window for a gulp of fresh air and breathed heavily for a few moments before continuing. "He had a nurse pull their files. Wouldn't let me look for myself, but he read through them. Then he said the women all maintained good records for check-ups and were healthier than most. Wished all his patients took such good care of themselves."

"Did he tell you if they shared any symptoms?" Lily asked.

"When I started asking for specifics, he got tight lipped. That's when he finally asked me if I was county or city law enforcement. I had to admit I'm private."

"What happened then?"

Bear chuckled. "It's a damn site easier getting thrown out of a doctor's office than working your way into one."

"Did you learn anything helpful?"

"Could be, could be. We're just getting started."

"Where to next?" Sam asked as he stopped at a red light.

"Home, Sam. We need to hit the senior centers, but Lily looks tired."

"I'm not t ..." Lily then noticed how Bear was rubbing his knee. "Yes, yes, I am tired, Sam. We'll save the senior centers for another day."

✦ ✦ ✦

That afternoon, Jessica and Rick lugged provisions from Costco into the kitchen. "A bale of toilet paper has the same dimensions as a bale of hay," she commented, holding the back door open for Rick with her butt. Her sightline was completely blocked by the immense white bundle in her arms so she didn't see Aurora and Frankie huddled over a huge cooking pot on the commercial-sized stainless stove. Folly and Furball both appeared from sources unknown to check what might have been purchased for them.

"And these could be weights," said Rick, doing curls with the jugs of orange, tomato and apple juice. His Alutiiq blood gave him bronze skin, dark eyes and shiny black hair, but his height came from some other source altogether. Maybe an Amazon passing through the Kodiak wilds, Jessica thought until her nose demanded her attention elsewhere. Taking in a deep breath of garlic, butter and herbs, she nearly moaned. "What smells so good?"

"Quiet, please," Aurora snapped. "We're working here."

"Sorry," Jessica said, winking at Rick. "We'll keep it down." They continued to unload in silence like downstairs servants in the presence of upstairs royalty. Everyone knew Aurora preferred the kitchen to herself. The only resident actually welcome was the suave octogenarian, Frankie Sapienza. The two of them bent together over their caldron in serious concentration. Then Jessica remembered.

Tonight's Sicilian Night. Yay!

Sicilian Night was a monthly extravaganza at Latin's Ranch. Everybody loved it. It had started when the old charmer smooth-talked his way into the formidable Latina's domain. Jessica had actually heard him whisper, "You are a Mexican blossom, but you cook like an Italian dream."

I wonder how Eunice would react if she heard that line of Italian blarney.

Jessica wanted to say as much to Rick, but she bit her tongue. She didn't like the staff to gossip, so it limited her fun, too.

Frankie had told Aurora of his bygone life under the sensual Mediterranean sun and described the tantalizing foods of his mother and his mother's mother. With mesmerizing tones and a deft hand, he'd urged her toward masterpieces from his island in the sea. The results were magnificent and became a regular celebration at Latin's Ranch.

Jessica took a peek at the menu board she had mounted on a wall in the dining room. Tonight's fare included plump twists of handmade fusilli baked with baby eggplant and sweet roasted peppers served with lemon garlic encrusted cod.

OMG.

That evening, Aurora bemoaned that she could not procure the fresh mackerel or bluefish of the Atlantic here in the Pacific Northwest. Nonetheless, everyone agreed the meal was luscious. As always, the five residents feasted with Jessica, Aurora and whichever aide was on duty. Tonight it was Chrissie. Jessica had invited Sam and Ben, but Ben couldn't make it. Those who could handle wine toasted with a full-bodied Chianti, while the others raised stemmed glasses of San Pellegrino mineral water.

"*Buon appetito*," Frankie proclaimed to the table at large, then added a bow toward Aurora, "*Bene*." Turning to Eunice, he added, "*Mangia*, my little dove." It tickled Jessica that Frankie kept his options open.

The group dressed in their finery for Sicilian nights so old gems and ruffles, ties and suits got a good airing. They laughed and argued and told tall tales like any big family. It was Charlie who made the mistake of asking, "Where's Ben tonight, Jessica?"

"He's missing some fine eats," Bear said, nodding his appreciation to Aurora.

"*Povero!* To miss such a bella meal ... such a bella woman." The Sicilian patted Jessica's hand.

"He's driving back from a Bellingham rehab center with Rachael in tow. She's been released again." Jessica took a sip of her wine and sulked. Once again, she was taking a back seat to Ben's ungrateful, uncooperative, unrelenting problem of a daughter.

"Oh dear. How is she this time?" Lily asked.

"Ben says she looks fragile but is nasty as a wolverine in a live trap. I invited him to bring her along. But he wouldn't." She felt her lower lip tremble the slightest bit at his absence.

But why? I don't want her here. Not really. She'd just turn a lovely evening sour for everyone.

"I guess that's what life is for an addict. A live trap," Lily observed.

Jessica nodded and tried to be kind. "I'm sure you're right."

I'd feel sorrier for Rachael if I wasn't busy feeling sorry for myself.

"Makes it lonely for you," Charlie observed. "And believe me, I know all about lonely."

"Oh, but how could I be lonely surrounded by all you guys?" Jessica managed a smile that sparkled more than the San Pellegrino. But she knew Lily's bullshit detector was the very top of the line. She didn't make eye contact with her old friend again until long after Chrissie helped Aurora remove the dessert cups left from the berries with zabaglione cream.

✦ ✦ ✦

Reggie's Tavern was a dog-eared watering hole known mostly to locals, except once when a movie crew was in town. That's why the wall décor included three signed photos of has-been actors amidst the antique timber tools. Logging must have been the original theme long before anyone remembered, at least judging by the hand hewn booths, and the split rail bar and tabletops. The bar was tended by another fixture named Dead Eye. He had one glass eye that always stared at you, regardless of where his real one was looking.

Will Haverstock found it spooky that Dead Eye always seemed to know when his customers needed refills or another slider. He was pleased to see Rick Peters come in. It came as a surprise when someone that cool seemed to like him. Rick took a chair at his table, one that still had most of the stuffing in its seat, then called to Dead Eye for a beer and a bag of spicy peanuts. Reggie's wasn't the type of place for free bowls of pretzels or mixed nuts.

Rick went to the bar to grab his order, then rejoined Will. While they drank, they talked about spring training and cars and women, but Will could only talk about women for just so long before his lack of knowledge became painfully obvious. He moved the conversation on to their jobs. He knew Rick had worked at a nursing home for a while and was glad to hear he was now at an adult care home. Rick called it Latin's Ranch.

"You must get along with old people, too," Will said, "to work with them and all."

"Yeah, but the ones I work with are still alive. I took the nursing home job because it was the only one I could get at the time I came down from Alaska. I mostly thought all those old fossils smelled bad. But I made some friends and found out they know a lot of shit I don't."

"Exactly," Will said, thrilled to have found a fellow enthusiast of such an exotic species as the senior citizen. His thought was interrupted when the door burst open and Sam came in, followed by Bear *kachunking* along on his quad cane. "It's not built for fucking wheelies you know," Sam was saying, clearly miffed.

"Yeah, yeah, but I wanted to floor it."

"It's not a stock car. It's just a golf cart." Sam doffed his hat at Doc McGrath, the veterinarian, who was flying high on his usual barstool. They crossed the room when Rick howdied them to the empty chairs at Will's table. After introductions were made and beer was served, Rick continued on the subject of nursing homes.

"Funny stuff happens all the time, for sure. Even weird sometimes," Rick said. "Like this cat at the nursing home that could detect who was going to kick the bucket next. He'd come curl up in bed with them until they died."

"How the hell did it know?" Will asked.

"It never told me," Rick said with a grin.

Bear knew Rick was talking about Furball. "Now that it's moved to Latin's Ranch, I don't want it in my room," he said.

"It can stay away from the barn, too," Sam added.

"Well, we get weird shit, too," Will said, not wanting to be left out. "Rick already knows I'm the embalmer at Chesterton's, right?"

"Yep. And I have to say, man, that sure as shit *is* weird."

"Not what I mean. What's weird is this. I work late sometimes. It's really quiet, you know? I mean it's just me and the dead people. But suddenly I hear the crematory oven starting up."

"What's weird about that? Don't you crisp corpses all the time?" Rick asked.

"Not when there're no bodies in the house with cremation orders. And not when nobody should be in the place to stoke up the oven. And it's happened more than once."

Rick, Sam and Bear stared at each other, then back at Will. Rick finally agreed. "That is pretty fucking weird."

Bear asked, "Have you ever gone to take a look?"

"Once. But nobody was there when I got there. Nobody living. I asked the boss about it the next day, and he said he'd look into it."

Will regretted bringing it up. He was running off at the mouth just to impress other men. He shook his head. "I shouldn't have mentioned it. I'm sure there's an explanation. Not my business what the other employees are doing. Or the boss either."

"But maybe it's not your boss that ..."

"Hi, guys," said a babe approaching the table with another girl following slightly behind. Will recognized the heart stopper as Rick's girl friend, Alita. The other one was tall with long straight hair. She slouched as if she were self conscious and wanted to fold in on herself. Next to Alita, she was like a little planet overshadowed by the sun. But when she cast a shy smile at Will, he suddenly took a renewed interest in astronomy.

He almost forgot he should never have mentioned the crematory and took a quick glance around to see who else might have overheard. The only one looking back was Dead Eye's one eye. And these guys right here at the table.

CHAPTER NINE

Case Notes
March 22, 3 p.m.
I'm having man trouble.
Chrissie met a guy named Will last night while she was out with Alita. She's totally forgotten how to do her job today. Blonde jokes would come to mind if she didn't have such dark hair. Chrissie's been lonely since that moron Mark walked out on her and the kids, so it's nice she met someone new. But she's so over the moon that she got the shower water too hot, the tea too cold, and nearly upset a bedpan.
"Chrissie," Eunice said to her. "We'll have to call this guy and ask him to return your brain."
Jessica's man Ben is giving me fits, too. He has to see that he's enabling his daughter, not helping her. I know he loves her, but she is an adult. It's up to Rachael to turn her own life around. Ben needs to take time for Jessica. Of course, it's not like Jess has an abundance of time to give either. Which is just the least bit my fault. She made big changes to take in my cohorts and me.
What if Jessica decides to close this place and take back her hours? That surely can't happen. I need to give it a serious think or two and come up with a plan that will work well for all parties. In the meantime, it's distracting me from the other man in trouble ... Charlie and his missing wife.
Just to catch up, yesterday Sam drove Bear and me to the three different senior centers where Catherine Blakely, Karen Oostrom and

Candi Kenilworth have been regulars. The fact that they all visit centers is one of the commonalities on our list.

They seemed like nice places. Friendly. Getting people to talk was easier than it was at It's Swell to be Well. Everybody we met was eager to help when they found out why we were there. These missing women are their friends. Well, maybe not Louise. There was some hinting about her being a man eater.

Bear gathered leads but nothing electrifying stood out. He got the names of men the women had dated and entertainment that had appeared at all three centers. Hard to imagine that one hunka hunka conned them all or that the Olde Tyme Tenors use senior centers to do their window shopping. But anything can be important, according to Bear, and I'm to write it down without any more lip. A fat one of which he's likely to get if he doesn't watch it with the attitude.

By the time we visited the second center, I discovered something all on my own. Maybe a real clue! As assistants go, I'm hot stuff.

- Lily Gilbert, Sharp-eyed Assistant to PI Bear Jacobs

"Look," Lily said, pointing a gnarled finger toward the wooden brochure rack. It hung on the wall just inside the front door of the second senior center they visited. The rack was orderly but loaded with brochures in tasteful, neutral tones, each about some senior affliction or requirement. The covers all had photos of oldsters with grins the size of comedy masks. From this, Lily presumed the portrayed patients were now affliction-free having consulted the brochures. All except one brochure fit the mold, and it had a different look altogether. "That's the third time I've seen it. I wonder what it is."

Bear sighted along her bony finger. "You mean the brochure on Kuykendall medical equipment rental?"

"No ... above it and over."

Bear began reading titles out loud. "*Wellbeing in Retirement* from Ludington Financial Services ... *Choosing a Care Center* from Driscoll Manor ... *End of Life Services* from Chesterton Funeral Parlor ..."

"Hey, isn't that where Louise Barker arranged services for Charlie? I'm sure it's the name that Candi Kenilworth used."

Bear gave Lily a hooded look. "I met someone who works there. Rick's friend. Will Haverstock, the embalmer."

Lily recognized the name as the guy who had invaded Chrissie's brain. "A new friend of Chrissie, too."

"They met when we were at Reggie's Tavern. Haverstock was talking about something going on at night. Something in the crematory. Wonder what he heard."

"Yeah. But first, keep going down the rack. The bright yellow brochure with the photo of the happy crowd. Grab that one."

"What's the big deal about that?"

"Well, look at it. All the people in that photo are young. Youngish, anyway. What's it doing here in Geezerlandia?"

"I don't know ... maybe a plastic surgeon?" He plucked a couple of copies with a massive paw and gave one to Lily, frowning at the other himself. He held it out at arm's length and stared at it.

"You need glasses," Lily muttered.

"You need to mind your own business," he muttered back, bringing the brochure closer to his nose. If he squinted, he could see it. The cover photo showed middle agers waving from the deck of a cruise ship. "Carefree Occasions," he read aloud from the cover.

Lily said, "I saw it at It's Swell to be Well and at the last senior center and now here."

Bear *kachunked* along on his quad cane and sat heavily on a sofa in the senior center lobby. He huffed a large sigh of relief. Lily knew this much walking and standing wore him down.

Bear spread the brochure open on a coffee table and ran his finger down the inside introduction, scanning the text. "Basically it says here that caregiving is exhausting mentally, physically and spiritually. Caregivers need to take care of themselves, too, if they hope to be any real help to their loved ones."

Lily had jumped ahead to the next section. "Carefree Occasions specializes in events and travel for anyone who's recently provided home care or placed a loved one in long term care or suffered bereavement." She looked up at Bear. "Kind of like group therapy with a view of the pool. There's a specialty tour for everyone, I guess."

Bear wrinkled his nose not unlike a grizzly sniffing the air for fresh scent. "Lily, we missed something on our list of similarities."

"We did?"

"Yep. Think about it. All the missing women had recently been called on to be caregivers. Sheila Blakely told us her mother Catherine had cared for her own mother until she died six months ago. Karen Oostrom took care of her husband at home until he needed hospice care."

"And Charlie's wife put him in long term care," Lily added, excitement adding a blush to her cheeks. Then she drooped. "But what about Candi Kenilworth? She didn't mention taking care of anybody when I talked with her."

"No, but she was concerned with Charlie's wife, helping her get along. Weren't they planning a trip together?"

"Yes! In the fall." Her eyes opened wider. "Wonder if it was a Carefree Occasions trip. Louise could have gotten them both involved." She flipped the brochure closed and looked at the back cover. It was an application for a home consultation.

"Wonder if this brochure was found in any of their houses. I think it's time to give Keegan a call. But first ..." Bear slapped around his body and this time located the Samsung in his pants pocket. He placed a call to Lia, the receptionist at Soundside nursing home where the gang had been housed before Latin's Ranch. After exchanging greetings, he asked Lia if they had the Carefree Occasions information in their brochure rack.

When he hung up, he nodded at Lily. "Lia says it's been popular with families of their residents. They received the first batch of brochures about three months ago."

✦ ✦ ✦

The late night phone call upset Bear enough that he couldn't sleep. He was in bed in the dark wishing he still smoked. It used to calm his nerves, help him focus. Maybe he should get up and climb the hill to Sam's place. See if the cowboy had any cigars.

"Damn it to hell," Bear growled into the dark room. The news from Keegan had distressed him. Now a man had gone missing.

He repeated the expletives loud enough to awaken even a deafening buzz saw like his roommate. Charlie snorted then stammered, "Wha ... what?" from his hospital bed on the other side of the room.

"Now a man. Old guy named Bronek Pokorski. Gone missing."

"Bron ... Poski ... missing?" Charlie sounded like an engine sputtering back to life.

"Shoots the shit out of my theory that old women are being abducted for sex reasons," Bear moped.

"You mean old *men* are being abducted for sex reasons?" Now Charlie was fully awake and sounded horrified.

"No, no. I mean probably not. This doesn't seem to have anything to do with sex."

"Well, okay. That's good then."

"No, Charlie. That's not good. That's not good at all. A lot more people may be in danger than I thought."

"You think we should all be scared?"

"I think I have more thinking to do." Bear rolled over. "Go back to sleep, Charlie."

But he could tell Charlie was lying awake, too. The saw mill didn't start back up again that night.

✦ ✦ ✦

The next morning, Bear stayed in bed late. Over a breakfast of crushed strawberries on waffles, Charlie told the others what Bear had said about men under attack. It put a pall over the morning.

Lily was tired, too, so she lay back down after breakfast. No, she was exhausted, she admitted to herself. Yesterday's tour of senior centers had drained her as much as it had Bear. Not that she would confess it to Jessica or anyone else who might say that she was doing too much. Only Chrissie seemed to really understand.

"You haven't been this active in a very long time," Chrissie said as she gathered the gauze, creams and bandages she needed to wrap Lily's leg after she cleaned it. Next, she removed the used compression bandage, fleece and gauze wrap. "You're loving it, aren't you?"

"I'm feeling useful again," Lily admitted. "And, yes, I love that."

"But you know the risks." Chrissie washed the leg with soap and water, scrubbing gently with her palm.

"Of course." Lily knew the next bad infection would likely kill her. Or, worse, strip her bit by bit. The other leg? Her hands? Eye sight? It was all possible. With diabetes complicated by neuropathy, Lily wouldn't feel an infection in her leg until it was far too late to save it. It took an eagle-eyed aide, watching all the time.

"Then I'm sure you will be careful," Chrissie said as she examined Lily's leg for flakes of skin, particles of plaque or minor lesions. Finding it free of these signs of infection, she rubbed it with safflower oil, then pulled a soft, thin stockinet over it.

Chrissie's trust in her made Lily feel a little guilty. Chrissie never treated her like an untrustworthy old person, even though she was more than capable of stretching the truth. She changed the subject. "Has he called yet?"

Chrissie's eyebrows lifted in an 'oh well' gesture along with a sigh. "Not yet. Probably won't. I don't want to get my hopes up." She wrapped a fleece strip around the leg from the toes up, smoothing it each step of the way since a wrinkle in the fabric could cause a break in Lily's delicate skin.

"You could call him. I hear that's what women do these days."

"Oh, no. I could never." Over the fleece, she wrapped a compression bandage, also from the toes up to move fluids out of the leg. It would help keep the leg from swelling.

"Well, he's a fool if he doesn't recognize a wonderful woman when he sees one," Lily said.

"I'd like him to call. But it's better if he doesn't." Chrissie stood straight and stretched, the legging wrapping complete for now. She did it every other day.

"Why on earth?"

"Because I'll probably fall for him, and then I'll let my kids meet him, and then they'll like him, and then he'll dump me like the other jerks I've chosen, and I'll have two little broken hearts to deal with. Along with my own. Easier not to get started with it at all."

Lily wanted to say there, there, look on the bright side, nothing ventured nothing gained. But Chrissie made a lot of sense. What young man wouldn't be afraid of a readymade family? "Chrissie, you are a whiz at your job. You are my one and only Wrapper Chick. You'll always be everybody's first choice for care, so you will always be in demand. Your kids will have you to rely on. Maybe you're meant to be like me."

"What do you mean?" Chrissie asked, placing her supplies on a shelf for the next time.

"After my husband died, I never found a replacement that looked good to me. As long as I had a man for the occasional short term relationship, I didn't need another long termer. I'm too independent for that."

Chrissie sighed again. "Well, the truth is I'd like a traditional family. But God knows I make poor choices in the man department. I thought my husband would be so different from my father, but it turned they were just alike. The next guy, same thing. Proof that I can't recognize the pick of the litter. So I'm done with trying – "

A loud bird chirp cut her short. She removed a latex glove and pulled the cell phone from her scrub pocket to look at caller ID. With a joyful yelp and a twirl out the door, Chrissie said, "It's him!" She sounded sixteen. Lily noticed that when she put her shoulders back like that, she even had a bust to go with that blissful new mood.

After Chrissie left, Lily decided to work on the problem of Jessica's free time. The idea came to her over a second cup of tea while morning sun splashed through her patio door. Furball ambled in to sit in the spotlight and give himself a thorough washing.

"Thoroughly disgusting," Lily said as he raised a hind leg skyward.

She outlined her thoughts on her laptop, making notes and revisions. Eunice came into the room and sat on her own bed. She pulled a little leather case from her nightstand. It looked like a manicure kit from the outside, but Lily knew it was full of tiny chain links, earring backings, tweezers, magnifiers, even needle nose pliers. With as much jewelry as Eunice owned, she was often in the repair business. At the moment, she was rebeading a bracelet with multiple strands.

By late morning, Lily talked Project Jessica over with Eunice, then they headed out to drive Sitting Bull to the barn. They explained the Project to Sam while he cleaned stalls, and he agreed with nothing more chatty than a nod. Lily then sent Eunice to discuss it with Frankie, who doted on his little dove. Just before lunch, Eunice gave Lily a thumbs up and a smile as bright as a shiny new dime. Finally, Lily placed a call to her daughter Sylvia.

CHAPTER TEN

Case Notes
March 23, 4 p.m.
My daughter Sylvia is in her forties, but she still surprises me occasionally. Just about the time I think she's as rooted in place as an oak tree, she up and accepts a new idea. "Mom, that's perfect. Let me see what I can come up with." Sylvia has money in Latin's Ranch, and of course she has me in here, too. So it's in her best interest to be sure Jessica keeps it open. With Sylvia on the case, Project Jessica is halfway home. Which clears my time for the case of Charlie's missing wife. This damn thing is like The Blob, getting bigger and bigger. Now Charlie's wife, three other women and at least one man have been sucked up into nothingness. A man, wouldn't you just know. Appears that we were wrong about sexual perversion.
Bear has 'bearicaded' himself in his room. I can hear him in there. First time I heard that throaty rumble, I thought it was a '68 Corvette or distant artillery fire. Now I know that's just Bear humming when he thinks. It can be contagious. Because of him, I've caught myself all day belting out, "I can't believe it's true that I am losing you." Which I guess is appropriate enough since there's no reason to assume the disappearances have stopped.
Bear better come up with a new theory soon. Or we'll all be humming "Who's Sorry Now?"

- Lily Gilbert, Musical Assistant to PI Bear Jacobs

Sylvia Henderson sat up even straighter, stretched her back and reviewed the final drawing on her monitor. It was her interior design for the lobby of a new pediatrician's office. She smiled in delight at her work. "Perfect!" she said.

Overall minimalist lines with child-pleasing brightness but nothing too splashy for moms and dads. A strong pure blue with accents of yellow in the fabrics, walls painted a fresh blue white, and the furniture in warm honey-toned wood. The big splashes of color on the walls were the limited edition prints of children by Bob Byerley.

"Well, yes, they are a bit sentimental now that you mention it, but if you can't do sweet in a baby doctor's office, where can you do it?" Sylvia was speaking to the desk photo of her husband Kyle. She'd chatted with it ever since his death. It was a comfort, as though they still shared an office, her space as Henderson Interiors and his with his real estate business, now as defunct as he was.

With her design complete, Sylvia had time for Lily's request. She couldn't be happier with her mother's improved health and outlook since moving to Latin's Ranch. She'd been so miserable at the nursing home before this.

"Miserable for me, too," Sylvia said to the handsome man in the photograph. "You remember those awful days."

Finding top notch caregivers for her mother had been a thankless chore even before the first nursing home was necessary. Lily had wanted no part of strangers invading her house, fighting it like a feral cat. She'd fired people nearly as fast as Sylvia hired them. Somehow the miracle that was Jessica Winslow had slipped beneath Lily's skin long enough to become indispensible to the old warrior.

Jessica had stayed close when Lily was finally forced into the nursing home by rampaging infection. The idea for Latin's Ranch had somehow grown like a healthy garden from those unpromising beginnings.

This time finding a caregiver should be a piece of cake because this time Lily wanted her help. Apparently they all did. Sylvia placed a call to Clarice, the Latin's Ranch bookkeeper, to ask her advice. "It's just two days a week, six hours each, maybe 11 to 5," Sylvia said. "Weekends would be preferable, I suppose, but we'll take the best person we can get and work out the days after that."

"I'll make a few calls. I still have contacts at Soundside," Clarice answered.

With the personnel search underway, Sylvia moved on to the second piece of the puzzle. "I know, dear," she said to the photo of Kyle. "Location, location, location."

✦ ✦ ✦

Bear liked puzzles. Like the one about the crematory chamber ablaze in the wee hours. What the hell was that about? Had the mortician decided it was a cheaper way to dispose of trash than garbage pick-up? Was an employee freelancing on the side? Maybe selling disposal to a veterinarian at a cheaper rate than taking animal bodies to a pet cemetery?

Bear tapped out a rhythm on his belly keeping beat as hummed, "We're Having a Heat Wave." He pushed himself back in the recliner that Jessica had found for his room, a recliner now butt sprung for his particular posterior. Could he connect the dots between a crematory at night and a bevy of missing seniors? Certainly a place burning too many dead bodies was just as whacked as a community missing too many living bodies. But he didn't know enough to make the dots create a visible picture. He needed to gather a lot more information. It was time to act.

He knew he should call Cupcake. But he had no proof of anything, and she'd get all fussy about little things like search warrants. As a retired PI, Bear didn't concern himself with such bothersome items. He charted his course. It would be dangerous. It would take manipulation and stealth and perilous risk.

He smiled. He called out for his aide, Rick. PI Bear Jacobs was back in business.

✦ ✦ ✦

Candi Kenilworth squinted at the elegant old man across from her. Together, she and Bronek Pokorski were trying to figure out what had happened. Her head still ached but she was finally able to sit upright on the straight back chair without an attack of nausea. He sat on one of the narrow beds in front of her. They leaned toward each other and spoke softly as if conversation might be breaking some unknown rule.

"I'm frightened, Mr. Pokorski." She clasped her hands to limit their trembling. Tears clouded her vision, spilling over onto her cheeks.

"Yes. Me, too. Please call me Bron, dear lady." His husky voice was thick with the accent from his native land. He was handsome although the years had left their wounds. Candi was attracted to his formal manner, detecting a chivalry she thought went extinct about the same time as the dodo bird. His posture was as straight as an old soldier, and he looked as though outdoor living might account for ruddy good health. If she wasn't so terrified, she might have flirted.

"I'm Candi," she said, her voice quivering. "Where are we?"

"I was here a few hours before you arrived, at least I think. I was unconscious, too, and there's no clock." The room they were in was bare of anything but beds, nightstand and the chair. "I pounded on the door, and I yelled for a long time, but nobody came."

"But, but how did we get here?" Candi asked. "I remember being in my house ... and going to my door and ... letting in a salesman." The memory was faint, as though projected on a gauze curtain.

"Same here," Bron said, nodding. His hands seemed incapable of stillness. One rubbed the nubbly blanket while the other wrapped around the metal bed frame. "I had an appointment, and the guy was right on time. Looked fine to me so I let him in."

Candi caught her breath. "You mean you contacted Carefree Occasions, too?"

"Yes! That's it. That's the name." His eyes snapped with excitement. "So that's the connection. How we both got here. I'd filled out an application on the back of a brochure asking for a visit. My wife died, you see.

She was sick so long with the cancer. I needed a little fun, so I sent in the information that they requested."

"It was something like that for me, too, Bron. My friend's husband is in a nursing home. She asked me to take this Carefree Occasions trip with her, a single seniors tour of New England. I filled out their form, too. Lots of questions. Almost like a dating service."

"So that's how they knew. They knew we lived alone from those applications. They knew a lot about us because we told them."

"My friend Louise disappeared, too." Candi felt tears form but wasn't sure if it was her fear or her humiliation. "I thought I was too smart to fall for scams on seniors. I'm always careful. But I walked right into this black hole."

A noise outside the door hushed them. Bron stood. He grabbed her hand and pulled her up. They were standing against the opposite wall when the double locks in the door clicked. Bron still held her hand. The door slowly opened, and their assailants entered the room.

The first man was so flabby around the gut that the scrubs he wore stretched tight at the seams. His size blocked their view of the second man's face.

Bron pushed forward and stepped in front of Candi. "Who are you?" He spit the words through clenched teeth, but the fat man didn't answer. Then the second man circled around him like a Chevy Volt passing an eighteen wheeler. It was Luke Carmichael, the nondescript salesman whose mild smile now looked like a gargoyle's leer to Candi. He was holding what she took to be a walkie talkie.

"Such a pleasure to see you two relics again," Luke said.

"What do you want? Let us – "

"For God's sake, shut up, old man," Luke snapped. "Both of you lie back down where you were."

For the first time, Candi noticed the beds weren't twins. They were gurneys.

"Let us go. I have money," Bron said.

Although terrified, Candi was aware the old man was trying to negotiate.

So smart, so brave.

It gave her strength. "I do, too. I'll pay you. And we won't tell a soul what has happened if you let us go now."

"Shut the fuck up. Both of you. On the beds now. I won't ask again." The leer was gone, and the voice was ice.

"*Świnia!*" Bron hissed, launching himself directly at Luke. Candi heard the zap then Bron fell like a rag doll.

Not a walkie talkie. A stun gun.

She leaped forward while Luke was distracted, aiming for the door. The fat man grabbed her arm, wrenching it behind her back but not before she'd seen into the next room. She battled as he marched her to the bed, turned her around and pushed her down. She reached for his face and connected sharp lacquered nails to skin, digging in like cat claws. He yelped, and slapped her so hard her head snapped back. She dropped, the fog returning as she watched the two men grapple Bron onto the other gurney. A nurse entered the room and gave him what Candi thought was a shot.

"Bron," she cried, doing her best to clear the fog and struggle back up.

A woman nurse and a man, both in scrubs. Scrubs. Like the hospital.

That's when Candi realized that the room next door, the one she had seen for only a fraction of a second, was an operating room. She'd recognized bloody linens in a pile and a stack of coolers like the little Igloo she had for picnics.

Ice water raced through her veins. The nurse, face protected behind a mask, turned toward her with another syringe. In that moment, Candi wondered who would care for her prize clematis from now on.

CHAPTER ELEVEN

Case Notes
March 24, 10 a.m.
Bear came out of seclusion, and told me he had a plan. Oh, he didn't want to tell me, but I overheard him shouting to Rick from the shower room this morning. The running water hid the words. Then Rick was sullen getting Eunice and me ready to start the day. He wouldn't tell us a damn thing, just looked worried. So I went to the source, once the source was available for an audience. The second we were alone in the living room I asked, "Bear, what are you up to?"
"What do you mean?" Mr. Innocent.
"You know damn well what I mean. What are you planning?"
"As you might say, madam, none of your bee's wax." He actually seemed to think that would shut me up, but I reminded him just who was keeping all these damn notes for whom, and who should show a little more gratitude, thank you very much. Finally, to shut me up, he spilled the beans.
"I'm going to Chesterton Funeral Parlor tonight. To have a talk with Will Haverstock, the embalmer."
Chrissie's beau? I didn't see that one coming. "Why go see an embalmer? Especially at night?"
"Because that's when he's hearing something happen in the crematory. Something that should not be going on. And I need to find out more since the Chesterton name keeps popping up. I asked Rick to tell Will I'll be dropping by, and Rick isn't real pleased about it. Says

the kid will be there if he asks him to be, but he thinks I'm too feeble to handle the trip on my own."

"What time you going?"

"Late."

"Dangerous?"

"Doubt it."

"Rick taking you?"

"Nope. Jessica would fire him. Right after she killed him."

"I'm coming, too."

"Oh, no you're not. In case it is dangerous. End of subject." He stormed out as fast as a man his size can storm on a quad cane.

"Okay. Anything you say," I called after him in my sweetie pie voice. As if one of his little snits could stop me. As I see it, the trick is to get out of here tonight without anyone telling Jessica. That means fooling the caregiver on duty. Good thing it's Alita. She's lovable as can be and learning all the skills an aide needs to know, but she isn't smart like Chrissie.

We also have to get out without Jessica's dog Folly raising a ruckus. An adventure!

- Lily Gilbert, Sneaky Assistant to PI Bear Jacobs

"Oh, I just love intrigue! Mystery! Suspense!" Eunice clasped her hands with delight when Lily explained her part in fooling the sweet youngster, Alita. "We should be ashamed, I suppose," Eunice added trying to look contrite. That lasted about a second before the glow of excitement was back. "When does the caper commence?"

"Bear won't tell me exactly when he's leaving," Lily said. Then she grinned like a Cheshire cat. "But I know he's meeting the embalmer at midnight."

"How did you find out?" Eunice asked.

"I told Rick that if he didn't tell me the time, I'd show Alita a few of the websites he looks at."

"What?" Eunice's eyes were as round as full moons. "Rick looks at porn?"

"No, I mean, not as far as I know. But he knows that Alita knows I'd never lie."

Eunice momentarily looked like a frownie emoticon with orange spiked hair. "Why, Lily. You threatened Rick. And used his girlfriend."

Lily shrugged. "The kids have to learn to be less trusting."

If Eunice tried to maintain a look of disapproval, she missed by a mile. "So what's the plan?"

"On his own, the only way Bear can get to Chesterton Funeral Parlor is by Sitting Bull. It will take at least a half hour to get there at the golf cart's blinding speed. So he'll leave here around 11:30. I'll be waiting for him."

The plan went off without a hitch. Almost.

Lily and Eunice used their own room to work the scam. One wall had a wide glass door that led to the patio and the pad where Sitting Bull was plugged in at night. Bear and Charlie had a similar exit from their room because these doors satisfied the fire code for alternative exits. Lily thought it was a slam dunk that Bear would be using it.

That night, Alita had the two women ready for bed by 10. She had come to Latin's Ranch as a housekeeper, but had just completed her CNA training course so she currently did a combination of both. "Funny," she chattered as she helped with nighties, put clothes on hangers, checked that the patio door was locked. "Bear went to bed early, too. Charlie always does, but the rest of you are usually night owls. Must have been a big day around here."

"Yes. Big. Oh goodness," Lily managed a massive yawn. "Guess I'll turn out my light right away."

"Not I," said Eunice the Drama Queen. "I shall watch television. An informative program, perhaps, on the Public Broadcasting System. Something regarding the health of the world's oceans or the misinterpretation of biblical prophecy. Alita, my love, would you pull the curtain? We mustn't allow the light to disturb Lily."

Jeez, Alita won't suspect a thing after that Oscar worthy performance.

And she didn't. Alita pulled the colorful curtain that was ceiling mounted between the two beds. Its only purpose was to provide each roomie with a little privacy. As soon as the girl said goodnight and closed the door, Lily sat back up. She transferred to her wheelchair and piled her pillows lengthwise in the bed, covering them with her blanket and quilt. She briefly wondered if that old shtick actually worked. Well, tonight it would just have to, in case Alita checked back. It was up to Eunice to head her off in case she did.

Lily couldn't manage every wardrobe item on her own, especially slacks. With only one leg, it was difficult for her to balance long enough to hop into them. So she didn't bother with it. She left on her nightie and covered it with the warm chenille robe that she had loved for years. Over that, she had a Pendleton plaid throw she wrapped around herself like a shawl. She put on a heavy sock and a rain boot to keep her foot warm, and a scarf for her head. By the time Lily was ready, Eunice had tiptoed over to the patio door.

"Coast is clear," Eunice said, peering through her cupped hands into the darkness. "Got a flashlight?"

"Check."

"The pork chop?"

"Check."

"Pepper spray?"

Pause.

"Pepper spray?" Lily asked.

"Take mine," Eunice said moving to her top dresser drawer, rummaging for a moment, and returning with a small can that looked just like a lipstick tube. "A girl can't be too careful."

"Thanks, Eunice. Now don't go to sleep. You're standing guard."

"How could I possibly snooze while *Tribes of the Upper Sahara* is on the television?" Eunice winked. She opened the door and gave Lily a little push outside. Lily was in her wheelchair with her walker folded over the arm rests. As soon as she was out on the patio, Eunice shut the door and pulled the window curtain. Lily was in the dark.

She listened for night sounds. Light traffic out on the road. The muffled TV. Charlie snoring from the next room. A barred owl. One of the horse's nickering. She fumbled the little Mag-Lite out of her pocket and turned it on. Directly in front of her a pair of wide eyes glowed in the light.

"Yikes!" Lily gasped.

Folly yapped a greeting of his own.

"Oh, Folly! Good boy. It's me, Lily. Look what I have for a good, good doggy." From her other robe pocket, she pulled out the napkin with the pork chop, the one that she had filched at dinner. "That's a good boy."

Folly sniffed at her hand, decided the prize had his name on it, grabbed up the chop and trotted away.

Guess a cocker/dachshund mix doesn't have strong guard dog instincts.

Lily smiled in the dark. Her plan was working. She rolled herself over to Sitting Bull, unfolded her walker and lifted herself out of the wheelchair. Now it was an easy transfer into the golf cart's passenger seat. Once seated, she reached out to fold the walker and swing it onto the floor of the back seat. The activity, and maybe her excitement, made her too warm in the mild evening so Lily slipped the wool throw off her shoulders and settled it over her lap. She removed her scarf, turned off the flashlight, and settled in.

Immediately, a crunching sound made her neck hairs come to attention. She turned her little light back on and aimed it at the back seat. Folly was curled up there, munching on his chop. Lily could not shoo him away, and didn't want to raise her voice to yell at him.

Oh well. Having a dog along can't be much of a problem. Can it?

Lily sat back and waited for Bear.

✦ ✦ ✦

Charlie hit rock star decibels as he snored his way through the night. Tonight, Bear was glad of it. The hacking and sputtering would cover any noise he made slipping out his patio door.

Very quietly he hummed, "Ain't Misbehavin'." The only other sound was the *kachunk* of his quad cane tapping the ground as he moved toward the spot he knew Sitting Bull stood at the ready. Not wanting to turn on a light, he walked like a blind man waving one hand in front of himself as he crossed the patio. Eventually, he felt the cold metal of the golf cart's snout. He unplugged it, circled the front and tried to put his cane on the back floor. Something metallic seemed to be in the way, but he finally was able to find a niche for the cane.

He swung himself into the driver's seat.

Lily said, "I told you I was coming with you."

"WHAT THE – " Bear yelped.

"Shhhhh!"

"— bleeding hell do you think you're up to?" he ended.

"Is something wrong with your hearing? Do you need your ears examined? I said I was coming with you."

Bear loomed over her, way past angry with his assistant. Hoping to intimidate her, he snarled, "Get out of here now."

"You can't make me."

"What are you, twelve? I said get out. This could be dangerous. You could get hurt. I won't be responsible for that."

It was too dark for him to see he'd made her mad. Really mad. But by the tone of her voice, it was obvious she was hissing out the words through clenched teeth. "You responsible for me? You're not responsible for me. The only one responsible for me is me. I do not choose to spend my last days huddling in fear of what's around the corner. I choose to meet it head on. I choose to take my own chances, and I'm as involved with this situation as you are, and don't you dare think you can shove me around, you big brute."

Silence except for an owl, a horse, a muffled TV and Charlie sputtering.

Eventually, Bear calmed his own temper enough to start Sitting Bull, and they swept away, bouncing up the drive toward the road. The cart's electric motor was quiet as it carried them away from the safety of Latin's Ranch.

In truth, Bear had to agree with Lily. You had to know that others were affected by the results of your actions, so you better ask yourself whether you might hurt someone. But you could not back down when your help was needed, or when your sense of self was on the line.

Yes, he had to agree with her. But that didn't mean he had to speak to her.

✦ ✦ ✦

By the time they'd cruised a mile or more, Lily started to cool off. There was almost no other traffic that late so being out on the open road wasn't as scary as she had anticipated. As she felt her anger drain away she even began to enjoy the moonlit drive, although she was glad of the heavy chenille robe over her nightgown. She pulled its faded powder blue collar tighter around her neck and snuggled into its softness. "Bear?" she asked.

No answer.

"Bear?"

No answer.

"You're only mad at me because you care."

He groaned. "Well aren't you just the Pollyanna."

Lily laughed. "At least it got you speaking to me. Besides, it's true. You do care. You worry about me. So I forgive you."

"*You* forgive *me*?" He shook his head. "I give up."

She patted his knee, and he jerked it away. She reached again, and he let her. They motored along, this time in a silence that was almost affable. As they turned from one sleeping street to the next, Bear paying little attention to stop signs or lights, their surroundings morphed from country to town.

On the outskirts, Lily saw Chesterton Funeral Parlor in front of them. It was a huge Victorian looking affair with gingerbread and bays and turrets. There might have been a time when it was surrounded by a wide and gracious lawn, but now it was the odd ball flanked on each side by a strip of modern stores and offices. Still, its slight rise gave it stature over its neighbors.

"Looks like a movie set if the Bates Motel suffered urban development," Bear observed.

"If I see a really sensitive looking young man, I'm out of here."

Bear drove into an alley that circled behind the commercial buildings. A handful of security lights revealed the backs of a small restaurant, real estate office, beauty salon and men's clothing store on one side of the alley. The other side was crammed with short driveways and single car garages behind boxy little houses. Sitting Bull passed trash and recycling bins, a pile of bald tires, alley cats on the prowl, fences and overgrown hedges that defined tiny backyards.

"Is that a kid peeing?" Bear asked, pointing to a child just visible in the glow of a yard light.

Lily squinted at it. "No, it's a statue peeing. Never could figure why people like those cherubs."

The funeral home was just past a clothing store on their left. Directly behind it was a wide cement pad with enough parking spaces for half a dozen vehicles, tucked up against a double garage door. The structure was attached to the funeral parlor but appeared to be newer in construction, without the Victorian frills.

A hearse and a somber town car occupied two of the parking spaces, each so large it overlapped the painted lines. Next to those two barges, a bilious green Hyundai looked like a kiddy car. "Will is meeting us here. The green slimeball must be his," Bear said. "I see the garage door is already open."

He drove Sitting Bull up to the opening and stopped. They both squinted ahead, but even in Sitting Bull's headlights, they could only see vague shapes. The interior space was poorly lit and dim this late at night.

"Is this where ambulances unload the bodies?" Lily asked, hoping there wasn't a backlog.

"I imagine they don't just heave them out on the front sidewalk."

She let his snarky remark pass. Either he was still irritated with her or edgy about the million things that could go wrong. She held the face of her watch toward the weak light leaking from the garage. "It's midnight now."

As if on cue, a young man appeared from the garage shadows and moved into the dim light. He waved them into the murky cavern where a single overhead florescent fixture hummed, doing its best to light the entire space, a cross between a garage bay and a storage area. Once Bear drove Sitting Bull inside, Lily thought how very much it felt like a trap. She shivered.

"You scared?" Bear asked.

"Oh, no. Just a little chilly." Planning to break and enter was one thing. Doing it, well, that was turning out to be quite another. Lily's sense of adventure was often in overdrive, but it always included the word *sense*. This was crazy. But she'd never tell Bear that.

As her eyes adjusted, Lily could see the outline of a second person in front of them. But Bear had only mentioned one. Sitting Bull drew nearer. The silhouette became clearer.

Is that a woman? Why it's ...

"Chrissie?"

"Lily?" the aide replied sounding just as surprised as Lily.

"Chrissie, why are you here?" Lily asked.

"Because when I'm not with you guys, I'm with Will. And he told me Bear would be here tonight."

"I wouldn't have trusted Bear if Rick and Chrissie hadn't told me I should," Will said. "Chrissie knows a good person when she sees one."

Lily evaluated Will, the embalmer with a slightly crooked nose and the hint of a limp. Kind eyes, a shy smile, unruly hair.

I've met a sensitive looking young man after all.

She wondered if he'd heard as much about her in the past couple days as she had about him.

"Quick, come inside," Will said, keeping his voice low. "I think someone else is here. We just heard a noise coming from the crematory. It's supposed to be empty at night."

"'Quick' is no longer one of my gaits, young man." Lily said, starting to lift herself out of Sitting Bull.

"And that's exactly why we need you to stay here, Lily," Bear said as he dismounted the golf cart. "I'm slow enough. You can help most by turning this beast around, getting it ready to leave."

Lily wanted to give him a fight but stopped herself. This was serious. They were breaking the law. Bear was right. She would slow them down. One leg.

Dammit all to hell.

"Fair enough," she said. Using her considerable arm strength she pulled herself over to the driver's seat. "I'll be here to drive the getaway golf cart. And I'll raise the roof if anyone else shows up."

Bear ducked his head in what might have been a bow to her. They both were wise enough to know the truth about their physical conditions. Sad but true, time is a thief. He reached in the back for his cane.

Folly, no doubt tickled to see his ol' pal Bear, yapped a hello.

"Holy crap!" Bear snorted.

"Shhhhhhhh! Quiet," Will said, voice taut as a high tension wire. "Whoever's inside will hear us." He stared at the door from the garage into the interior of the funeral home.

"Oh, dear," Lily confessed. "I forgot Folly was still in the back seat."

Outside, two alley cats began a vociferous love tryst. Folly's little head whipped around, his long nose quivered, and suddenly he shot out of the cart and away on his short doxy legs.

"Oh, no! We have to catch him. We can't lose Jessica's dog!" Lily felt a flash of panic even scarier than this spooky garage.

It was Chrissie the Caregiver to the rescue. "Don't worry, Miss Lily. I'll get him." She took off like a filly out of a starting gate, galloping after the cockadock and down the alley.

"Okay, Will, let's go," Bear said. "We need to move ahead. Lily, keep your eyes open."

"But Chrissie," Will started to protest.

"Moving at that speed, she'll be fine. Gets her out of harm's way."

That seemed to calm the embalmer. "You're right, Mr. Bear." Will opened the door to the interior.

Looking over Will's shoulder, Bear could see a wall of refrigerator units dead ahead. It pulled him up short, this room where all the clients were dead. His nose wrinkled from the reek of chemicals, and his eyes narrowed at all the evil-looking metallic implements.

Jesus. What a place.

"This is where I work most of the time," Will said, moving forward into the workspace with the pride of a tour guide. "The crematory is down the hall, through that archway. Stairs there go up to the viewing rooms above us." He pointed to the far side of the cool, antiseptic room.

Before Bear *kachunked* into the room, another noise stopped him. It sounded like footsteps coming down that hallway, moving fast. A man in a dark cardigan burst into the room as Bear shrank back into the darkness of the garage.

"Will," he heard an angry voice snap at the embalmer. "What the hell is going on in here?"

"Ah ... ah ... Nothing, Mr. Chesterton. I mean I was working late, but I'm – "

"I was upstairs in the office, and I heard a woman yelling. Something about folly."

"Oh that. I'm sorry. I was listening to my TV."

Bear, still hidden in the dark, thought way to go, kid. He wouldn't have guessed that Will had it in him.

"Definitely a woman yelling. And a dog barking." Chesterton sniped.

"Ah, it's a mystery movie, lots of action --"

Bear pushed himself against the garage wall behind the door just as Orlo Chesterton blew through it, staring straight ahead.

"See? See? Goddamn it, Will, the garage door is wide open!"

"I must have forgotten to close it when I came in, Mr. Chesterton. I'm sorry."

Will limped behind the funeral director as Orlo Chesterton went to the alley and peered both ways into the dark. Bear hoped Chrissie wasn't right outside with a dog too friendly to be any protection. Apparently she wasn't, because Chesterton spun back around. That's when he noticed Sitting Bull.

Bear worried about Lily, but trusted her to baffle 'em with bullshit. He made his move while Chesterton was diverted. The big man crept into the embalming room, across the white tile floor and toward the hall that led to the crematory. He could no longer see the garage, but he could hear Chesterton sputtering above his own heavy breathing. Bear wasn't much better at sprinting than Lily, and rushing offended his knees.

"What the hell is this, Will? A golf cart?"

"Yes, yes, that's what it appears to be, all right."

Bear soldiered on as quickly as he could. He wouldn't have long before Chesterton threw them out. Or had them arrested.

"You must be Orlo Chesterton," Lily said in a voice loud enough for Bear to hear.

"Yes, I ... who the hell are you? Will! What's an old woman in a bathrobe doing in the garage?"

"Why, that's not a very friendly way to greet a prospective customer, Mr. Chesterton," Lily said. "And here I've heard such good things about your operation. Now, I want to ask all about your deluxe services ..."

Bear hurried through the archway and saw a staircase to his left, a door to the right. He could no longer hear her chatter, but he knew Lily was buying him time. Will was there if she needed physical help, although Lily could deliver quite a wallop if she had to.

Bear opened the door, peered inside and saw the oven gleaming directly ahead of him. In his mind he'd pictured a crematory chamber as a brick oven like the ones in Grimm's grimmest fairy tales. But this was enormous, sleek as diamond plate, all the more ominous for its pristine exterior and digital control panel. The wide oven door was shut, but Bear could hear a deep rumble like the sound of a forest fire from within.

A heavy duty trolley sat in front of the chamber holding a huge corrugated cardboard carton. Bear had a bizarre image of a giant's shoe box without its lid. He assessed the trolley's infrastructure and realized it could be tilted to tip the box into the oven. This must still be the preheat phase.

"Quit gawking," he muttered to himself. Whatever was in that box, he needed to see it and get the hell out of here.

He needed to see it, but he didn't want to. He wanted to turn back now. Bear forced his legs forward against their protest. They ached from the effort to move fast. They wanted to stop. He wanted to stop.

He reached the box. With a deep breath, and no more hesitation, he stared inside.

There were two of them nestled together. An old man and an old woman. Their naked bodies were huddled side by side, one's head to the other's toes. Each had been sliced collar bone to pubis, the torsos cracked wide open. Puddles of blood had pooled and dried inside. Other than that, each cavity was empty. The organs had been removed. Hearts, livers, kidneys. All gone. Patches of skin were missing, too. Bear saw gory remains that he couldn't identify tucked between the box walls and the corpses. This close, the odor of putrefying flesh and blood overcame the chemical scents. He made a little noise that was part cry and part fear and part repulsion.

Left overs.

His own insides threatened a revolt as he looked at the remains of each pale face. Both pairs of eyes were missing. Backing away, tears jeopardizing his own vision, he noticed a tattoo of a delicate vine curling around the woman's upper arm. It was the only pretty thing left to her.

Adrenaline gushed through his system, fueled by rage and horror. He stomped from the room, intent on getting to Sitting Bull, leaving with Lily and calling Keegan. He kachunked back through the embalming room and into the garage just in time to hear Lily snap at Chesterton, "Don't you touch me, or I'll have you for assault."

"I'm calling the police," Chesterton said. He held Lily's arm and was trying to drag her out of Sitting Bull.

"Leave her alone, boss, and I mean now," Will said, wedging his scrawny self between the two.

Chesterton turned on him. "And if you think you still have a job here – "

"Back off, Chesterton," Bear growled.

Chesterton yelped and turned. Bear thought he looked like a red faced Mr. Rogers.

"Now who the hell are you? Is this an open house for gimps?" Chesterton made a move toward Bear, but the old sleuth raised the quad cane and slammed it into the funeral director's shoulder.

Chesterton went down with a cry of pain, writhing on the floor.

"He'll be back up in a minute," Bear said, then added with no remorse whatsoever, "But I might have broken his collar bone."

"Maybe he won't move all that fast," said Lily giving the funeral director a shot of pepper spray from a lipstick tube. "Let's get out of here."

"You have pepper spray?" Bear said with a certain pride in his assistant's preparedness.

"Eunice has my back."

Will helped stash Bear's cane in the back of Sitting Bull while Bear pulled himself into the passenger seat. Then the boy said, "I have to find Chrissie." He sprinted ahead of them out of the garage.

"He's not limping now," Bear observed to Lily.

"Funny what love can do," Lily said as she gunned Sitting Bull toward the alley. Then she hesitated.

"Look down there," Bear pointed at a light-colored panel truck to the left. "It's blocking the alley." Lily turned right, heading back the way they had come.

"We're here, Lily!" Chrissie yelled, appearing in the headlights. She had Folly in her arms and was running with Will toward the golf cart. Where the alley met the street ahead of them, Bear saw a sleek dark vehicle cruise past. They weren't the only ones still up at this time of night.

The first shot hit Sitting Bull in its candy apple butt. Bear turned and saw Orlo Chesterton staggering out of the storeroom and heading their way, one shoulder drooping.

"Is the crazy bastard really shooting at us?" They couldn't outrun bullets so Bear yelled for Will to help get Lily out of the cart. Together they all stumbled away to hunker behind a tall wooden fence that bordered the alley along the back of a yard. As they hid, several more shots split the night.

Bear didn't get it. Orlo Chesterton was either the world's worst marksman, or he wasn't doing the shooting. None of the shots was even coming close to the Latin's Ranch gang. Bear peered between fence stakes just in time to see the funeral director fall. Several more shots were fired, and Chesterton's body jumped two, then three times.

Finally, the shooting stopped. They heard the sound of feet running away. Lights were coming on in several of the little houses along the alley.

"They weren't shooting at us. They were shooting at Chesterton," Bear told the others.

"But if they were shooting at Chesterton, then he isn't the bad guy. So who the hell is?" Lily's question had them all looking at each other wide eyed, heads turning like members of a meerkat colony.

"We gotta move," said Bear as a backyard light suddenly spot lit the fence where they were clustered. "Cops will be on their way."

Will helped Lily get back into the alley. Bear followed with Chrissie who was still holding Folly. The little pooch appeared to be having a ball, his tongue lolling happily. The humans watched a light blink on and off inside the panel truck down at the end of the alley. It roared to life, backed onto the street, and squealed away.

Will said, "I better go help him." He sprinted toward the lump in the alley that was his fallen boss while Bear struggled back into Sitting Bull. Chrissie gave him Folly to hold, and she helped Lily into the cart. Then she ran after Will. As she went, she called 911.

Lily turned the golf cart around and drove to Will and Chrissie. By the time Sitting Bull arrived, the two were on their knees next to Chesterton, and Chrissie was listening for a heartbeat. Blood spattered the two of them as well as the funeral director and the pavement. Will glanced up and said to Bear, "He looks bad."

"He looks like Swiss cheese," Bear answered, observing the bullet holes. Then he looked at Lily. She was ashen and her hands trembled on the steering wheel.

"We need to get home now," he said patting her shoulder gingerly with his enormous hand. He put Folly on the back seat and muttered, "Stay put, you little piece of mange." Then he pulled Lily's Pendleton throw off the floor and wrapped it around her shoulders. "Will, can you and Chrissie wait here for the medics? The shooters are gone. You'll be okay."

"What about the cops?" Lily said.

"We won't wait for the cavalry to arrive," Bear replied, "or we'll be here all night. I'll call Keegan on our way home. I'd rather talk at Latin's Ranch than in this goddamn alley."

They heard sirens approaching as Lily drove Sitting Bull onto the street. Bear had her pull off as soon as they could onto the grass in a city park, letting police cruisers and sheriff cars and a fire department ambulance tear past. None of the officials saw the golf cart in the darkness under the drooping boughs of a madrona tree. At least none stopped to take a look at it.

But Bear noticed the Caddy. It cruised past, slow and menacing. Black as a panther. It was the same one he'd seen from the alley. It stopped briefly, then picked up speed and purred away. He wondered how long it would be before he encountered it again. And just how dangerous that encounter might be.

For now, he was far too upset to worry about it. Hidden there in that park, he finally had time to recall the harrowing site of those two fragile bodies, or what was left of them. No dignity, no artifice. Terrible things had been done to those two people.

In the quiet and the dark, Bear tried to stifle a sob. He failed.

"Tell me what you found," Lily said somberly. "You don't keep things from your partner. Tell me all of it."

And he did. The bodies, the gore. He ended with the lovely tattoo on the woman's arm, a gentle flower so out of place in the gore.

Lily caught her breath. "That tattoo? Everyone in the garden club has seen it. It's a clematis vine. The woman in that box is Candi Kenilworth."

CHAPTER TWELVE

Case Notes
March 25, 2 pm
I'd like to say that Bear, Folly and I snuck back in with no one the wiser, but Latin's Ranch was lit up like a carnival ride. Everybody was standing out on the patio waiting for us when I pulled Sitting Bull into its recharging spot. They clucked and flapped like a flock of distressed chickens until they were sure we were all right. Well, Sam and Alita might have been more like seriously pissed off chickens.
Eunice had worried when we'd been gone longer than she thought we should be. She'd gone to Frankie. He'd alerted Sam who let Alita know. Normally, he would have awakened Jessica ... that's the procedure if something out of the ordinary happens at night. But it turns out Jess wasn't home herself. Probably doing a little night dancing at Ben's house. Usually I'd be pleased that they found a few minutes alone together.
But last night I was way passed pleased that she wasn't home. She'd told both Alita and Sam that she'd be gone and to be extra watchful that all was well. Her absence gave us time to talk the two of them down, to make them feel they were in no way responsible for our clandestine breakout.
We were still up wagging our chins when Jessica came tiptoeing home not long before dawn. None of us wanted to fess up to our night's events, so we managed to make her think we were worried about her *what with people going missing left and right. She got*

all huffy even saying that the missing people were OLD which she wasn't and we were. She ordered everyone back to bed. The only one who slept through the whole damn thing was Charlie.

We might have gotten away with it if Deputy Keegan and her partner Deputy Eye Candy hadn't turned up first thing this morning. Aurora served us all corn fritters and country ham. Maybe that's why the cops actually went pretty easy on Bear and me when we talked in the living room after breakfast.

Now that she knows the truth about our adventure last night, I'm not sure how long it will take Jessica to speak to me again.

-Lily Gilbert, Contrite Assistant to PI Bear Jacobs

Lily could tell from the way Bear was blinking his beady obsidian eyes that he was trying to look wrongly accused as he said to the deputies, "Sounds like Will and Chrissie gave you a good rundown of events last night. I did, too, when you finally answered your phone. I can't fathom why you're so upset with me."

"Don't give me that 'couldn't reach you' crap, Al Jacobs," Jo Keegan snarled. "You were heading for home before you even tried."

"You know, Cupcake, they wouldn't call it *cop* an attitude if you people weren't so likely to do just that."

"Don't call me Cupcake."

Deputy Detective Clay Galligan was not pleased either. "After Will Haverstock said you'd been there, the officers sent a squad car out looking for Bonnie and Clyde in a golf cart. You wasted police time."

Yep. Even frowning he's smoldering hot.

Lily smiled at the young investigator. "They didn't find us because we left the road and hid whenever we heard a car coming. Behind bushes or trees. A golf cart has its advantages."

"So you admit you were trying to avoid us." Galligan smoldered at her some more.

"No, officer," Bear said, the voice of reason. "We were trying to avoid a light-colored panel truck full of murderous gunmen."

"And, seriously, young man. Are you going to arrest a seventy-something lady merely because she wants to be out of the line of fire?" Lily batted what few lashes she had left at Galligan.

Bear made the low growly sound that passed for a laugh.

"Let it go, Clay," Keegan said with a sigh. "We can't win." She then told Bear and Lily that Orlo Chesterton had not died, but he was in intensive care. None of the bullets had been a kill shot, but there were at least four separate wounds for his body to grapple with.

"Better put some guards on that room," Bear said. "Somebody wants him dead."

"It's already done," Clay said.

"Will you arrest him if he survives the hospital?" Bear asked.

Keegan answered, "You know, big guy, there's not much evidence that he actually committed a crime. But there's plenty of evidence that you broke into his property in the middle of the damn night and that maybe he felt the need to defend it."

"But what about those bodies? With their innards missing?" Bear asked. Lily was surprised that Keegan had to be reminded of the gory sight.

The investigators cast a glance at each other before Keegan said, "Tell us again about those bodies."

Bear had described them in detail the night before when he called Keegan. Lily had heard him. But everyone who watched cop shows on TV knew they asked the same questions again and again to get witnesses to remember more details or to trip over themselves. She figured that was why they wanted Bear to repeat the story. Then she added her own explanation of the clematis tattoo.

"You saw the bodies, too, ma'am?" Galligan asked.

"Well, no. I was waiting in the getaway golf cart."

Bear would have sworn Keegan's lips nearly lifted into a grin. But she sobered when she asked, "You sure organs were actually missing? Or were the bodies mutilated? It could look a lot alike."

Bear lost patience. "The torsos were cut open and empty. The organs including a lot of the skin were gone. Go to the morgue and take a close look for yourself if you don't believe me."

"But that's the thing, Bear," Keegan answered. "We can't. The bodies might have been in the room when you were there, but by the time the cops got there, they were in the crematory chamber burning away at 1800 degrees. The first cops on the scene didn't know to stop the oven."

"What? But who put them in the oven after I saw them? Will?"

"According to Chrissie she was with him from the time you left."

"And Chesterton sure didn't do it because he was out in the alley being shot," Bear said. "So somebody got in there and destroyed evidence."

"Evidence of what? All we have is your statement that bodies were butchered. We won't even know who they were unless something is left of any recent dental work. Some of the newer resin fillings can survive that kind of heat but not much else will."

"Yeah," Clay added with an air of disbelief. "And why the hell would anybody cut up old people anyway?"

✦ ✦ ✦

"Why would anyone cut up old people?" Eunice asked. Now that the deputies had gone, the other residents gathered around the game table. Bear had been bringing them all up to speed.

"Good question, Eunice," Bear said.

Charlie was dealing with the idea that his missing wife may be dead. He knew it was likely. But the horror of this was too much. "Did that happen to Louise?" He asked in a pitch even higher than usual. "My Louise? She doesn't deserve that. Nobody deserves that."

"Charlie, there's no real proof. Not yet. Not for Louise." Bear patted his roommate's bony shoulder. He knew Charlie was grieving. He'd seen him in the afternoons, out on the patio alone with a box of Kleenex.

"But Candi and she were friends."

Lily tried to help. "They like fresh young organs for transplants, Charlie. Innards without a lot of mileage. Younger than Louise. That's what I've read. Maybe we're on the wrong trail."

Lily was trying to comfort Charlie. Bear knew that. But she was proving to be the best assistant he'd ever had in the brains department. Her comment made him wonder why anyone might want body parts way beyond their best years. He followed that trail. "Maybe someone's experimenting with youth serums or geriatric medications, and they need organs for research. Or could there be a reason for old stem cells? Something old cells are actually better for?"

It was quiet while they thought about that. They looked like a séance for seniors only. From other rooms, Bear heard Aurora unloading the dishwasher and Chrissie singing some damn love song by one of these modern divas who warbles around a note instead of actually hitting it. The canaries, always glad of a tune, joined in.

Bear broke the group's silence. "Are there cults that mutilate old people?"

Lily added. "Or one lone madman who tortures them, um, us?"

"*Testa di cazzo!*" Frankie muttered as he put a protective arm around his little dove. Bear, not for the first time, reflected it was just as well none of them could translate a lot of Italian.

Jessica came in with a pitcher of iced sun tea, five colorful tumblers and a plate of sliced apples and pears. Bear hoped it was a peace offering of sorts. He'd made his own apology to her, and that was enough for him. But he knew Lily was exceedingly distressed at having hurt her.

After Jessica left the room, Bear poured the tea and asked, "Frankie, any other thoughts about this?"

The old Sicilian gave him a long, calculating stare. But he only said, "I know nothing. I saw nothing while I was knowing nothing."

Bear gave him a good long look back. But finally he moved on. "The doctor at It's Swell to Be Well made a point of how healthy his patients are. Candi Kenilworth was one of them. Maybe it has to do with being in unusually good shape for your age."

"That's right, Bear," Lily said, her face brightening with his idea. "On our list of similarities, all the women exercise at gyms and like to take walks. Sounds like they work at staying healthy."

Bear felt a need to caution his assistant. He held up a paw like a traffic cop making a motion to stop. "Still, we don't know anything about the male corpse we found, healthy or otherwise. Don't even know for sure he's the missing Bronek Pokorski."

"Has to be more than a coincidence."

"I agree it's unlikely. And this 'healthy' thing is promising. But I don't want to start down the wrong path again. We need more information."

"How do we get it?" Lily asked.

"By paying a visit to Orlo Chesterton."

"Didn't you say he's in intensive care?" Eunice asked.

Bear's old knees ached like a son of a bitch. But still he replied, "Like that could stop me."

✦ ✦ ✦

Lily needed to set things right with Jessica. Their friendship had sustained a blow, and the wound must not be allowed to fester. She had her chance when she saw the caregiver sweeping the dregs of winter off the back patio. A drizzle had finally given way to an afternoon sun shower. Lily opened the door from the kitchen and rolled herself outside. She was too tired for her walker today after last night's escapade.

For a while neither said a thing. Jessica appeared inordinately involved in her clean up, her body language as stiff as the broom. Lily's pride was equally stiff as she pretended to concentrate on new shoots in the container garden.

Finally, Lily realized that even though Jessica was the far more conciliatory of the two, she wasn't going to give in this time.

Can't say as I blame her. Dammit.

Like it or not, it was up to Lily to open the collective bargaining. "Looks like shoots are starting to appear now it's not so cold out here."

Jessica swept with the concentration of a professional curler.

Lily tried again. "It'll soon be time to get the patio furniture out."

Brush, brush, brush.

Stop being such a stubborn old fool.

"Jessica, I can't stand it that you're mad at me. There. I said it. Can you forgive me?"

Jessica finally stopped sweeping. She turned to Lily, her streaked blonde curls bouncing in the fresh breeze. "Mad? I'm not mad. I'm disappointed."

"Disappointed? But that's even worse." It cut as sharp as a knife. Lily worried she would cry.

"I thought I could trust you. Maybe not Bear. But you." Jessica's lip trembled.

"You can trust me. You know that," Lily said. "But you can't give me a curfew or lock me in. I'm not a child."

"Lily, I do know that. I know you need personal space. But I need some help here. I can't do this if I have to keep an eye on every damn thing every damn second." Jessica sniffed. Lily could see this confrontation was costing her plenty.

"That's just it, my darling girl. I don't want to be watched. I love your concern because it means you are family. But I have to feel free to live what years I have left with as much control as I can. I told Bear the same thing when he tried to get me to stay behind last night. Which he did. It wasn't his fault."

"If you feel too restricted, then you should have come to me long before this happened. What you did wasn't fair to Sam or Alita. They were in charge, and you disappeared." Jessica didn't yell, but Lily wished she would. Then she wouldn't feel so wretched.

"I know. I'm sorry about that, Jess."

"And I'm responsible for your welfare whether you want to admit it or not. I try very hard to stay out of your way. I rarely butt in. But allowing me the right to watch out for you is the price of staying here."

"I know. And it's a fair price. I just hate to have to say that I need it." Lily heaved a huge sigh. "I don't want to admit that I'm vulnerable. But I know I am. I know that I'm still alive because you've been there for me when I've needed you most."

Jessica's posture lost its starch as she gave Lily a wan smile. "My God, if Sylvia knew what happened last night, she'd have me locked up for elder abuse. And she'd commit elder abuse on you."

Lily saw the attempt at humor for exactly what it was. Jessica was offering an olive branch. Lily had to reassess personal freedom. Hers needed to end where Jessica's guardianship needed to start. This was a complex dance and it would take them both more than one lesson to learn all the steps.

"All right, Jess. Here's a promise. If I feel the need to go out in the middle of the night again, I won't sneak out. I'll tell whoever is in charge."

"And here's my promise. I might try to talk you out of it, but I won't stop you. I'll just go with you."

Lily laughed and held out her hand. "It's a deal. High five?"

Instead, Jessica dropped to her knees and leaned over the wheelchair to hug the older woman. "I can't lose you, Lily. Not after it took so many years for me to find you in the first place."

The loss of a little personal freedom was nothing if it meant the salvation of a friendship. Lily never wanted to frighten Jessica again.

✦ ✦ ✦

Lily and Jessica made peace just in time for Eunice to declare open warfare on Frankie. Lily was aware that Eunice had had her suspicions for some time regarding Aurora, Sicilian Nights, and Frankie's true interest. Eunice felt his love of the cooking was a little too close to love of the cook.

It came to a head the evening Aurora waltzed into the dining room to serve the evening meal with a hunk of bling clasped to her ample bosom. Dazzling yellow diamonds surrounded a thumb-sized opal to create a sunflower supported by green emerald leaves. To Lily, the damned thing looked nearly the size of a real sunflower. She wondered what kind of cast iron undergarment it took just to support its weight.

"What is *that*?" Eunice took one look at the brooch, blanched to Shaken White then flushed instantly to Raging Red. She turned to the old smoothie seated next to her, and hissed "How dare you?"

Many years in a dangerous business had taught Frankie Sapienza when to duck, so the teacup hurtling toward his head missed by a millimeter. "My dove! What is wrong?" he asked. He looked truly befuddled.

"Your *dove*? You two timing cad!" Eunice spit out the words like ack ack fire. She levitated out of her chair, swung her own sequin-encrusted shawl over her shoulder, and flounced from the room.

"But what have I done, *cara mia*?" Frankie asked. Lily knew that every woman older than the age of twelve had seen that look of wrongly accused innocence on a man's face at one time or another.

Frankie began to rise but Lily waved him off, quietly counseling him to give it time. She thought she should follow Eunice to offer any comfort that she could. But the door to their bedroom slammed with such fervor that it vibrated in its doorframe. She could hear things inside being hurled against the walls. Maybe a visit right this moment wasn't such a wise idea.

An enraged tigress isn't picky about her next victim.

Lily rolled her wheelchair into the kitchen where Jessica was trying to calm an overwrought Aurora. The cook was in tears over upsetting Eunice and was blubbering something about her pin. Lily could overhear Bear, Charlie, Frankie and Sam where they lingered at the dining room table, no doubt hoping that a meal would be served by someone sooner or later.

"Women," Bear said at last.

"In my younger days, I found it wise to have more than one at a time," Charlie said. "Then one of them was always speaking to you."

"I never speak to any of them if I can avoid it," Sam said. "Safer than way."

"But what did I do?" asked the Sicilian.

"You know you don't need to commit a crime to be punished for it," Bear said.

"Eunice will come around one of these days, and then you'll never hear the end of it," said Charlie in his current role as the old philosopher.

"My dove es not like that. She good and kind." The old man's hands shook as he tried to hoist his water glass to his lips.

Bear said, "Well, Frankie, I'm thinking it had to do with that pin Aurora was wearing. Know anything about that?"

Frankie cocked his head. "Pin? You mean like to hold something together?"

"No. Like a brooch. Flashy as a spinner hubcap." He patted himself on the chest in the general area a brooch would be worn.

"Yes! I give Eunice earrings that look like that. Only small, more delicate."

"I got no evidence or anything, but I think that might just be your problem, Frankie."

The light dawned in Frankie's face as surely as the sun rises in the east. "You mean ... my dove think I give this pin to the cook? And this pin is bigger than her earrings? She es jealous for Frankie?" He raised his heavy white eyebrows and flashed a grin that revealed more than one gold cap. "This is a good thing, no? It mean she love me."

"Well, it's probably not all that easy. First you have to get her to listen to you."

"Should be no problem, no?" Frankie looked overjoyed. "Bear, you some great detective."

Bear said no more. Lily figured he realized it would still be a problem, yes.

CHAPTER THIRTEEN

Case Notes
March 26, 10 am
It used to be easy. You could just call and ask almost anything about a patient. Now hospitals have fewer leaks than the CIA. Even I couldn't worm a thing out of them. So we had to take whatever we found once we got there.
Bear went out to the barn to ask Sam if he'd help us talk to Orlo Chesterton. He told me Sam gave him some serious crap about the other night. Sam is pretty protective of Jessica. He made Bear promise to do something nice for her. Bear says he promised, but wouldn't tell me what. Said it didn't involve me.
Can you imagine such a thing?
Anyhoo, Sam agreed to give us a hand with Bear's plan. This was a big concession on his part. Instead of just dropping us off on his way to Man Land, he had to play an active role at the hospital with us. He pushed my chair, and Bear walked beside us.
It was slow going, the big man kachunking along on his quad cane at half speed. I think he's aching after all the activity lately. Hope he's not pushing himself too hard. He looks good, but he did have that heart thingy, and I wouldn't want a repeat performance. But I can't give him orders if I want to keep him from giving them to me. Hard though it may be for me to button it, I kept my big yap shut about it.

- Lily Gilbert, Muzzled Assistant to PI Bear Jacobs

The trio rode the elevator up toward the ICU, keeping quiet whenever another passenger got on or off. Otherwise, Bear hummed *Que Sera Sera.* Lily could tell Sam was nervous because he kept tapping the rhythm on the handles of her chair. Finally the old cowboy muttered, "I hate hospitals. Never even been to an ICU."

"Nothing to worry about, Sam," Lily said, reaching around to give his hand a pat. "I've been here lots what with one leg infection or another. I know the place inside and out. More important, I know the people. If there's a guard, the head nurse Geraldine will have demanded he stay outside the ICU door."

"Yeah, but why would cops listen to her?"

"You don't know Geraldine. Nobody gets in her way in the ICU. John Q. Law will be cowed."

Bear growned. "You gotta spend less time around Eunice."

Bear's plan depended on Lily's friendliness with the staff. She tried to reassure him. "Believe me, it would be harder to break out of ICU than into it."

The elevator inched its way from the first floor to the fourth. "Okay, boys, almost there." Lily glanced over at Bear who was wearing a plaid flannel robe circa WWII over a hospital gown. His hairy legs were visible from his knees down to his mukluks. He unleashed an eerie moan more lupine than ursine.

"You okay?" Lily asked, startled.

"I'm practicing."

"Practicing what? Howling at the moon?"

"I need to seem weak enough to be a patient."

"Well, take it easy, hambone. You sound like a werewolf."

The elevator door opened on four. Sam pushed Lily out, and Bear limped along behind them, moaning at a more or less controlled level. The place was just as Lily remembered, a small waiting room to the left and the ICU door dead ahead. Sure enough, there was a uniformed deputy in a straight backed chair just to the right of the door.

Lily smiled to herself when she saw how young the kid looked. And bored. Sitting in a hospital all day had to be damn dull if you'd joined the force expecting to hunt down murderers and thieves. This kid had nothing to do but bide his time, with not so much as a video game or cell phone to keep him company.

His inexperience along with her familiarity would be their ticket in. Lily knew that Bear and she looked like nothing more than sick old people, nearly invisible to young eyes. This rookie wouldn't think of them as a threat to a fly, much less to Orlo Chesterton.

Sam leaned forward and pressed the buzzer next to the ICU door. He and the boy cop exchanged nods. Lily, clutching her sweater tight over her breast, manufactured a tremble. "Oh, my goodness. Are there bad guys on the loose?"

"Nothing to be afraid of, ma'am. I'm just here to keep an eye on a patient."

"Oh my! How exciting!"

"Yes, ma'am," said the guard, stifling a yawn. "Exciting."

A stern and jowly face like a grouper appeared in the glass inset in the ICU door. It glowered at Sam before looking down at Lily. Suddenly it erupted in a big toothy smile. The door whooshed open. "Why, Ms. Lily! It's so good to see you."

Lily was just able to say, "You, too, Geraldine," before she was squashed tight to the woman's ample scrubs.

Geraldine eventually stood back and beamed at her. "You look wonderful!"

ICU nurses didn't always see happy results. Just *living* must look good to them. Lily replied, "I came by to say hello to everyone and tell you all about my new digs."

"Well, you come right on in." Geraldine looked at Sam and ordered, "Wheel her right on in to the nurses' station. Everyone will want to say hello."

The cop stood and said, "But they—"

Geraldine cut him off. "Sit back down, young man. This is my business, not yours. Lily wouldn't bother anybody."

Ha!

Lily felt a moment of panic as Sam pushed her inside. Bear was supposed to scoot in behind them with nobody the wiser. She wanted to turn and see if he made it. But she stuck to the plan, chattering away about Latin's Ranch, to draw the nurse's attention away.

✦ ✦ ✦

Bear slipped through the door behind Lily and Sam. It worked not because he was stealthy but because the cop was sulking. The nurse had him intimidated, like a pooch told to roll over and play dead. Bear limped in behind Sam and Lily in full sickie mode, moaning all the way.

The ICU door shut automatically behind him. Bear could hear Lily nattering on and on. "I felt good enough to leave Soundside and go to adult care at Latin's Ranch, and let me tell you all about my ..." In the meantime he slipped into the first patient room on the right.

Bear's luck was holding. Really good luck would have been if Orlo Chesterton was in the room. But at least there wasn't some other sick bastard with a call button at the ready. The room was empty. Bear peered back out into the Intensive Care Unit's central core. It was a circular space with patient rooms around the nurses' station like spokes around a hub. Lily was parked there, with nurses and aides listening in.

"I was so weak at Soundside, but then I met a physical therapist who helped me build up ..."

Sam was virtually ignored as the nursing personnel chatted with their one-time patient. Bear watched the cowboy lean casually against the high front of the station and peer over it. His job was to find Chesterton's room number if he could. His battered old Stetson hid the direction of his eyes. While Sam scanned the desk for information, Bear scooted from the first room to the second. He went in far enough to see a woman flat on her back with a leg in traction. She was drugged, asleep or dead. Whichever, she paid no attention to an old man in a bedraggled robe and slipper socks.

When Bear peeked out of room two, Sam was watching for him. The cowboy held up six fingers and jerked his chin forward. Bear looked ahead. He took off, going from the second room to the sixth, nearly cutting across the full diameter of the circle.

"... I found some excellent CNAs there but have to say the food service was even worse there than here ..."

General laughter and agreement among the nurses that, yes, the hospital food was pretty bad.

Bear felt like a runner going for home.

Well, maybe not that fast. And there'll be no sliding.

He scuttled into Room Six and nearly smacked into a buxom redhead who was coming out, carrying a tray with a used disposable syringe and its wrappings.

"... that should help you with the pain for a while," she was saying, removing a surgical mask when she looked up, directly into Bear's chest. Her gaze climbed to his eyes. "Goodness! Who are you, and what are you doing here?" Years of working a stressful job were written on her face, but her green eyes made Bear's blood run a little bit hotter.

"I'm Harvey Chesterton, ma'am," he lied with ease from years of practice in the PI trade. "Have a room down the hall, where the nurses are nowhere near as pretty as they are right here. Just came in to howdy to my baby brother, Orlo."

The green eyes narrowed a bit as she looked him over. "But should you be out of bed yourself?"

"Yes, ma'am. They told me to walk as much as I can."

"Well, if the cop didn't stop you, I guess I can't. But don't stay too long. Mr. Chesterton needs his rest."

"I won't take long, ma'am. And might I say, you are vision enough to make a sick man well."

"You and your brother may not look alike, but your bullshit is identical," she said, putting a hand on his chest to gently push around him.

He breathed deep of her spicy scent as she left the room then turned his attention to the man lying so quiet and still. Orlo Chesterton's bed was surrounded by monitors and IV racks and eerie machines making beeps and sucking sounds. Scarier than the sight of Orlo was the sight of Deputy Detective Josephine Keegan sitting in the visitor's chair.

Holy crap!

"Fancy meeting you here." Bear eased himself into the only other chair in the room. Awkward as it might be, he was glad to see Keegan here. It meant that law enforcement was taking a genuine interest. While a bunch of hearsay about missing seniors might not get them motivated, they could really sink their teeth into an attempted murder.

"How'd you get in here? You ... you ..."

As Keegan sputtered in search of the perfect word, Bear now understood the ease in passing the cop at the ICU door. It wasn't just that the kid was bored. He'd known the detective was here. "The kid on the door must figure Chesterton is safe as long as you're here."

Before Keegan could answer, the funeral director interrupted. The bruises around his eyes were so dark he looked like a frightened panda. "I've seen you ... who?" His voice was far weaker than the last time Bear had heard it while breaking into the funeral home. One of his hands wore a fiberglass cast. The rest of the man was under the covers, but Bear knew his chest would be bandaged from the multiple wounds he'd received in the alley.

"Yes, Mr. Chesterton, he is a suspicious looking character," Keegan said then whispered to Bear, "I will deal with you later. Get out."

Bear figured she wouldn't quibble in front of this very sick man. So he held his ground. "I saw the bodies, Mr. Chesterton."

"Funeral home ... viewing rooms."

"No. Mutilated bodies in the crematory. And then they were gone. Who did that, Mr. Chesterton?"

"Not my fault. Blackmail," he whimpered.

Bear and Keegan stared at each other in surprise.

"You're being blackmailed?" Keegan asked.

"Scared." Chesterton closed his eyes.

"You're under police protection now. Tell us who's blackmailing you."

"And what you did to lead to blackmail. Start with that," Bear said. He leaned forward, hands on his quad cane.

Keegan fumed and mouthed, "Just you wait."

"They paid for bodies ... then made me do worse. Said they'd tell." Chesterton spoke slowly, his breath becoming shallow.

"Paid you to do what?" Keegan asked.

"Didn't embalm. Or cremate ... told families I did." He sounded even weaker. Bear noticed that his pupils were contracting to pin points.

"He looks bad. I'm getting the nurse back," Keegan said. She stood and reached across the invalid's bed to grab up the call button and poke it.

"You sold families cremation services, but you weren't really cremating the remains, were you?" Bear asked. The guy was a cretin but not a murderous one.

"Yes ... I cheated them. But no killings. Ask Driscoll ... not ..." His breathing became ragged. Bear stood up, next to Keegan. One of the mysterious machines began a frantic alarm. Nurses and aides came rushing in. They started CPR.

Bear put a massive paw on Keegan's shoulder and pulled her back. They created as much room for the crash team as they could, flattened themselves against an inside wall of the tiny room. Bear, taller than anyone else, could see that the CPR was failing. Chesterton's lips turned blue as he sunk into unconsciousness.

"He's dying," Bear whispered to Keegan, but not quietly enough to go unnoticed.

A nurse frowned at them and ordered them to leave. Almost immediately another said, "He's flat lined." One by one the machines stopped their frantic beeping. As the medical personal called the time of death, the room went dreadfully silent. Orlo Chesterton was now in need of a funeral service for himself.

The silence was broken by a low angry voice, one with a bear-like snarl. "Find the Redhead, Keegan. She did a fucking hit right here in front of us. We watched her kill this man."

✦ ✦ ✦

Lily was cold. She'd been waiting with Sam and Bear in the bleak interrogation room at the Sheriff's office. They hadn't been offered as much as coffee. Other than the table and chairs in the center of the room, and the large mirror on one wall, the room was devoid of décor. Regardless of the damp coolness to the room, Bear was hunched over the table, snoozing. Sam leaned back on his chair's hind legs, his own long legs sprawled forward, one boot over the other. His hat covered his eyes.

Since neither of them was interested in chatting anymore, Lily's mind wandered.

This place could really use Sylvia's touch.

Does anybody not know that's a two-way glass?

Maybe Eunice is right. The coppers are dusting off their thumbscrews and waterboards.

Lily recalled the last moments in the ICU which seemed like decades ago. She'd been asking the nurses their opinion of a prosthetic when Keegan's partner Clay Galligan came through the ICU door. All the nurses looked up and stared at him.

Moths to a flame.

When he noticed Lily he did a double take. "What the hell are you doing here?" His eyes shifted to Sam. "And who are you?"

"Name's Sam Hart. And watch your language around all these ladies."

"The guard let us in," Lily said quickly as the testosterone level in the ICU threatened to rise. "I'm just visiting my old friends."

Detective Cutie didn't buy it. He squinted at her. "Did Keegan see you?"

"You mean she's here, too? With Chesterton?" Lily was thoroughly surprised. She hadn't heard Keegan shoot Bear or even tongue-lash him to death.

That's when the alarm went off in Orlo Chesterton's room. Things got exciting fast. Nurses pulled their attention away from Galligan and rushed to the room. Keegan rushed out, screaming into her mobile. Bear came shuffling out behind her.

"Get them out of here now," Keegan ordered Galligan when she saw Sam and Lily. "Him, too," she added, pointing at Bear. "Then lock down that door."

The next thing Lily knew, the rookie who'd been guarding the ICU door was driving the threesome to the Sheriff's department. He dumped them in the interrogation room. And there they sat.

They waited over an hour before they heard Keegan outside the door. "Jesus, Galligan, I didn't mean to have them brought here. I meant to get them home."

Bear snorted awake, and Sam brought his chair down on all fours.

Lily heard Galligan reply, "But we need them to talk. They're guilty of something."

"That may be. But they're old, you chucklehead. Show a little kindness."

Lily and Bear grinned at each other. If things got too rough, they'd just play the geezer card with Keegan.

Of course, Keegan showed very little kindness herself as she burst through the door and took a seat across from them. Galligan slouched in the chair next to her. The two of them frowned at the Latin's Ranch three. Keegan must have noticed Lily tremble because she left the room and came back with a jacket.

As Lily gratefully slipped into the coat, Keegan said to Bear, "Orlo Chesterton had been receiving Versed and morphine for sedation and pain. Looks like Nurse Redhead administered a fatal dose of it. He was dying while we were talking to him. How did you know?"

"I didn't," Bear said. "But when I saw his pupils contract and his skin start turning blue, it looked like an O.D. to me. Did you catch her?"

"She's gone. Must have walked out of the ICU right after she left Chesterton's room. Nobody noticed because they were all busy with Little Miss Chatterbox." Keegan turned an accusatory eye at Lily.

Sam said, "I saw her go. Has some mileage on her but still a good looking filly. She pranced out of the room, set a tray with a syringe on the counter, frowned at me and kept going out the main ICU door. Probably won't find prints since she was wearing latex gloves," said Sam. It was quite a speech for a man who hated to talk to women.

"We'll find her. But about Chesterton. You knew what he was talking about, Bear. About charging families for bogus cremations. How'd you get that? I couldn't understand what he was saying."

"I've had more down time to think about this than you. I've been doing some online research. First thing to know is the black market for body parts is huge, like up to a fifth of the kidneys are found that way. People on waiting lists get too desperate to wait any longer. The shortage of organs is because they're illegal to buy or sell in every country but Iran. So more than one funeral director has gotten involved in scams."

"I still don't get it," Galligan broke in.

Bear turned his head toward the young detective. "They tell a family that the loved one has been cremated as requested, but it hasn't really happened. The going rate for morticians to sell a corpse to cutters who'll harvest parts for transplant or medical research is a thousand a body."

"Jeeez-us," Sam breathed slow and low, either a curse or a prayer.

"But ... but organs have to be fresh, don't they?" Galligan asked.

"Well, funeral parlors have lots of refrigerator space. And lots of body parts last longer than others. Bones, skin, tendons."

"Wouldn't the quality be compromised?" Keegan asked.

"Absolutely. Recipients could get diseased tissue. I mean, the body was dead for a reason. And a place that would buy parts this way wouldn't be too picky about spreading disease. Maybe cancer, maybe HIV."

Everyone in the room looked pale as they contemplated the magnitude of Chesterton's seedy practice. *Alleged* practice, Lily reminded herself. But she grappled with the grief of families who thought they had done right by their fathers or daughters ... or transplant patients who hoped for a healthy new knee, not one with leukemia.

Keegan said, "If Chesterton was selling bodies, we need to find out who was buying. There must be records of some kind. Clay, let's get a warrant for the funeral home."

"You think the buyer wanted him dead?" her partner asked. "Seems like killing the golden goose."

"Maybe the goose was about to squawk. At least it's a place to start. Then we better talk to any family who might have found out what he did – "

"Or received a diseased organ," Galligan added.

"Those are some pretty righteous motives for murder."

Bear added, "Nurse Redhead didn't want him talking to us. Find her, and you'll find the motive to kill Chesterton. But that won't necessarily explain the disappearance of seniors around the county."

"First things first," Keegan said.

Bear nodded. "Now I think it's time for us to go home."

"But we're not done here."

"I am," Lily said, not kidding around. Either the thought of stolen bodies had sickened her or her blood sugar levels were going haywire. "I'm a diabetic, you know. I need my blood meter."

"And I'd like to get dressed." Bear was still in his robe and slippers.

"Okay, we can resume this later. But one thing before you go." Lily expected Keegan to yell at them, but the deputy surprised her. "You guys have done a helluva job. Without your help, we would never have tumbled to this so soon. We're very grateful. Aren't we, Clay?"

Detective Galligan looked more grumpy than grateful. "Yeah, I guess."

"But it's time you to start being careful. I won't tell you not to investigate because I know it would do me no good. But I want you to avoid dangerous situations. Leave that stuff to us. The research you're doing is the biggest help of all. So I'll make you a deal. If you keep out of the line of fire, we'll keep you in the loop."

"Fair enough," Bear said as he began to stand. Lily gave back the jacket, patting Keegan's hand in the process.

"You okay with that, Galligan?" Keegan asked her partner.

A breath-stopping smile crossed his lips. "Fair enough ... Cupcake."

Lily could hear Keegan swearing at Galligan above Bear's laugh all the way out to the patrol car that took them back to Sam's pickup. But Bear went silent as Sam drove through a McDonald's to get Lily an orange juice before continuing toward home. Finally Lily asked, "You've got more on your mind don't you, Bear?"

He glanced down at her where she was nestled on the bench seat between the men, sipping juice through a straw. "The cops will dig into Chesterton's murder and who was buying the bodies he was stealing. They have the forensics to back them up and manpower we don't have." Bear paused to give his head a shake. "But they won't be thinking about the missing seniors now. Hell, there's no rhyme or reason. But, Lily, healthy old people are being kidnapped, murdered and cut to pieces. The confusion word being *old*."

"So that's what we'll keep working on," she said with a resolute nod.

"Chesterton referred to a Driscoll and being made to do something worse."

"Driscoll ... Driscoll ... Like Driscoll Manor Assisted Care maybe?"

"Maybe," Bear nodded. "As screwed up as stealing parts from corpses might be, it's not as bad as killing for them."

It was a long sad ride home for the Latin's Ranch three.

CHAPTER FOURTEEN

Case Notes
April 2, 1 pm
For the next few days, nothing much happened which is fine by me. I'm pooped. Besides, I've been feeling equal parts weepy and pissed and frightened about what Bear is thinking now, that old people are being murdered for their body parts.
I know the need for organs is desperate and that waiting lists for transplants are years long. I shudder at the pain of parents who watch their children suffer while they wait and wait. But what I've been reading online appalls me.
There's a big market for human hearts, lungs, kidneys, bone, skin and eyes taken in shady circumstances. That includes foreigners selling their own organs, not always by choice, poor souls. Or bodies of prisoners. Or homicides like young guns cut down in gang wars. The need is so great that not all the clinics purchasing tissue are as careful as they should be. They sure as hell don't look too closely at documentation.
I understand the desperation, even though I don't understand why anyone would want an old person's old tissue. But surely nothing should be harvested by killing the donor. Not even to save another life. And how much more horrifying if we're playing loose with death for no better reason than skin to enlarge penises or plump up lips. That's just insane.
I'm sick at heart and need time off, so my dear friend Eunice booked

the free Afternoon of Beauty she won on the radio. She was the only caller old enough to correctly identify the name of Tom Mix's wonder horse. Most callers couldn't even identify Tom Mix. Eunice said if Sylvia would take us, she'd buy an Afternoon of Beauty for each of us, too. I'm glad to see her happy about something since she's still not speaking to Frankie. She's one stubborn little warrior.

Anyhoo, the detective agency is closed today. We're on our way to Shear Elegance Salon and Spa.

Oh, and about Bear. He hasn't heard from Detective Keegan for a couple days. I don't know where he disappeared today, but he headed out on Sitting Bull just before lunch. Not like him to miss a meal. At least he had the good sense to tell Aurora he wouldn't be here, or he'd have muchos jalapeños in his stew tonight. Of course, the old hot head might like that.

-Lily Gilbert, Soon-To-Be-Stunning Assistant to PI Bear Jacobs

---

Bear had a cheeseburger at Reggie's. The food at Latin's Ranch was better – and safer – but sometimes a guy didn't really want *good*. He wanted grease and salt. Bear had saved up enough of his Personal Needs Allowance to pay for Ben's bowl of chili and a couple of beers apiece.

Ben Stassen sat across the butt-burned, knife-scarred table. Bear figured the guy was what women would refer to as a dreamboat. Or maybe a hunk these days. Stud muffin? Hottie? Women bitched about the euphemisms men had for them, but the girls had a pretty colorful lingo of their own.

"I hurt Jessica the other night," Bear began when they'd both been served. He told Ben the story of breaking into Chesterton's Funeral Home. "Not sure she'd give a juicy fart about me, but I took Lily with me. And she really loves Lily. It scared Jessica pretty bad."

"I know, Bear. She told me about it. But why invite me to lunch? Seems you owe it to her, not me." Ben glanced at Bear with his brows raised in a question as he added a handful of broken crackers to the chili.

Bear looked around the seedy bar and at Dead Eye's dead eye. Somehow he couldn't picture Jessica really enjoying a lunch date here. "Well, that's the thing. You're my penance." Bear explained that Sam had made him promise to do something nice for Jessica.

"Okay. But my question stands. How does lunch with me pay your debt to Jessica?" Ben took a bite of the chili. He gasped. His eyes watered. His nose dripped.

"They don't call it ass-burning for nothing," Bear observed.

Dead Eye appeared with a couple more cold beers.

"Thanks," Ben squeaked.

Bear put on his 'this is serious' countenance. "I asked you here so we could talk like a couple of girls. About feelings and shit. Invade your privacy some. On Jessica's behalf."

Ben looked perplexed. As well as red in the face. "Well, thanks, but my business is my business."

"Not when you're running your business off the fuckin' rails," Bear said with as much heat as the chili. "So shut up and listen to an old guy, for cripes sake. God knows I've made mistakes, and I wish someone with balls would have talked to me."

Bear watched Ben's posture stiffen, and even though he maintained a pleasant enough expression, ice formed in the younger man's eyes. Before he could protest, Bear held up an enormous paw. "I don't talk about my background much. Don't see the point most times. But you should know I've found a lot of runaways in my time. Brought kids home to parents willing to pay a PI to do it. One little shit even took a shot at me before I removed the gun from his hand and ... but that's another story.

"The point is, once they were home, some made it. Their parents and they found common ground that didn't shake under their feet. But most of them? They just chewed up the family and spit it all away. The likelihood that runaways will go for good is higher the older they are, especially when drugs are involved. Which brings me to your daughter, Rachael."

"Sounds like you're about to hold an intervention," Ben said in a voice cold as granite.

"Nope, not really. The thing I'm trying to say here is that Rachael isn't going to make it just because you want her to. And you sure as hell know it by now."

Ben stared into his still-full chili bowl and set down the spoon. "Well, I guess I could say, yeah, I know all the bullshit about enabling. And yeah, I know about just saying no. And I could say what the hell business is it of yours anyway -"

"You'd be within your rights."

"- but the truth is, I just don't know what the fuck to do, Bear." He slumped but not from booze like most of Reggie's patrons. "You bring a person into the world, you have some responsibility to man up, don't you? You don't leave just because it's hard."

Ben looked bleak enough to make Bear sorry he'd launched into this, even for love of Jessica. But he soldiered on. "Maybe not. But it seems to me you're trying to fix damage you didn't cause. That just won't fly. The way I hear it, your wife dumped you both. Not your problem to solve no matter how hard you try. It's between the Mrs. and her daughter."

"Yeah, well, that's not going to happen. She's long gone."

"Then you can't repair the missing link. But I'll tell you what you can do. Not because I'm applying for sainthood, mind you. It's because Jessica's wellbeing is important to mine. That makes yours important to mine, too."

Bear told him about Lily's Project Jessica. "Right now, in addition to everything else she does, Jessica works part time as a CNA. We're going to take two days of that work away from her."

He said Sylvia had found a senior center where the Latin's Ranch five could go for Friday and Saturday afternoons as long as they had someone to watch out for their needs. All of them were willing, and Sylvia would pay the tab for an assistant to go with them. Rick, Alita and Chrissie would cover duties for Friday and Saturday mornings and nights. That meant Jessica was off the hook from Friday morning all the way through until Sunday. The only thing they still had to arrange was transportation, and Bear had an idea about that.

"Jessica will have two days off in a row. Enough time that a man might close his office on Fridays and leave town with the lady. Or hole up with her. Or whatever."

Ben stared at Bear. "And this relates to my daughter how?"

"Are you as blind as Dead Eye? Take two days a week for you and Jessica, for the love of God. If the cops call about your daughter, you just won't be available to go rescue her. Let her problem be her problem. You might find she learns to handle it if you're not always there to wipe her ass. She's not a kid anymore, Ben. She has to take part in saving herself."

"Damn," Ben said with the bite of satire. "Most people tell me that's the way to handle all days, not just two."

"While I'm inclined to agree, it's not my concern. You want to be a patsy the rest of the week, be my guest. I just want two good days for Jessica that she knows she can count on." He stopped and took a deep draft of the beer. Then he reached over for Ben's forgotten chili and downed a mouthful.

Finally, Ben spoke. "I might be willing, Bear. But who's to say she wants to spend her free time with me?"

"Holy shit, man. We can only create the sunshine. It's up to you to make the hay."

✦ ✦ ✦

Sylvia Henderson smiled at the gorgeous man sitting across the tiny table from her at Starbucks, each of them enjoying a six-adjective coffee. She'd probably be over the moon if he weren't gay. As it was, Tony Sapienza had been her friend for a long time, and she cared not at all about his sexual orientation. He didn't hide it, but he wasn't flamboyant either. Tony was expansive and funny and free, where Sylvia was reserved and serious and elegant. They saw in each other the virtues they could have used in themselves.

They were planning another trip to Paris. While they chatted about French cuisine and wine, her attention wandered to the front window of the Starbucks. "My goodness, look at the size of that Cadillac pulling in. Looks like a mobster car."

"It is." Tony said. "That's Vinny." Tony had introduced his grandfather Frankie to Latin's Ranch on Sylvia's recommendation. "He works for my grandfather."

"Your grandfather knows mobsters?"

"My grandfather is a mobster."

Sylvia knew that Lily and Eunice had guessed it, and now it turned out their gossip wasn't so idle after all. Not that it should be such a surprise. Mobsters get old, too. At least the ones that don't end up in car trunks.

"What's he doing here?" Sylvia watched Vinny leave the car and approach the coffee shop. He didn't appear to be carrying unconcealed or to be bulging in the wrong places. In fact, he looked good. Damn good. He was bull shouldered and narrow hipped, kind of like a cartoon superhero. His suit was a beautifully tailored dark pinstripe. The shine on his Italian leather shoes was as flawless as was the glossy wave in his thick black hair. Large dark glasses hid his eyes but as he entered the coffeehouse, Sylvia could see the scar on one cheek that curled down and under his square jaw.

This was the type of man a nice woman like Sylvia never met. Merely by looking at him, she didn't want to be a nice woman at all.

Vinny stopped at the entrance and seemed to look toward them. The dark glasses hid his sightline. Tony excused himself and went to hand over a small box he pulled from his jacket pocket. Sylvia noticed it was the unmistakable Tiffany blue. Vinny took the box, nodded at Tony then bowed to Sylvia. At least she thought it was at her. Mr. Magnificent left the store, but when he got to the Caddy, he bowed again before ducking inside and driving away.

Sylvia breathed a quiet, "That's amore."

"What?" Tony asked.

"Nothing." She sipped her latte, glad it was now cool.

"Are you feeling well? You're flushed."

"Am not. I'm fine." Then she had a startling thought. Was Vinny gay, too? "Is he a new guy in your life?"

"Who, Vinny? No way," Tony said with a shudder and snort of laughter.

Sylvia felt elated with his answer. "Then who is he, and why are you giving him a gift from Tiffany's?"

"Vinny's straight as an arrow, or he'd be unemployed. He's my grandfather's capo, uh, companion. Bodyguard. Helps out with errands. Some of them are even legal." Tony told her about the battle raging between Eunice and Frankie. Hoping to appease his darling, Frankie had asked Tony to purchase something uniquely right for her. "Apparently there was some fiasco regarding yellow DiamaLite that Frankie ordered on a TV shopping channel. So I got Eunice the Tiffany dove charm on a chain. That's what he always calls her. His little dove."

"That's perfect." But the image in Sylvia's mind had more to do with Vinny's perfect butt.

What on earth is wrong with me? Am I going to need smelling salts?

"Frankie sent Vinny here to pick it up from me so he could give it to her right away."

"Well if anything can bring peace, a dove ought to do it."

"Yeah. Especially one that's 18 karat gold."

"I hope your grandfather sends Vinny to let me know. I mean us. To let us know. If Eunice likes it."

✦ ✦ ✦

"Give us the works," Eunice chirped to Monsieur Alain at Shear Elegance. "Mani, pedi, color and cut."

"Would a pedicure be half price for me?" Lily asked. Before she left Latin's Ranch, Chrissie had unwrapped her leg and proclaimed it free of wounds. She would wrap it again when Lily returned. Chrissie had consulted with a home health nurse and been told that the swirling bath that went with a pedicure would be good for the leg.

"Doesn't matter. I'm buying. Get whatever you want."

Lily and Sylvia consulted the list of services offered by the spa and salon. For the first time in her life, Lily chose a facial wax.

"And that'll be the last time," she huffed afterwards to her daughter. "They ripped off my cheeks! I'm red as a raspberry." She had to admit that the soothing crèmes, perfumed towels and gentle massage of the facial that followed made up for the wax. "If I had any cheeks left, they would be exceptionally soft."

When they moved to the pedicure chairs, they passed Eunice on her way from a stylist's station to the wash basins. She wore a voluminous tropical patterned cape, and her head was a gleaming bouquet of foils. "I'm getting my orange streaks even brighter," Eunice beamed then went on her way twitching her fragile hips to a rhythm all her own.

"She doesn't appear to be missing Frankie much," Sylvia observed.

"Oh, I don't know. Mention his name and she utters some old world curse she learned at her granny's knee."

As they relaxed their feet in swirling water, Sylvia told her mother about Vinny and confirmed that Frankie was indeed a man with a past. "He'll be giving her a gift soon that might help the situation."

Then they talked about Project Jessica. "I've found the perfect senior center," Sylvia said. "Lots of activities as well as a big lounge just to relax in."

"Sounds lovely, dear," said Lily. She was thumbing through an old issue of the local newspaper she'd found in the stack of even older hairstyle magazines.

"And more good news. Do you remember Babs? The activities director from Soundside? She agreed to spend Friday and Saturday afternoons as your assistant at the senior center. That should please Jessica since you all liked her."

"That's wonderful, dear." Lily was half-listening as she read through the obits, pleased that nobody she knew was listed there. The facial followed by the foot bath was relaxing her frayed nerves. She had dutifully passed on Chrissie's instruction to the pedicurist. "Be sure it's good and dry before you use any lotion. Moisture increases the chances of infection." All in all, this was just the day away that she had craved.

Eunice, Sylvia and Lily were at Shear Elegance the whole afternoon, braiding their way from station to station. Eunice took part in gossip whether she knew the participants or not. Sylvia eventually zoned out with her iPad, developing a new decorating idea. But Lily perked up when she overheard a conversation between a woman getting a French manicure and another having a nail fill.

"Did you hear that Bruno Brockman died?" asked Ms. Frenchie.

"No!" exclaimed Ms. Acrylic.

"Yep. He was at that hoity toity assisted living place over in Edmonds."

"The one up on the cliff? Right on the Sound?"

"That's the one."

"Just old age?"

"An OD of his pain killer so I've heard. Must have gotten confused. Or downed the whole bottle to get away from that miserable wife of his." Ms. Frenchie held a manicured hand in the air to examine the stark white tips.

Lily hoped the wife had better friends than Ms. Frenchie, but that wasn't the bit that brought her out of her salon-induced haze. Bruno Brockman was the name in one of the obits. And the hoity toity place on the cliff in Edmonds must be Driscoll Manor. The place that Orlo Chesterton mentioned on his death bed. Another suspicious death? She had to report to Bear.

✦ ✦ ✦

Will Haverstock sprayed disinfectant on the body before him, then placed a sheet over the parts that would have embarrassed the dead man to expose in life. He stared at the face for a moment. The cadaver looked a little like Will's grandfather, raw boned and whippet thin. Will smoothed the old man's thin hair back from his forehead. "Looks to me like you had a haircut recently, Mr. Pickard. Don't think we'll need to call in a barber."

Calvin the janitor was just crossing through the embalming room with his cart of supplies. As he headed on through the archway, he said, "Fuckin' weird how you speak to the stiffs, boy."

Will didn't care what Cal thought. It personalized things, making it easier to perform the tasks an embalmer must do. Before he began to shave the corpse, Will explained to it, "Did you know you can get razor burn even after death?" He began wielding the razor. "But there's less chance if I shave before the embalming chemicals firm the skin."

As he worked, Will thought he was damn lucky to still have a job. After all, he'd been there when the boss was shot. And Mr. Chesterton had technically fired him. But nobody here knew that. So he'd just reported for work as usual.

"I'm glad the boss is still at the morgue, you know what I mean, Mr. Pickard? Not looking forward to working on his remains." The job was harder when he'd known the person in life and especially grisly after an autopsy. "Maybe Mrs. Chesterton will choose a cremation instead."

The funeral parlor was still open for business. Chesterton's widow had called an impromptu staff meeting the day after Orlo's death and assured them all that it was business as usual. Will figured that the boss had died before he'd been able to tell his wife about Will or Bear or anything else that happened that night.

Millicent Chesterton hadn't looked deep in mourning to Will, but you could never really tell. "Grief makes some folks gnash their teeth and pull their hair," he said to the corpse as he began to assemble the eye cups, mouth support, needles, thread and glue he'd need to set the facial features in a pleasing expression. "Others climb deep inside themselves and shut the lid as tight as a hatch on a submarine. That's the kind of thing you learn working in a funeral home. Mr. Chesterton taught me a lot."

Will hadn't exactly liked his boss but respected his knowledge of mortuary science. He doubted the widow would be as knowledgeable. Will hoped she meant it when she said she wouldn't close the place down.

Did any of his co-workers know the cops thought Chesterton had been selling bodies instead of cremating them? Will shook his head as he worked. "I don't know anything about that, Mr. Pickard. I only embalm. And rest assured, nobody but you will want your parts when I'm done."

He wasn't usually the observant type and mostly kept his nose to himself. If he hadn't heard those night noises, Will would have never believed anything like that could have been happening. "I wonder what Bear thinks," he said to Mr. Pickard as he picked up a scalpel. The room was silent for a time while Will cut an incision into the body's neck to begin the injection of embalming fluids and the draining of blood. Will knew embalmers who listened to iPods or even played radios as they worked, but he found it disrespectful. Maybe if he knew what kind of music Mr. Pickard had liked in life ...

The door from the crematory banged open, and Cal marched back in. "If the cops fucked around with that oven, they've got me to answer to," the beefy janitor declared. Cal was responsible for maintaining the oven between uses. "Damn! It stinks in here."

Will had long since grown inured to the heavy odor of the embalming chemicals. He was grateful that the stench usually made Cal clear out. But now, Cal strolled over to peer at the body. "What brings gramps to Motel Deep 6?"

Will grimaced. "Mr. Pickard's heart gave out. Unlike you, he had one." Will disliked Cal. He was a slob, dressed in old clothes that smelled of sweat. Today he had a couple scratches on his neck that appearing to be festering.

Probably clawed while teasing some poor kitten.

"You're a real comedian, Wierdo. You got any road kill on tap for me today?" Cal picked up bodies from rest homes and other locations around town when Will was too overloaded with embalming to do it.

"No deceased orders at the moment."

"Then I'm out of here." Cal slammed the door to the garage on his way out.

"Sorry about that, Mr. Pickard. I dislike Cal's slang and he knows it." Will massaged the corpse's limbs to be sure the blood was flowing out and the formaldehyde solution was pumping in. Finally Will used a specialized hose to suck fluids from the organs, sutured the incision he'd created, and placed the body in storage.

Will removed his paper gown and blue latex gloves. He would do Mr. Pickard's make-up in the morning. It was getting late, and he was tired. But he had to return a call first. Unfortunately, Millicent Chesterton had been in the office and taken the message. "A Bear Jacobs asked you to call," she'd said. "And, please Will, limit the personal calls from now on, okay?"

He hoped she had no idea who Bear was. As he punched in the number Will wished that right about now, *he* had no idea who Bear was either. But this time, the big man's request wasn't as hard as breaking and entering.

"Yes, we pick up bodies at Driscoll Manor," Will said. "Most funeral homes are on call to most assisted living places. They like to spread the business around."

"Did you receive a guy named Bruno Brockman a while back?"

"Sounds familiar. Unusual name."

"Anything strike you as ... irregular about it?"

Will paused. Maybe professional ethics should keep him from talking to Bear. His boss would have said yes, but then Bear was looking into his boss's murder. Considering that, Mr. Chesterton would probably be all for it.

"When Cal picked up Mr. Brockman, the administrator told him it was an OD. I suppose it could have been a suicide, though."

"Has it happened before? A questionable death from Driscoll Manor?"

"Once that I know of. A body came in with petechial hemorrhaging."

"Interesting. Thanks, Will."

After the call, Will headed for home, eager to check in with Chrissie. All the way there he worried whether he'd said too much. He recalled the boss telling him that the deceased, the family and the doctor would not be well served by too many questions.

Would his big mouth get him in hot water at Motel Deep 6?

CHAPTER FIFTEEN

Case Notes
April 3, 2 pm
Bear must have been a force to reckon with when he was a cub. He's taller than most, still well over six foot although I imagine he's shrunk some. His shoulders are broad enough to have been a tackle in the Black and Blue Division, and there are telltale signs of a rough past. Like the jagged scar high on his forehead that wanders for two inches before it disappears into his hairline. Looks to me like that had to hurt.
He's no push over, but let's face it. He's seen better days just like the rest of us at Latin's Ranch. Every morning is its own little tragedy of aches or leaks or gasps as our bodies discover new ways to let us down. Bear must have been feeling a little vulnerable. That's the only way I can explain enlisting help from Vinny Tononi.
Every now and then, one of us has seen a long black Cadillac slink real slow across the driveway entrance. I never thought much about it. I mean, it isn't like anybody can drive this twisty road at Indy speeds so a car that big should take its time. Maybe it was just one of those limos that shuttles people who live in the neighborhood down to SeaTac.
Then Bear and I saw it the night we broke into Chesterton Funeral Home. After that, I figured it was up to no good. But Bear figured different, and he's the big shot detective. He took his inquiries right to Frankie. None of us knew much about the old paisano before he

came to live here, but we've had our theories. Turns out we're right. Frankie told Bear he still has Sicilian acquaintances who might be happy to see him whacked before he succumbs to natural causes. So Frankie has his goombah Vinny Tononi keep an eye on Latin's Ranch from time to time. Even had him check up on Bear and me that night outside the funeral home, after Eunice told him we'd been gone too long. And Vinny's ride is a long black Caddy. Mystery solved. And confirmed by Sylvia after a coffee date with her friend Tony, who is Frankie's grandson.

Now the old smoothie has loaned Vinny to us for the day. God only knows what all he's armed with, but he makes little clanking sounds when he walks. And I don't believe that chain under his collar is a necklace.

Vinny scares the snot out of me. But Bear won't let me go with him to Driscoll Manor unless Vinny takes us. The old fart says we owe it to Jessica after our promises that we'd be more careful. He's right, of course. I need to suck it up and hope if anyone gets hit, wasted, clipped or iced, it won't be me.

-Lily Gilbert, Nervous Assistant to PI Bear Jacobs

Riding in the Caddy was a lot cushier than Sitting Bull, but the golf cart was more fun, maybe because it didn't need to be driven by a thug. Lily shared the ample back seat with Bear and stared at the back of the driver, Vinny Tononi. A neck that size was rarely seen on a human being.

"Do you really think we'll need so much muscle?" Lily whispered to Bear.

"Enemy territory, Lily. We're entering enemy territory."

"Is someone going to shoot at us again?" She tried to sit up straight, but the soft cushioned seat sucked her back.

"Don't think so. We're going to an assisted living facility in the middle of the day, and they usually aren't locked and loaded. I just think a show of strength can get some types to talk. And it can't hurt when you don't want to be thrown out on your keisters."

Bear had made an appointment at Driscoll Manor, pretending an interest in possible admittance. It was beautiful, looking like it might have been built as a mansion in the early days of Washington timber fortunes. The architectural style could be called National Park Lodge except it had been updated and modernized through the decades. Now, as an assisted living residence, rooms were transformed into apartments. Elevators had been added. If animal heads had once hung on the walls, they'd been replaced with lovely landscapes by local artists. A massive river rock fireplace which had once burned wood now flickered with a low gas flame.

As they waited for the administrator in the lobby, Vinny hulked behind them like a threatening Mount St. Helens.

"Driscoll Manor is definitely not for the Medicaid set," Lily concluded, glancing around at the sumptuous décor. "It would take plenty of moolah to hang your hat here."

When the administrator finally appeared, he looked at them as though mutts had invaded Westminster. He didn't exactly raise his nose higher in the air, but his friendly countenance morphed to guarded caution. His name was Russell Driscoll. Lily figured he was the son of a son of an ancestor who was of far sturdier stock. Like a hybrid plant that loses its vigor through the generations, this Driscoll appeared pallid and soft.

When he took Lily's hand in greeting, she nearly recoiled from his limp grasp. He didn't shake Bear's enormous paw at all, opting instead for a slight bow, and he ignored Vinny other than a slight widening of his eyes. He ushered the trio into a snug alcove off the main lobby, taking a wingback chair for himself.

Lily was pleased the Manor no longer carried out its lodge motif with furniture made from elk antlers. Nor was it the heavy duty vinyl in lesser facilities whose residents were so classless as to occasionally dribble. Instead, the upholstery fabric was a lovely muted brocade.

In fact, the whole place seemed muted, with no resident chatter, as if to speak loudly would destroy the ambiance. The only sound was a piped-in track of great songs arranged to be dull as mush. All in all, Lily far preferred the sunny hubbub of Latin's Ranch.

Bear pushed Lily's wheelchair next to a love seat, then sat. Vinny stood dead still in the alcove, his hands crossed over the general area of his genitals.

Why the hell do men do that?

His presence would intimidate anyone else from joining them. Lily had to admire Bear's pre-planning.

"Now, Mr. Jacobs, what might I do for you?" Russell Driscoll asked. He cast a glance through immaculate thick lenses toward Lily. "Were you thinking of living quarters for Mrs. Gilbert? Or yourself, perhaps? I must warn you that Driscoll Manor rarely has an opening. And when we do, there is a waiting list that is years long." He executed a 'what can you do' shrug of his bony shoulders.

Bear nipped the small talk short and played loose with the truth. "You can confirm the information that Orlo Chesterton passed on just before he passed on."

Driscoll lifted his eyebrows. "While I was very sorry to hear of Orlo's death – and let me say what a dear friend and consummate professional he was – why on earth would I know what he had on his mind at the point of death?"

Liar, liar, pants on fire.

Lily started to speak but the slightest lift of a finger from Bear convinced her to hold her tongue.

Bear said, "He told me to ask you, Russ. Ask you about the people who die here prematurely."

Now Driscoll and Lily both stared at Bear. She thought it must be that entrapment wasn't an issue for a private dick.

"What on earth are you talking about?" Driscoll protested. "And just who exactly are you?"

"I'm a detective, Russ. I detect bad guys. And I think I'm looking at one right now."

Driscoll looked the big man up and down. "You're no detective. Not for any law enforcement I know."

"Didn't say I was."

Lily found the administrator's skepticism reasonable. Maybe he doesn't think a cop would be walking with a quad cane and hauling an old lady around with the help of thug.

"Well, I'm calling them right now. You're verging on slander, Mr. Jacobs, and I won't have it." As Driscoll stood to go, Vinny took one giant step forward. The administrator retreated two baby steps back to the beautiful chair. The choreography was masterful.

"Thank you for reconsidering," Bear said when Driscoll reseated himself.

"Just get on with it. What do you want?"

"I have reason to believe that at least two people died here under questionable circumstances." Bear described the bodies that Will had told him about, one with petechial hemorrhaging and the other with signs of an overdose.

"Who told you such things? Is someone at that funeral parlor telling tales?" Driscoll scowled as if he were taking role of the funeral home employees. "Surely not Mrs. Chesterton. Or any of the office staff. What would they know? Maybe the embalmer. Of course. He'd see the bodies."

"That's not the question on the table." Lily knew Bear would never name Will as his source, but she worried that Driscoll had guessed it.

"You have no proof that either death was avoidable. If you did, you'd go to the authorities. You don't scare me. You're nothing but a toothless old bully."

Bear's mass occupied more than half of the love seat. Somehow he gathered himself together and leaned forward on his cane. He went from 'at ease' to 'attention' in a split second. Even Lily felt the hairs at the back of her neck prickle as Bear began to speak. "No, I don't have proof, Russ. But just the taint that you're lending death a hand could close you down. Don't think I won't spread the word."

"No legitimate press would publish such rot." Driscoll wasn't yet backing down. Lily had to admit he was pluckier than she would have guessed. But Bear was wily. She was surprised his next gambit involved her.

"You really want to go head to head in a press conference against this sweet looking lady here who'd be claiming you offed a dear one a little too soon?"

Driscoll looked at her and scowled. She offered a smile so wide it would make her dentist proud.

Bear went for the kill. "And we won't stop there. I'm talking internet, Russ. Viral wildfire about how your residents had better live in fear. Negative publicity is murder in the health care business."

Driscoll sat stock still, nothing moving but the rapid blinking of his eyelids. Finally, whether due to Bear's threat or the massive goodfella in his lobby, he folded.

"All right. I'll say this much. Sometimes, we may have a resident who feels his time has come. It is up to him how – intensely – we scrutinize his demise. If his family is at peace and his doctor signs a death certificate, I don't ask a great many questions. Orlo Chesterton understood that and didn't question either. It was not our job to –"

"Oh, cut the crap," Lily snapped, unable to keep still any longer. "If we spill the beans to the media, I'm betting your waiting list will evaporate pdq."

Driscoll snapped. "And you'd do it, too, wouldn't you, you old b – "

"Driscoll," Bear cut him off. "We're not here to publicize your weaknesses. It's not our goal. Frankly, I agree that what a resident wants for himself is largely his own business."

"Then I've given you everything you need."

"Not quite. I want to know what other special services you offer. You tell us about that, and we'll keep silent about your willingness to assist residents on their way to meet their Maker."

"What more do you want to know? What do you mean by special services?"

"Do you help residents live as well as die? Are you in the body parts business?" Bear reached into a pocket and handed over a crumpled brochure from Carefree Occasions.

"Ah." Driscoll stared at the brochure for a long time. Lily thought he might have gone to Carolina in his mind, but he finally began in a soft monotone. "I'm breaking no laws, you understand. Driscoll Manor has served the best interests of our seniors for many decades and will continue to do so."

"I'm sure you have. Go on."

"Many of our residents are what I call healthy seniors. They could have a dozen active, happy years ahead of them. But maybe one malfunctioning organ stands between them and those years. It is very difficult for seniors to rise to the top of transplant lists. They have to wait so long that their general health may begin to fail, while they watch fresh healthy organs go to younger people who have more years to live. By the time an organ is available for one of these people, his or her general health may have disintegrated to the point that surgery is now out of the question."

At last, the penny dropped for Lily. She finally understood why seniors would take organs from seniors. "Old people like me don't need organs that work for decades ... we just need a few years."

"Exactly," Driscoll said, actually casting a small smile in her direction as if she were a particularly apt student. "Seniors can do fine with older organs. Take a kidney, for instance. If it is from a person over 55 it won't function as many years as those from younger donors. But that's all a senior needs."

"So a second waiting list is growing," Bear interjected. "A B-list."

"Yes. A second list of candidates willing to accept older, higher-risk donors. Organs considered too chancy for young recipients are acceptable for seniors who can't face a long wait." Driscoll squared his shoulders. "I offer to put residents who are in this predicament in touch with an organization that may be able to help them. It's the company that owns Carefree Occasions."

Bear took the brochure back and peered at the mouse type on the bottom of the back page. Next to the copyright he found the name. "BioTetics, Inc?"

Driscoll nodded. "Yes, that's it. They try to help families who can afford it find the kind of donor organs that residents like ours need. I consider it a valuable service."

Lily wondered if Bear's gut felt as queasy as hers. She glanced at Vinny. She thought even Mr. Stoneface was frowning a little.

Bear asked, "Do you know where they are getting these higher risk organs?"

"No, I don't."

"Did you know healthy seniors are disappearing from our community?"

Driscoll paled. "You mean ... No. I don't want to know any more. I have nothing to do with anything like that." He stood, his hands clutching each other as if they might otherwise fly away. His distress looked real to Lily.

"I would like you all to leave now. I've told you what I know." He looked around as if expecting to see someone else. "You would do well to go lightly with BioTetics. You and your thug won't frighten them so easily."

"Thug?" Bear asked. "Vinny's just our driver."

"Of course he is. I trust you will keep your word ... that I will see no mention of Driscoll Manor in the press. It would be unpleasant to have to sue."

For the first time since she had met him, Lily heard a noise from Vinny. It sounded like water running over rocks until it broke into an actual laugh.

"He sue. Es funny, no? I tell joke to my *Padrino*."

Lily had watched enough mob movies to know that wasn't a good thing. Apparently, Russell Driscoll had, too. He got paler still as he hustled from the room, leaving them to find their own way out.

Once Vinny had helped them back into the Caddy, Bear leaned back, closed his eyes and began to hum. Lily thought it was *Anything Goes*. She waited as long as she could before the feeling of exclusion made her burst.

"Bear?"

Nothing now. Not even humming.

"Bear?"

Nothing.

"BEAR!"

"What the hell are you yelling for?" His beady eyes snapped open.

"Are you hibernating?"

"I'm thinking."

"Think and talk at the same time. Tell me what you think of Driscoll."

"I'd guess there's more to his involvement with Chesterton Funeral Home than he's admitting. Orlo agreed not to ask him too many questions about deaths here. Stands to reason, Driscoll knew Chesterton was selling bodies instead of cremating them."

"They kept each other's dirty little secrets."

"Yep. Maybe Driscoll even paid Chesterton to turn the other cheek. Or maybe Chesterton paid a fee to Driscoll for particularly usable corpses. Ones with minimal collateral damage to healthy organs. Don't know. That's for Keegan to look into."

"But not us?"

"Nope. Our focus needs to be on following the missing seniors. The ones disappearing while still alive."

"So what we've learned is that there's a company that is coming up with body parts for seniors who can afford them."

"Right."

"And they're called BioTetics."

"Right again. BioTetics owns a company called Carefree Occasions with brochures in every senior center and nursing home we visit."

"And one was found in Candi Kenilworth's home."

"Exactly."

"So what does that mean?"

"Well, as a no-proof, wild-ass guess I'd say Carefree Occasions is a source for BioTetics to find a large batch of organ donees who nobody will miss any too soon."

Lily felt like she'd been slapped in the face with an evil but undeniable truth. She was appalled that she had not seen the connection earlier. "Oh, Bear. Oh. What do we do now?"

"I'm working on that. If someone would leave me alone long enough to come up with a plan."

He shut his eyes again and leaned back against the head rest once again.

"When we get home, maybe the rest of the gang will have some ideas, too."

He rolled his great head in her direction. The solemnity she saw in the set of his jaw startled her. "I don't think so, Lily. Not this time. I think we should keep it to ourselves for a while."

"Really? Why?"

"We got involved in this whole mess to look for Charlie's missing wife. He may have been a player, and she may only have been his most recent plaything, but he actually loves Louise."

"Poor Charlie."

"If I'm right, she's as dead as Fluffy-san. I'm not ready to tell him that her pieces have been sold off to the highest bidders. Not without more proof."

Lily blanched and turned away. For a while, she watched the scenery go by. The tinted windows dulled the colorful buds of rhodies finally ready to burst into full bloom. When she looked back at Bear she asked, "You don't think that it would soothe Charlie to know that her life has given new hope to others in need?"

Bear smiled. Lily saw sadness in that grin, but fondness for her, too. He patted her hand and said, "I think he'll think that's crap. And I think you think so, too."

✦ ✦ ✦

It was early morning. Jessica and Ben were failing at phone sex.

"Ben, I can't do this. I feel silly."

"Why?"

"I live directly above five curious old people, four of whom suffer from insomnia. That impedes my ability to play with sex toys."

"Oh. Well, how about I come right over?"

"You live a good thirty minutes away."

"Nonsense. I can cut that time in half."

"I don't want you to set an all time land speed record. Besides, my shift begins pretty soon."

"Easier to get to the moon than get on your calendar."

"Poor baby. Come for dinner Thursday. It's Sicilian night. Plied with enough Chianti, I may have a special dessert just for you."

"The cannoli as sex toy?"

"It would work better for me than a smart phone."

✦ ✦ ✦

Eunice continued to avoid Frankie. Lily had never known her to act this way. She would not allow his name to be spoken in her presence. If it happened, she made some noise halfway between a spit and a hiss then left the room. She sat as far from him as possible at meal time while he made cow eyes down the length of the dining table. Occasionally he even whimpered a few tragic bars from *Pagliacci*. It was getting on everyone's nerves.

"With so many hearts bleeding all over the table it's hard to concentrate on missing body parts," Bear was heard to growl.

Lily decided to take matters into her own hands. The next day she and Eunice were puttering along the edge of the woods where the columbine and harebells were waving in the breeze. When Eunice stopped to peer at a clump of bitterroot, Lily reached over and switched off Sitting Bull's ignition. She pocketed the key.

"Now listen here, Eunice, we all love you but you're being a major pain in the ass."

"Me? Me?" Eunice sat up tall, or as close to tall as she could manage.

"Yes, you you. You loved those earrings from Frankie until you saw the brooch on Aurora."

Eunice's lips quivered between a pout and a tight knot of fury. Finally, denial won out. "Not true. I've merely lost all interest in him. It's my prerogative." She shot an angry glare at her old friend. "And it's my business."

"Say what you want, you crazy old bat, but you think he bought that pin for her. And he didn't."

"This is none of your ... he didn't?"

"He didn't. Aurora admired your earrings and talked about them so much at home, her Julio bought her the pin. She told Jessica, but you wouldn't let her tell you."

"Julio? She has a Julio?"

"Yes. And he gave it to her. Frankie is innocent." Lily cocked her head then added, "I admit that is a phrase not often heard, but in this case the godfather is clean."

Eunice cupped her face in her hands. "Oh, oh dear. I must apologize to Aurora. And I must go to my Frankie. Will he ever forgive me?"

"I'm thinking that's a safe bet." Lily handed her the keys and Eunice set Sitting Bull on fly.

By that evening at dinner, the lovebirds were back together. The billing and cooing was almost as irritating as the cold shoulders had been. Eunice was not only wearing her yellow DiamaLike earrings, but a golden dove with very real diamonds dangled from her neck.

Lily guessed that Frankie's little dove had eaten a fair amount of crow.

CHAPTER SIXTEEN

Case Notes
April 5, 10 pm
I wouldn't want to be in Ben Stassen's shoes. Or shoe as the case may be. Jessica is pissed at him. Somehow, I can't help but feel it is partly my fault. I came to bed soon after dinner so I could collect my own thoughts instead of chatter with the others.
Tonight was Sicilian Night. Aurora used chicken in her osso buco, because some of us won't eat veal, and Jessica can't afford it on what we pay anyway. But it was still so rich and savory that the aroma grabbed us by our noses and assembled us in the living room long before Aurora was ready to serve. Frankie was still allowed in the kitchen with her, but his charm failed him when his critique began. "Not with risotto, amica mia," we heard him mourn. "Polenta is the tradition."
Aurora is touchy with Frankie since the brooch fiasco. She told him that a man his age should try something new every century or so, and if he wasn't willing to do that, he could just cook it himself next time. Shortly after Frankie vacated the kitchen, she sent Furball packing, too. He'd yowled his hunger while braiding his fat self around her legs once too often.
Finally, it was time. We assembled around the table. Ben and Sam joined us. As a treat for me, Sylvia did, too. Much to my surprise, Vinny was also there. Guess he's part of the family now. He smiled at Sylvia which is a facial expression none of us knew he could make.

What's up with that?

We were all dressed to the nines. Jessica even reached a ten if you ask me. Her little black dress didn't have the drama of Eudora's tiger-striped kaftan, but the emerald earrings Ben gave her last Christmas were all the glitter she needed. The rest came from the sparkle in her eyes. She radiated good humor.

Everything was festive up until dessert. That's when we sprang our big surprise on Jessica. Over hazelnut gelato – with a glass of sweet Marsala for those who wanted it – we revealed Project Jessica. Then everything went to hell in a hand basket the size of Sitting Bull.

-Lily Gilbert, Woebegone Assistant to PI Bear Jacobs

Lily tapped her water glass with a spoon to focus everyone's attention. While chatter came to a halt, she looked around the table at the expectant faces glowing with the secret she was about to reveal to their caregiver. "We have an announcement to make, Jessica."

Charlie beat a drum roll on the table with his fork and spoon.

"Starting tomorrow, you will have *more free time*." Lily drew out more free time the way Bob Barker would have said *brand new car*.

Jessica looked bewildered. The fire from her emeralds danced on her ears as she glanced around the table.

Eunice beamed a smile that was lighthouse bright.

Chrissie and Aurora applauded.

"Here, here," said Bear raising his glass.

Sam, Sylvia and Ben clinked with him.

Jessica narrowed her eyes as her gaze landed back on Lily. "Okay, okay. What's going on, you guys?"

"You know, dear, that all of us love you. We depend on you, and you never let us down. But we worry about you. We want you to have more time to enjoy your ranch and your horses and, well, everything you love." Lily gave a vaudevillian wiggle of her eyebrows in the direction of Ben.

Jessica's eyes narrowed a bit more. "Uh-huh. And just how are you going to manage that?"

Lily explained that Sylvia had found a senior center that would welcome them on Friday and Saturday afternoons. She'd even hired a person to go along with them. Lily gave Sylvia credit for doing the work and paying all expenses. When Lily wound down, Jessica's jaw had dropped. She seemed speechless.

Filling the void, Chrissie piped up. "Rick and Alita and I worked out a schedule to give you Friday and Saturday mornings and evenings off, too."

Jessica finally spoke. "But ... that adds up to two whole days. In a row."

"That's right. You would have never worked it that way for yourself."

"And you know Babs Sloane," Sylvia said. "She was the activities director at Soundside before she retired. She'll be with them the whole time. She knows everyone's ... limitations ... and welcomes the challenge."

"We'll be safe with Babs," Eunice said. She cast her eyes in Frankie's direction. "She's cheery to a fault, but you'll get used to her." Lily thought there must have been a time when Eunice had enough eyelashes to bat them.

Even Sam spoke up. "I'll be just up the way at the barn. They can call me if they need me to come help them."

Lily could sense the cogs begin to turn in Jessica's fertile brain. The caregiver looked less amazed, more intrigued. "How will all five of you get there? Does Babs have a van?"

Frankie puffed out his chest like a sage grouse in a courting ritual. "I have it handled, cara mia. My Vinny Tononi, he take us and bring us home. No worry. We come to no harm."

Vinny managed a very slight bow toward Jessica.

Jessica picked up her dessert spoon then set it back down. "How will you get lunch?"

"I make it for them to take in the morning. Like a picnic but for indoors," Aurora said.

Jessica nodded, then turned to the big man. "Bear? Are you going along with this?"

"Sure. They have a chess championship."

"Charlie?"

"They got Wii."

Jessica's lip quivered. Puddles formed in her eyes. Her complexion darkened, not to a pretty pink but to blotches of red. "But ... but, aren't you guys happy here?"

The dam burst, and Jessica overflowed with a mighty sob.

The rest of them looked flabbergasted. Lily had not anticipated this at all. Was Jessica jealous? Did she feel unwanted? "Oh, my dear, of course we're happy here. We love it here."

All the residents confirmed their happiness at once. It was a flash mob of coos and affection and solidarity.

Next, they tried logic. Chrissie hit all the mental health buzz words. "Social outreach is enriching for them, Jessica. Verbal interaction. Cognitive stimulation ..."

"Lots of gossip," Eunice said.

Bear took the no-bullshit route. "You work too hard on our behalf. If you don't get some relief, you'll end up kicking our sorry old asses out in the street where at best we'd become road kill."

By now, Jessica had dried her tears. Then Lily added the cherry to the top of the sundae, driving home her earlier point. "We want you to have more time for yourself and for Ben. Right, Ben?"

Ben flashed Jessica a grin that could melt a woman's underwear. "I'm taking time off from my job, too. We can be together. "

A clock ticked. *O Sole Mio* soared from a CD. A couple coffee cups clinked against saucers. Everyone stared at Jessica in anticipation.

Jessica stared at Ben. Then at the others. Then back at Ben. Even without a meteorologist, Lily could see the storm clouds gathering.

"Let me get this straight," Jessica said in a flat voice. "You all think I need help running my own life, so you're taking over the job for me."

"Jessica, that's not – " Lily began.

Jessica raised her hand in a cop-like gesture to stop. "I can understand that, and I thank you for your thoughtfulness although I would have preferred you allow me to be part of the plan." She favored the residents with a small smile and a loud sniff.

Then she rounded on Ben. "But you, Ben Stassen. You can't find time to be with me without their help? It had to be someone else's suggestion? Not your own?"

Ben looked sideswiped. "Well, actually, Jess, no, I couldn't do it without their help. It depends on their willingness to create the time. This will give us a chance to –"

"— to make a plan only to have your daughter break it almost every damn time?"

Ben's jaw tightened. "To have you think of me as a priority. For a change."

Lily could feel Storm Jessica about to level the Pacific Northwest. She could think of no way to stop it.

"For a change? So I have to make changes in my life while you--"

"Jessica, this isn't the place for this." Ben looked toward the crowd that was avidly looking back.

"It's the place you chose to bring it up."

"Well, now I choose to leave it alone until you can be more reasonable."

"I'm perfectly reasonable right now." Jessica crossed her arms and narrowed her eyes all the more.

Ben's chair scraped across the floor as he pushed back and stood. "And I'm perfectly sure I better leave right now until you've calmed down."

Lily was afraid that would take a century or two. "Oh dear," she muttered to Eunice who was seated next to her.

"Nobody's stopping you," Jessica called to Ben's departing back. Then she stood and threw her napkin on the table. As he slammed out the front door, she turned to look at the group. Lily watched her grapple with emotion, trying to talk herself down the way she would a frightened filly.

"Thank you so much for thinking of me. It will be wonderful. I'll love having time for the horses and for ..." She sniffed. "For ... oh ... goodnight, everyone." Jessica headed in the opposite direction from Ben, clattering up the stairs in her fancy evening stilettos.

The rest of the dinner party sat in silence looking as woebegone as a bunch of elderly orphans. Finally Charlie held up the wine bottle and said, "Anyone for more Marsala?"

✦ ✦ ✦

The next Friday, Latin Lover was watching Jessica clean the stall across the barn from his own. His mahogany coat shone with health and care. Down the line, Gina Lola's big gray head was sticking over her stall gate – and Folly's little snout under it – so they could observe the action, as well.

"Life is a big old pile of shit," Jessica said to the livestock. "What a way to enjoy my day off."

Her flock had flown the coop for their maiden voyage to the senior center. Vinny Tononi looked too much like a mobster for her to feel totally comfortable turning her residents over to him. She'd told Sam to follow along behind the Cadillac until they were safely at the senior center and then to take the afternoon off. Now Jessica was alone with her chores. She'd relished the idea of physical labor today, wanting to be sweaty and exhausted and sore. She needed to release the high tension that had her wired. To be too tired for yet another sleepless night. To act as bad as she felt without prying eyes to see it.

The idea of hard work had sounded better than the reality of it. Now cleaning her sixth stall, she was still waiting for endorphins. "Just where are the little shits? I'm supposed to feel like a million bucks by now."

The stallion looked wise. He knew about mares and how sometimes they could deliver nasty kicks. Leave them alone until they're ready. Then be there. That's what his horse sense said to him.

Lifting another forkful of road apples into the manure cart, Jessica began to cry. It started as a tightening in her sinuses, a sting in her tear ducks, then a great gulping of air. She felt petty, but didn't give a damn as long as no one was around to hear. The horses would never tell.

"How can I be so fucking jealous of his daughter? I mean she's his *daughter,* for the love of God. Of course, she comes first. I get that. I mean, that's how parents have to be, right? But, damn it to hell, when do I get to be first? Answer me that."

Latin Lover and Gina Lola looked on, each munching a shock of orchard grass hay.

"Ed always did whatever the hell he wanted, whether I agreed or not.

He didn't listen." She thought about the night she'd asked her husband not to go out. The night his truck jackknifed on the black ice. The night her life had collapsed. She'd worked like the devil to make a comeback after his death. She'd suffered the losses faced by anyone who works with livestock. She'd trained other people's horses, taught others to ride, took on the management of an adult family home just to keep going. She'd at long last pulled a nose ahead of financial doom.

Her tears stopped dripping and her nose began, but her sinuses would soon be as stuffed as a Christmas turkey. Then she'd be a mouth-breather.

Thank God everyone's gone.

"I love Ben, I do. I know it isn't just gratitude. He's a wonderful man. And he's had enough heartache. I just can't ask him to put me ahead of his daughter." She spread fresh pine shavings around the clean stall. "But I can't play second fiddle, not again. It's my turn to matter to somebody."

"Yes, you can ask it, Jess. It's time we talked it through."

Jessica froze.

Is Ben here? Is he with his horses? Is he standing behind me? Please let me die right here.

Ben must have come in to groom his animals, expecting to find Sam. Instead here she was, blubbering out words she would not want him to hear until she sugar coated it, rewrote and edited her script.

She turned. She stared.

Blame him!

"How dare you sneak up on me?" She ran to the tack room at the end of the barn stripping off her work gloves. She put her hands over her Rudolf nose and swollen eyes. She smelled like the wrong end of a horse.

Ben followed. He grabbed her and held on as she tried to pull away.

She didn't try very hard. "Don't look at me," she said. "I look awful."

"Not as bad as you smell."

"How much did you hear?"

"The only part that mattered. That you love me."

"But I can't have you." She showered tears onto his shirt.

"Jessica, you didn't want to listen at dinner, but you're going to listen now. I had a man-to-man with Bear not long ago. He helped me see a few things more clearly. About Rachael. About how I'm doing her as much harm as good by clutching hold so tight. Maybe more."

"B-B-Bear?"

"Seems he's had some experience with situations like these."

Sniff. "What did he say?"

"I can't reconstruct exactly what he said, but I can tell you what I heard. And what I am going to do. I'm going to loosen the tie to Rachael."

"Loosen the tie?" Jessica's head was pounding as hard as her heart. She couldn't seem to form a complete thought.

"If Rachael wants a relationship with her father, she has to work for it, too. I'm doing this for me, Jess. With or without you, I am not going to be on call for that girl all the time anymore."

"I can't ask you to do that, Ben."

"I'm doing it whether you ask or not. This isn't your fault. It's not mine. You don't have to ask me to put you first. I want to."

Relief began to flood her system and restore her senses. "At least let me be part of the decision-making, okay?"

"It may take a little practice. But I'll get good at it. That's a promise."

Her eyes and nose and heart all felt washed and new. She walked with Ben, arm in arm, back to the empty house. Even Aurora was gone, having said she'd be back in time to prep dinner. Jessica put in a quick call to Lily who assured her all was well at the senior center. "There are some scrabble players here who are real patsies. We're having a ball. And you. How are you doing?"

"I couldn't be better."

Jessica and Ben hit the shower together to remove the eau de horse. They made love there and again in Jessica's bedroom.

"No insomniacs downstairs to overhear us," Ben said, a bit out of breath. "Project Jessica is off to a helluva start."

By the time the Latin's Ranch gang returned from the senior center at dinner time, Jessica and Ben were gone. They did not return until Sunday. Nothing and no one had come between them.

But then, Rachael had not yet called.

✦ ✦ ✦

Sunday afternoon, Bear and Detective Keegan sat on the patio behind Latin's Ranch. Everyone else was napping or watching the Mariners lose to the Twins. Furball was making every effort to reach the hummingbird feeder, launching his massive proportions like an overweight space shuttle. He missed the mark every time.

"Have you found Nurse Redhead yet?" Bear asked after updating Keegan on his visit to Driscoll Manor.

"Not yet," the detective answered. "She got out before we locked down the ICU. Several hospital staffers remember seeing her, but none knew her." She looked from Folly asleep in the sun off toward the barn and horse pastures. "It's nice here."

"They don't know their co-workers?" Bear glanced at her. "And, yeah. This is a nicer place than a lot of old farts call home." He could see the spring sun was having the same curative effect on the energetic cop as it had on the dog. He'd never seen Keegan look relaxed before. Her face had fewer lines. She looked softer, like she'd been drawn with pastels instead of ink. Bear approved, not that he'd ever tell her such a thing.

"Hospitals use specialized temp agencies when they have shortages. New faces around all the time. Employees aren't to blame for not recognizing them all. We're going through all HR records to see what we can match up."

"Jessica uses an agency here when she's in a jam. We had some bad luck with that at Soundside, though." Bear remembered the sexual assault on an elderly woman by a temp worker. "Criminal background checks aren't all they're cracked up to be. They only reveal convictions, not accusations."

"Agencies provided five temps that day to the hospital. All accounted for. Red must have slipped under everyone's radar. Came in, did the deed, got out."

"She was wearing a surgical mask when I first saw her."

"Probably so we couldn't identify her when she gave Chesterton the drug."

"I don't think so. Other people saw her in the ICU, too. And she took the mask off while she talked to me. So why'd she have it on to begin with?"

"Curious, Bear."

"Curious, Keegan."

They sat for a while letting spring do its magic. Then Bear said, "Okay. Let's review. We have five missing seniors. The glue holding them together is pretty weak. They're all healthy, they've all recently been caregivers, at least some of them have connections to Chesterton Funeral Home and have been approached by Carefree Occasions."

Keegan took the next chapter. "On a tip from an embalmer, the Latin's Ranch Old Fools break into Chesterton Funeral Parlor. You claim to find two eviscerated bodies, but they're in the oven before the cops can get to them to identify. That same night the funeral director is shot."

"You and I both turn up at the hospital in time to see a red haired nurse murder Chesterton right in front of us."

"Just before that, he admits to us he's been selling bodies instead of cremating them. Clay and I start looking for Red. I pay a visit to the employment agency while he interviews funeral home employees, looking for any ties to a company in the human body aftermarket."

"Lily and I continue on the trail of the missing seniors. It leads us to Driscoll Manor where we're told about BioTetics offering old organs to old patients."

"Our paths intersect, Bear. My murderer and your missing seniors lead us in the same direction. BioTetics. We're tracking the same bad guys."

"Or bad girls. Somehow Red has to be involved in the missing seniors, too. Otherwise half the population of the county is picking off the other half. Too much coincidence."

Keegan's phone blatted, startling them both. "Yeah." She listened. "Shit. On my way." Instantly, she was all business again, softness evaporating. "Have to go meet Clay, Bear. There's been a shooting." She pushed open the door with such force it banged against the wall. He could hear her cross through the kitchen into the living room and toward the front door, moving at speed.

"And they're off," Bear said to himself imitating a race announcer. He crossed his hands over his belly and sat back in the extra sturdy deck chair. He listened to a Western Tanager go through its repertoire. He was so deep in thought, he was still as stone. Minutes passed. Then he steepled his fingers and tapped the tips together. A smile inched across his face as he hummed the opening measures of *Some Enchanted Evening*.

Bear lifted himself, leaning heavily on the quad cane. He quaked with the effort, but once upright he was fairly steady. "Work it, work it," he muttered, mocking the exercise DVD he heard playing in Jessica's apartment some mornings. He began the long walk toward Sam's trailer. But Sam wasn't there.

Bear had a choice. Take Sitting Bull or walk all the way to the barn. He hadn't walked that far in years. His body had suffered a more abusive history than his mind.

Can I make it?

Bear made his choice and started on his way.

CHAPTER SEVENTEEN

Case Notes
April 7, 8 pm
Don't expect much happy talk from me tonight. I was so worried about Chrissie and Will it wore me to a frazzle. And now, Bear's plan for Sam has me scared to death. I hadn't counted on this 'assistant to a private investigator' stuff getting so life and death. But I'm getting ahead of myself.
This afternoon, the big man walked up to the barn to see Sam. You read that right. Walked up to the barn. He called me to come get him in Sitting Bull. He didn't even ask please. I nearly told him to have his buddy Vinny Tononi haul his big ass home. But it's so pretty outside now in the evenings – what with everything a crazy quilt of spring color – that I kind of wanted to go. Besides, if Bear really needs my help, well, you know.
At the entrance of the barn, my eyes were sun dazzled until they adjusted to the lower light inside. I stopped Sitting Bull, waiting for my sight to clear, and inhaled deeply. I love the odor of the barn, the horses, sweet hay and the pine shavings Sam uses for bedding. Even the aroma of horse manure is tolerable. But it's a good thing Jessica isn't a pig farmer.
When I could finally see, I noticed Bear with Sam down at the far end. They were sitting on hay bales with clear plastic cups of liquid gold that looked like 90 proof. Neither glanced up at my approach. Maybe they were telling a dirty joke or some other man secret. I how-

died Dancer, Gina Lola, Latin Lover and the rest of the horses as Sitting Bull purred through the double row of stalls.

Once close enough, I could see that Bear looked poorly. His skin was damn near the same ash gray as his cardigan. I stopped right in front of him and said, "Your ride has arrived, good sir."

Sam had to steady Bear as he stood, but the curmudgeon shook off the help as he clambered into the cart.

"You tried to do too much, didn't you?" I asked as he settled like a sack of meal beside me. I couldn't help being put out. He'll be thinking he can climb Mt. Rainier next. He surprised the crap out of me by taking my hand and patting it. Can't think of a faster way he could have shut my pie hole.

"It's not that, Lily." His voice was so scratchy I swear he was fighting tears. His head sagged toward his chest.

"What then? You're scaring me." I dug a Kleenex out of my pocket in case he really did start to drip. I decided to keep the tissue myself when he said, "Will Haverstock was shot today. And Chrissie was with him."

-Lily Gilbert, Desolate Assistant to PI Bear Jacobs

"How bad? Is he dead? Is Chrissie okay? How'd it happen?" Lily's mouth was moving faster than her brain. She grabbed tight to the Kleenex and began shredding it into fluffy bits of confetti. Her body was instantly cold as a glacier, and her hands looked just as blue.

"Chrissie's fine. She wasn't hit. In fact, she was staunching Will's blood when the cops arrived.'

Lily felt a rush of relief. "Oh, thank God." But the relief was short lived. "How's Will? Is he going to be okay?"

Bear wagged a maybe-so-maybe-not gesture with his hand. "He'll survive, according to Keegan, although he's lost a lot of blood. But it's my fault he was wounded at all. I dragged him into this." His head sunk lower. When Lily saw his tears, she realized he wasn't merely tired from the walk. His body language shrieked guilt. "Who the hell do I think I am, trying to be a detective again? Oldest story in the book, a has-been trying to reclaim his glory days. That boy will recover, but he's in pain and has me to thank for it."

Lily didn't interrupt Bear's blame fest, although she had many questions. She let Bear rant. Sometimes that's just what a person needs in order to work out his misery. She sat in the driver's seat next to him, fretting in silence, wanting to put her arms around him but knowing he needed space. Sam, sprawling in the back, poured a shot of Jack Daniel's for her, too. She was glad of the warmth as it burned its way down her throat and thawed the ice.

Finally Bear calmed enough to tell Lily what had happened. "Keegan got a call about a shooting when she was at the house with me this afternoon. She called later to tell me it was Will."

Lily figured Keegan must be feeling a little guilt herself. The detective knew that Will was on the scene the night Chesterton was shot. That Will told Bear about the questionable deaths in the funeral home. Hell, Driscoll up at the manor had even guessed he was their source of information. They should all have realized he might be in danger.

"Will was hit coming out the back door of Reggie's Tavern along with Chrissie. They'd been watching the ballgame on TV. Apparently, he leaned down to kiss her just as the bullet grazed him. Otherwise, his head would have split like a casaba." Bear paused for a sip of the whiskey. "As it is he has a divot along the side of his skull, and he's lost the top of his right ear." He'll be hearing ring tones for days."

"Poor boy," Lily cooed.

"At least the second bullet missed them."

"Second bullet?"

"A guy tackled the love birds and dumped them down on the ground with himself on top. The second bullet missed them. Then the tackle pulled out a gun and shot the shooter."

"Somebody else just happened to be in the lot behind the bar with a gun?" Sam tipped his hat a little further back. Lily could see his eyes with one brow raised when she turned around to look at him.

She turned back to Bear, and poked him in the arm. "A good Samaritan. You happen to know anything about that?"

"He got away," Bear said. "Everyone did. But there was blood on the concrete where the shooter must have been waiting next to the dumpster. Will's little green car was parked in the lot so it was no mystery where he was."

"Witnesses?" Lily asked.

Bear gave his head a shake. "Not according to Keegan. Apparently Will and Chrissie were so into each other they wouldn't have noticed a buffalo herd. Doc McGrath says a white panel truck burned rubber out of there just as he was pulling in. Dead Eye doesn't exactly maintain sophisticated surveillance equipment so there's no video."

"A white panel truck. That's what was behind the funeral home when Chesterton was shot." Lily visualized it parked at the far end of the alley. "This all ties back to that, doesn't it? To bodies in the crematory."

"Keegan has a crew behind Reggie's looking for the bullets. Maybe they'll match some that hit the mortician. She sent Will to the emergency ward along with Chrissie doing her Florence Nightingale bit and snapping at the EMTs."

"Then he's in good hands," Lily said.

"But I should never have involved him in the first place," Bear answered.

Sam said, "Not your fault, Bear. That boy involved you, not the other way around. I was there at Reggie's when he brought up the crematory in the first place."

Lily was weary of his breast beating. "Besides, you did what you could for him. You saved his life by having Vinny look out for him. At least I assume the good Samaritan was Vinny, and that you sent him there."

If a Bear could look sheepish, he did. He confessed he'd enlisted Frankie's help to shadow Will in the evenings. Vinny – or another paisan like him – had chased off the shooter with a load of lead as a *buon viaggio*.

"I couldn't tell Keegan who Vinny was because Frankie's friends aren't exactly tight with the law. They don't worry about little things like permits to carry or concealed weapons."

"Will won't blame you for getting him involved. He'd lend a hand whether you asked him to or not. But you better be ready for a load of shit from Chrissie," Lily said. "I'd like to head back so I can call her and see how they're doing." With no objections from the men, Lily circled Sitting

Bull around and left the barn.

As she drove she decided to clear a little air. "Just one more thing. Why the hell didn't you tell me you were having Will tailed?"

"If Keegan flat out asked, I didn't want you to have to lie about Vinny. Lying isn't in your nature. Besides, I didn't want you to worry about Will if it turned out there was no reason."

"Not good enough, Bear. Do you need my *we're-in-this-together* lecture once again?"

"Please God, no." Bear rolled his beady eyes skyward.

"All right then. No more secrets."

"Yes, ma'am. No more secrets."

When Lily stopped at Sam's trailer to drop him off, his parting words were, "Bear? If there are no more secrets, maybe you better tell Lily what else you have planned."

✦ ✦ ✦

Lily and Bear were bickering when they plugged in Sitting Bull at the patio and made a slow procession into the living room, his cane clattering in syncopation to her walker slamming up and down. She was too angry with him to even feel the exhaustion in her bones.

"You tell me."

"I won't."

"You will." Lily was so focused that at first she didn't notice Will and Chrissie standing in the room with Jessica, all three staring at the quarreling oldsters.

"Chrissie!" Lily yelled when she finally saw something other than the object of her fury. She picked up speed on her walker, tottered over to the aide and took her hand. "I'm so glad you're not hurt, my dear."

"You really love my Chrissie," Will said in a woozy singsong, his arm slung across his girl's bony shoulders. A bandage wound around his head and over his right ear like a gauze sweatband. "You're a wonderful person."

Lily considered his dopey grin and dilated pupils. "And you, young man, how are you feeling?"

"I really love my Chrissie, too." He wobbled a bit until Chrissie wrapped her arm around him in support.

The homely aide smiled and blushed such a lovely shade she looked prettier than a bride. She said, "His drugs are turned up pretty high, but he'll be fine after a good night's sleep or two. Jessica said I could bring him here."

Lily had no doubt that Jessica would open her arms to yet another orphan of the storm. At the moment the caregiver was toting a bundle of sheets and blankets plus a pillow. "I still have the empty room so it'll be easy for her to keep an eye on him. Come along, you two."

Bear put his hand on Will's shoulder. "Glad you're safe, boy."

"I really love you, too, Mr. Bear." Will beamed up at him and lurched forward for an awkward embrace. Chrissie eventually peeled him away from Bear and followed Jessica to the private room she hadn't yet rented to another senior resident.

That left Bear and Lily alone.

As soon as the others were out of earshot, she rounded on him. He wasn't getting off that easy. "I love you, too, you big old pain in the ass, but you better tell me the plan, or I'll show you just how accurate a one-legged lady's kick can be."

The canaries in the living room quit singing and took shelter under their seed cup. Furball slunk from the room, looking for safer ground. Bear huffed and fumed and made sounds that couldn't be called real words. Finally, he caved. He plopped heavily into the seat of a sturdy wingchair and sighed. "You remember Carefree Occasions."

Lily stood in front of him like a wraith, assuming a wraith could lean on a walker. "Of course. You think I'm demented? The place that offers respite for caregivers."

"Right. Well, I filled out a form online. Gave them all kinds of information about how I'm a healthy sixty-something living alone and ready to get back into the world to party."

Lily reversed to a sofa with the precision of a long haul trucker backing into a dock. She sat while saying, "Healthy? Sixty-something? Pardon me for mentioning it, but they're going to know that's hogwash the second they lay eyes on you."

"I used the name of Sam Hart. Sam is healthy and sixty-something, and according to the form I filled out, he's quite a wild man."

Lily stared, mouth agape. "Did you even ask him first?"

"Well ... he knows about it now. That's why I went up to the barn to see him. They think he lives alone."

"He does."

"I mean here at Latin's Ranch, not in the trailer. They're coming Friday afternoon to meet him and explain all about their program."

"But everyone will be gone on Friday. We'll be at the senior center. The place will be empty. He could be in danger." Lily knew she was sputtering and tried to calm herself with a deep breath.

"That's the point. I want everyone else gone. If they make a move on Sam, I'll be here to stop it."

"You crazy old bastard!" Lily grabbed the arms of the chair to stop the trembling in her hands. "Then I'll be here, too."

"I knew you'd say that. That's why I didn't tell you." Bear struggled to stand. "You'll go to the senior center with the rest of the gang, and that's that." He drew himself up and marched from the room, his cane tapping a *kachunk, kachunk* with the precision of a military band.

When no one else was around to hear except the canaries, Lily had the last word. "Sure I will, Bear. Sure I will."

✦ ✦ ✦

Bear tromped into his bedroom and was about to slam the door, but Charlie was already snoring in that mulish bray of his. Bear closed the door gently, then plopped down on the side of his bed and faced the patio, watching the night deepen outside. He could see little but the silhouettes of the planters and the humped shape of Sitting Bull parked far to the right. If there were any night sounds Charlie drowned them out.

Bear wasn't really mad at Lily although she was plenty frustrating. Mostly she just poked him in a spot that was already sore. He despised endangering other people. When he was young, he could take on the physical stuff himself. It was nearly impossible to admit it, but he couldn't do it all anymore. Lily was right. He couldn't convince anyone he was still vital and healthy. He could see no way to end this without involving someone who was. Sam was the only candidate he had.

Bear had known it might happen ever since Dr. Flannery at It's Swell to be Well had said all three of his missing patients were healthier than most for their ages. Not really old yet since they were all under seventy. "Let's call them *youthful seniors*," Bear muttered to himself, just to give his new demographic a name.

Bear's first surmise had been that the doctor might be involved. But no. Flannery didn't connect to everybody. Candi Kenilworth wasn't a patient of his. He couldn't be the source of unsuspecting organ donors, at least not the only source.

When Bear had seen Kenilworth's violated body in the crematory it had been so dismembered that he could tell nothing about her other than the clematis tattoo. He'd had to depend on descriptions from Charlie and Lily to even know she fit his profile of a youthful senior.

Her disappearance at first supported Bear's idea of a sexual predator on the loose, but that theory was shot to shit when she was found at the crematory along with a man's body. Bear presumed the male corpse was Bronek Pokorski since no other senior male had been reported missing. With a man now in the mix, Bear had needed a new cause. That's when he'd started to toy with the idea of youthful seniors murdered for their organs.

Bear didn't have proof, but he'd gathered enough facts to believe it himself. Hearts and kidneys got all the publicity, but eyes, muscle, bone, connective tissue and more could rectify birth defects and congenital disease, provide burn and accident treatment, or even make periodontal surgery possible. The demand was ever increasing while the legal supply stayed nearly stagnant.

The biggest market for questionable organs might well be transplant survivors who were prone to redevelop the condition that made the transplant necessary in the first place. They'd need to get in line for yet another heart which was virtually inconceivable.

Was it so hard to believe that senior citizens were a market as well? If you need corneas to last you just a few more years, do you really care if they came from a donor with heart failure? Wouldn't you gladly pay to jump the line? Bear had received all the confirmation of his theory that he needed when the administrator of Driscoll Manor told him about Carefree Occasions, the front for BioTetics. After reading their literature one more time, he believed they were gathering data on caregivers, a group old enough to be in charge of ailing loved ones, but fresh enough to still be active. In other words, a whole crop of youthful seniors to harvest.

Still, he had no proof. And Keegan had her hands full with investigating Chesterton's murder. The rest just sounded crazy. "No law enforcement would believe this shit without any proof," Bear muttered.

"Talking to yourself?" asked Rick, coming through the door with a stack of towels.

"More like yelling at myself," Bear answered the aide. Rick handed him his evening meds, then got out Bear's pajamas. "Want a shower tonight?"

"Sure. Something else I can't do on my own anymore."

Rick helped him into the handicap shower where there was no high step to enter. Bear could use the rails, the handheld nozzle and the plastic shower chair to sit if he needed the support. Afterwards, Rick helped him maneuver to the toilet and then into his pajamas.

While Bear clambered into bed, Rick said, "I heard about Will."

Shit.

"Sorry about your friend. My fault."

"Are you kidding? I'd say you did him a favor."

"How do you figure that?"

"Will's the talk of Reggie's. Great for his image." Rick gave Bear a sly glance. "Course, Chrissie's willingness to jump his bones helps with that, too."

Rick's strange logic made Bear feel better. But after the aide said goodnight, the darkness descended again. Bear thought about his conversation with Sam in the barn earlier in the evening.

"It could be hazardous to your health. No way around it. You'd have to face at least one thug, maybe two, both most likely armed," he had said to Sam. "And that's if everything goes right."

The old cowboy had nodded and taken another sip of Jack.

"We'll record it," Bear continued. "That's not really admissible evidence, but it's something to play for Keegan."

Sam nodded.

"I'll be there, with the rifle. As soon as you give me the sign or they make their move, I'll come in ready to blast the bastards."

After draining his glass, Sam said, "Sounds good."

"You can say no, Sam. Keegan would just tell me to keep looking for real evidence."

"People might keep dying before we find it. And they should pay for what they've done to Will." They'd just heard Lily enter the barn on Sitting Bull. Sam leaned closer to Bear and said, "So let's do it your way."

Now, in bed late at night, Bear realized that the whole time he'd been reconstructing this conversation, he'd been softly humming *I Did It My Way.*

CHAPTER EIGHTEEN

Case Notes
April 11, 11 am
I was in my wheelchair on the patio snapping beans for Aurora. A breeze perfumed with lilac swept through the open door to the kitchen, and I could hear her in there singing something Spanish about being kissed a lot. I'm sure everybody's seen calendar art of sweet old ladies on porch swings happily recalling the good old days to the young'uns while they perform this honest earthy task. Personally, I hated it as a kid, and I hate it now. Back then, I tried to get away with snapping off the stem and nothing more. I remember my mother chiding me that if I left beans that long they wouldn't fit in the Mason jars.
I mention the beans because they got Bear and me to talking again. I gave him the cold shoulder all day yesterday and at breakfast. I heard him coming through the kitchen and onto the patio behind me. You can't mistake that quad cane as the four little feet hit the ground, two by two. Kachunk. Kachunk.
After observing for a time he pulled a deck chair next to me and sat. He reached into the bag, snapped the head off a bean and dropped it into the mixing bowl on my lap. Then another.
"They're too long," I said.
"Yes, Ma'am," he answered and started breaking the beans into thirds.
"Better."

"Does this mean you're speaking to me again?"

"There're too many beans here for me to ignore you the whole time."

Snap, snap, snap.

"I thought you might want to know Keegan called."

He knows I can't resist that. "And?"

"The gravel in Reggie's parking lot didn't allow for tire tracks. Doc McGrath thought that maybe a C and a 1 were in the license of the panel truck. But it could have been a G and an I. Keegan will run it anyway but doesn't expect much." Snap, snap.

"What about the blood they found where the shooter stood?" I asked.

"Type O positive. Narrows it down to a third of the US population." Snap, snap. "Keegan said Galligan talked with Dead Eye and the half-pickled locals who were there at the time, but nobody noticed a stranger. Most of them wouldn't go out of their way to help a cop anyway. How come I'm snapping more of these beans than you are?"

I had taken a break. "You'll eat more of them than I will."

"Oh. Is Will still recovering here?"

"Nope. Went home this morning. Said his grandparents shouldn't be alone too long."

"I like that kid."

"Might even be worthy of Chrissie. Are you still feeling responsible for what happened?"

"Yep."

"Well, I guess you are, Bear. Me, too. Once this is all over, we need to decide whether we can keep going with stuff like this. I don't know that it's possible to do detective work that never endangers anyone."

Bear picked up another bean. "On the other hand, nobody else is as worried about all those old people as these two old people right here snapping beans."

-Lily Gilbert, Snappy Assistant to PI Bear Jacobs

Late Friday morning, Lily cruised over to the Menu Board on her walker. Ever since the gang started going to the senior center twice a week, the white board just outside the kitchen had taken on double duty. It was now their message center as well. A handful of markers were cupped in the tray below it.

"Where's everybody going to be today?" Eunice called through the archway from the living room where she, Frankie and Charlie waited for Vinny to drive them to the senior center. Sun poured through the picture window, making the bold prints in the overstuffed chairs dance with life.

"Let's see. Jessica and Ben trailered two horses and went to Whidbey Island for a couple days," Lily read aloud then turned to look through the archway at Eunice. The sun sparkling in her old friend's orange spikes made her head look on fire. "Hope they can work a little romance in around the trail rides and kayaking."

"He's getting pretty far afield for that daughter of his to reel him back," Eunice observed. "That's a good sign."

Lily continued to read. "Bear wrote that Sam's taking him to an air show at that little field in Arlington."

"That's right. He's abandoning us for the day," Charlie said sounding petulant.

"Didn't know he was a fan of flying machines," Eunice said.

"He's just full of mysteries, he is," Lily muttered before reading on. "Aurora will be here by 4:00 to start dinner. Grilled salmon and fresh green beans. And Alita is the aide for the evening."

"*Andiamo*," said Frankie when Vinny's big Caddy purred to a halt out front.

As Eunice, Frankie and Charlie settled into the Caddy, Lily said, "Oops, forgot my book." While Vinny folded Charlie's wheelchair into the trunk, she went back inside and reappeared a few minutes later with a bedraggled paperback.

"Didn't think you'd be reading now that the Scrabble championships have started," Eunice said.

"I have an appointment with the lymphedema specialist. After Vinny drops you all off at the center, he'll take me there. She always makes me wait a long time, so I need something to read."

Lying to my friends is coming a little too easily these days.

She averted her eyes to the couple on the cover of the book. They were on the last book she'd read, too. Only this time, they were dressed as pirate and serving wench instead of settler and Indian maiden. The guy's chest was naked on both. "Bear says I have to start getting ebooks so nobody will see these romance covers."

Eunice harrumphed. "He may know a lot of things, Lily, but the man knows squat about art."

✦ ✦ ✦

Bear *kachunked* out of his room and watched the Caddy ooze away, dark as an oil slick, taking the rest of the residents to the senior center for the day.

Thank God they're gone. Now we can get serious.

He placed a call to Sam. When the barn manager picked up, Bear said, "The coast is clear." He'd always wanted to use that line. "Follow that cab," was still on his bucket list. He went out back to the patio and waited for Sam to walk down to the house from his Airstream.

✦ ✦ ✦

Will parked his kiwi green Hyundai in front of Latin's Ranch. He hadn't liked the color, but neither had anyone else so he'd gotten a great deal on the car. It might not be a looker, but today it was his chariot of fire. He reached over to kiss Chrissie's cheek. Now that he knew there was an extra bed at Latin's Ranch for another resident – and now that his ear didn't throb so painfully where the tip of it had once been – he knew just what he wanted to do with that bed.

"Everybody will be gone for hours. Nobody will hear us. We can have afternoon delights until Aurora arrives," said Chrissie. She patted his knee then worked her talented hand higher up his thigh.

Mercy.

✦ ✦ ✦

Out back on the patio, Bear watched Sam walk toward him from the mobile home. Sam's stride was long and determined. He moved like a hunter, the Winchester cradled under his right upper arm and over his forearm, barrel pointed downward. The last time Sam had used the gun was to shoot a feral dog that had attacked Latin Dancer.

I may be shooting a couple of mad dogs with it myself.

Bear would have preferred a handgun, but the Winchester was the sum total of their armory. He didn't know a lot about bolt action rifles, but at the range he'd be using it, that didn't matter much.

They'd already talked it out. There wasn't a lot more to be said. Sam waited for Bear to stand, then they went through the door into the kitchen. The kitchen connected with the dining room. The men stood there for a moment, looking through the archway into the living room. A medical supply closet was at the far end of the living room, just inside the door that led to the resident rooms. Before the renovation from private home to adult care home, it had probably been a coat closet.

Bear considered the floor plan one more time. "You wait over there," he said pointing to a chair and end table in the far corner. "They can't get behind you if you're there."

Sam nodded. He solemnly handed the rifle to Bear, and Bear gave him his cell phone.

"Set it on the end table, aimed toward the front door. Turn it on when they get here. If we don't get the picture, we'll at least have sound."

"We've been all through this, Bear," Sam said then walked into the living room to take up his stance.

"Just a reminder, Sam. I'll be in the supply closet right behind you. Speak loud, and I'll be able to hear." Before he left the dining room to take up his position, the menu board caught the corner of his eye.

"Shit," he said, then read aloud the message Lily had written there: "Boys, Vinny will bring me back by one o'clock. Don't want to miss the fun."

Bear had heard her call to the others that she'd come back in for her book. She must have written the message then. He let out a roar. "That woman's going to be the death of me. If not, I'm going to kill her."

✦ ✦ ✦

"Hey, Cal. The Korean kiddy car is parked there. Doesn't it belong to that embalmer? What's his name?" Luke Carmichael slowed the panel truck to a crawl and the occupants stared at the little car in the Latin's Ranch driveway.

"Will Haverstock. Maybe. 'Course maybe someone else drives a puke green cracker box."" Cal, the janitor from Chesterton Funeral Parlor, rubbed at the festering wound he'd received when Candi Kenilworth had scratched him.

Luke had teased him about his success with babes when he first saw that wound. He'd made even more fun when the janitor was winged by a big Italian-looking stranger after he'd failed to kill Will behind that lowlife bar. To Luke's way of thinking, Cal was a loser all around. But the boss seemed to trust him. Probably figured the lout was too dumb to plan anything on his own.

"We'll take him out if he's here," said Luke. "Bag two for the price of one."

"Pleasure," said their boss from the back of the panel truck. It was fitted out as a mobile ER unit on the inside. "But be careful. This could be a set-up. If not, we'll look for him after we take this Sam Hart person."

"Maybe you should come in with me this trip, Boss." Luke usually went into the homes by himself while the other two waited in the truck to subdue the victim if need be. Sometimes they even prepared for surgery right away if they had a backlog of orders.

"Agreed. Begins to feel like there are several mouths that need to be closed," his boss said and opened the truck's back door.

✦ ✦ ✦

Chrissie whispered in Will's ear, "Shhhh! Who's that? Is Aurora early?" Will had just unhooked her bra and buried his face in breasts softer than jumbo marshmallows.

He looked up and listened. "Shit. I think that's Mr. Bear. Growling about something Lily did."

"Oh, no! They're all supposed to be gone!" Chrissie pulled her hand out of Will's pants.

He zipped up, although it wasn't easy to convince his hard on that it was the thing to do. "You stay here. I'll go see what's going on."

✦ ✦ ✦

"They're here," said Sam loud enough for Bear to hear. "Three of them. Getting out of the panel truck."

"Three? I figured on two." Bear's anxiety jumped a level. Hiding in the medical supply closet, he couldn't see the action, but he knew that Sam was keeping watch through a small opening in the drapes over the picture window. With three of them, Bear wished he had his cell phone. He'd have called Keegan after all.

"One's a big guy. Fat. He's moving out of sight. The other two are coming to the door."

"One a woman?"

"I'll say."

Now Bear was sure. "Recognize her?"

"No, I ... Well, I'll be damned. It's – "

The door bell rang.

"Be careful. Act like a real party animal. Start the video on the phone. Then open the door."

Sam did as he was told, judging by what Bear could hear. He hated having no sightline. He heard the front door open.

"Mr. Hart?" A young man's voice.

"How the hell's it hangin'?" boomed a happy-go-lucky voice. The reserved Sam Hart was pouring himself into the role of asshole. "Get on in here, young fella."

"I'm Luke Carmichael from Carefree Occasions. We have an appointment to talk about ways for caregivers to join each other in stress free travel and group events."

"And to meet babes, right, amigo?" asked Sam, the newly minted womanizer.

"Yes, that, too."

"Who's this good looking filly with the Red Hair and flashy emerald eyes?" Sam bellowed. Bear got the identification.

"This is my boss – "

Luke was cut off by a husky female purr. "I've seen Mr. Hart before, Luke. Give up the bumpkin act, cowpoke."

Sam suddenly sounded like Sam again. "Yes. At the hospital. You're the nurse who murdered Orlo Chesterton. I'm afraid your bedside manner needs some work."

"And I'm afraid this means trouble, Luke. Especially for Mr. Hart."

The door to the supply closet banged open. "Drop the gun, Fucker," Bear growled in his outdoor voice at Luke. He listed heavily to the left on his quad cane. But he had the Winchester in his right arm, cradled by the strap, aimed right at Luke's testicles. Luke dropped the Colt Python.

Bear glanced at the splendid woman who showed no sign of fear. If anything, he thought it was humor dancing in her eyes. He said, "Hiya, Red. Or should I say Mrs. Chesterton? Figured you had to be one and the same."

"Yeah, big man? How's that?"

"Only thing that makes sense. Something has to connect the murder at the hospital to the shenanigans at the funeral parlor. You didn't hide from any of us behind that nursing mask ... you wore it to conceal your identity from your hubby. Orlo. He was so feeble it worked. No cry for help from him, no thought that his wife was about to finish the job. I was right there to see you do the hit – "

"— and to give me that line of crap about being Orlo's brother. I knew right then you'd be a problem."

"I had Will describe his new boss for me. Have to give it to you, Red, that hair and those eyes burn a memory into a guy's brain."

Bear saw Luke's left hand make a move into a pocket. "Hold it right there if you ever want that hand to pick your nose again." Luke left his hand in his pocket.

Then Bear's plan totally unraveled in a complex choreography of everyone dancing at once.

"Hey, guys. What's going on?" Will entered the room from the hall directly behind Bear and Sam. Folly bounced through the door along with him.

Sam spun around and yelled, "Will! Get out!"

Instead, Will froze.

Luke leaped forward, removed his hand from his pocket and smashed Sam in the head with a short, flexible sap. The weapon, a devastating combo of leather and lead, could easily crush a man's skull.

Bear hoped Sam's old hat softened the blow as he, leaning hard on his cane, kicked Luke's gun off the playing field.

Red drew her own gun when Bear nearly lost his balance.

Sam folded like a jack knife and hit the ground.

Will lurched forward to catch Sam. For a heartbeat, he blocked Bear's bead on Luke. That heartbeat was just enough time for Red to aim her H & K snub nose at Will while Luke scrambled to pick up the Colt.

Millicent Chesterton spoke to Bear. "You've heard the old joke about *Shoot at Will*, haven't you? That's just what I'll do if you don't drop that rifle. Do it now."

Bear did what he was told, lowering Sam's Winchester to the floor.

Luke slammed Sam in the head a second time. "He's for sure in la-la land now."

Folly loved Sam. He snarled then bit into Luke's lower calf, the highest a cockadock could reach. He ripped away a piece of pant leg and a piece of the leg inside.

"Son of a bitch!" Luke shrieked and flung the sap at Folly. It hit him on the front right shoulder. The little dog yelped and limped away.

✦ ✦ ✦

Finally, everyone was still. The Redhead chuckled at the little performance then turned her attention to the embalmer. "Surprised to see you here, Will. Disappointed, too."

"Mrs. Chesterton? What are you doing here? Why did this guy attack Sam?" Will looked dumbfounded.

Luke was rubbing his leg where the dog had bitten him. "She's too close to miss, corpse cutter. I see Cal only winged you."

Will raised a hand to his bandaged ear. "*Cal* shot me?"

"He did a lousy job of it, but the boss won't. And even if she destroys your head, the rest of your scrawny body can be reused. Not all full of formaldehyde like when you're done with it."

"Mrs. Chesterton, what's he saying? You're not part of this?"

Red said, "You should have just minded your own business, dear boy. We'll miss your talents at the parlor. Get in here, Cal." When the fat man appeared he had his own gun in hand. Red told him to hold it on Bear.

Will said to Bear, "This guy's our janitor."

"I'm a lot more than that, gimp," Cal said.

With Cal and Luke now on guard, Red began to look around the living room and dining room. "What is this place? Some kind of nursing home?"

Bear said nothing.

"Anyone else here?"

"No one," Will said quickly.

Bear said nothing.

Red walked into the dining room, glanced at the menu board, then peered into the kitchen. "How many others know about us?"

Bear said nothing. This time, neither did Will.

"What are we going to do now?" Luke asked, sounding anxious.

"Answer the question, Big Man," Red said.

Bear said nothing.

Luke's bland face screwed itself into disgust. "He's old meat. Nobody wants his body parts. Let's just kill him and get out of here."

"Not until he tells us what we need to know. But you're right. We have to get moving before someone else shows up. Cal, you and Will carry the cowboy out to the truck. He's a perfect specimen. Luke, you keep the gun on Bear and follow along." She replaced the snub nose in her jacket pocket, turned and walked out of Latin's Ranch ahead of the rest.

✦ ✦ ✦

Well, this is a helluva mess. Where did Will come from? Is Sam even alive?

"Move it," Luke said, poking Bear in the back with the gun.

Bear continued forward slowly, leaning on his cane. He watched Red climb into the passenger compartment of the panel truck. She disappeared into the back.

Will struggled next to him, walking backwards carrying Sam's shoulders. He stumbled and fell. Cal hung on to Sam's feet but kicked Will. "Get up, Lurch." Will labored to his feet and picked up his end of the cowboy once again.

By the time they got to the truck, the Redhead had opened both back doors. Cal and Will climbed in to deposit Sam on a gurney inside. Red told Cal to get Will's car, and as Will turned to get out of the truck, she slammed him in the head.

Bear didn't see the weapon she used, only saw the kid buckle and collapse. He tried to move forward, but Luke grabbed his shoulder and moved the Colt to his ear. "Careful, old man. He's going with Sam. The more guts to sell, the better."

"Now for you," the Redhead said. Bear saw she had a syringe as she stepped out of the truck, down its ramp, and moved toward him.

He was close to panic. "What's your play, Red?"

"I'm taking you back to the funeral parlor for a nice little chat. Right outside a two thousand degree oven just in case you choose not to talk to me."

Bear couldn't let her use the drug. That was endgame. She'd told Luke not to shoot earlier, so maybe he would hesitate just long enough ...

With enormous effort, Bear threw himself over backward, slapping into Luke. As they fell, like one domino on top of another, Bear struggled to get the gun. Luke was pinned beneath him, but Bear's massive paw closed on the weapon in the younger man's hand. He was yanking it free when Red jabbed him in the neck. He tried to carry on, but his strength drained away. In seconds, Luke was able to push himself free and take control of the handgun once more.

"You must still think you're a guy to be scared of," Luke scoffed, but Bear could no longer answer.

By the time Cal pulled the Hyundai alongside the truck and got out, he and Luke had to manhandle Bear into the little car. Red slipped into the driver's seat. "Good thing green's my color," she muttered.

"You can handle him okay, boss?" Luke asked.

Bear began to float on a cloud above the scene. In some dreamy part of his brain, he heard her say, "He's no danger to me now. You take the cowboy and Will down to BioTetics. Have the doctors there by three. We'll meet you in the OR before then.

"Cal, you stay here. That sign inside said someone named Lily would be here at one. That's any minute now. Kill whoever shows then join me at the mortuary. I'll need your help to cremate Bear's body."

✦ ✦ ✦

Folly didn't know why his leg didn't work or why it hurt to run. But he did know he wanted to be in the safest place for injured dogs. He tucked his tail between his legs and began the long journey, made even longer with only three legs to count on.

He felt woozy when he finally limped through the big barn door. But he kept going until he slipped under the gate into Gina Lola's stall. She put her massive head down and snuffled at him. He dropped into the deep pine curls that Sam used as bedding to make the Percheron's enormous feet comfortable. Folly leaned against Gina Lola's front leg and closed his eyes.

The big horse stood just where she was, munching her hay. Whether she knew it or not, she was on guard, protecting the little dog from further harm.

✦ ✦ ✦

Lily sat in the luxurious backseat behind Vinny. Looking at the size of him made her feel very small. But today, she was glad of it. Today, she needed protection. Today, she was nervous about Bear and Sam.

She was still leery enough around the mobster to give him a minimum of backtalk. Only when they approached Latin's Ranch did a complaint force itself from her lips. "Well, I can see damn all from back here. What just pulled out?"

Vinny turned into the drive, while the dust from the other vehicle was still settling. "A delivery truck."

Lily gasped. "A white panel truck? Like the one in the alley?"

"Yes, Signora Lily."

"Oh no! Hurry, Vinny." She began pounding on the back of his seat. She'd gone from nervous to terrified in under sixty seconds.

"Stay calm, Signora Lily."

"Get the lead out, Vinny!" She felt nearly hysterical.

Vinny stopped the car in front of the house. They both stared at the front door and the wide front porch. No movement inside or out. No Bear. No Sam.

Lily said, "Let's go in."

"No."

"No?"

"I go." He turned around and looked at her. "You stay."

Some kind of invisible rays shot from his eyes and pinned her to the seat. Quickly, she recovered. "Oh for heaven's sake. I'm going, too." That's when she saw the gun in his hand. A very big, very nasty looking gun.

"You have to stay in the back seat. Because your walker stay in the trunk."

"Why you ... you ... bully!"

Vinny turned away, ignoring her. He opened the car door. As he stepped out, the house door blasted open. A fat man burst onto the porch firing at the Caddy. Vinny dropped down shielded by the front door of the car.

"Vinny!" Lily yelled.

"Is okay, Miss Lily. This *cafone* a very bad shot. But you get down."

Lily scrunched until only her head from the eyes up was over the window ledge. The Caddy's darkened windows hid her from the shooter. Maybe. She peered out, hoping to see Bear appear behind the fat man and clobber him.

Where is he? Where's Sam? Are we too late?

Another, sharper blast. The fat man took flight sideways across the porch. A second hit jerked his body even further.

Vinny shot him? Sideways? How the hell ...?

Lily saw Chrissie come around the end of the porch, holding a Winchester rifle. It was very literally the smoking gun.

CHAPTER NINETEEN

Case Notes
April 11, 7 pm
Chrissie stood there like Annie Oakley. "Hurt my honey will you, Ass Wipe? Threaten my friend Lily? Take that!" She shot the fat man again. She was magnificent.
Chrissie told me later that her father had taught her to hunt when he wasn't slapping her mother around, so the Winchester was nothing new to her. Would a born nurturer like Chrissie mourn using the shooting lessons on a human? Maybe, if Cal hadn't been so brutal to Will. But the three kill shots didn't strike her as the least bit excessive. It frightens me that Detectives Keegan and Stud Muffin might not see it that way.
Vinny wouldn't get me my damn walker until he checked the house for more bad guys. He ordered Chrissie to sit in the car with me and wait for him. He took the rifle away from her and disappeared around the house as stealthily as a guerilla.
"If he'd just asked, I could have told him everyone else is gone." Chrissie said.
"Gone? You mean Bear and Sam are gone?" Why and where?
"Will's gone, too." Chrissie's lip trembled. "They took them all away. Will and Sam were unconscious. Bear was drugged."
I put my arms around her as she cried, and soon she put hers around me. Then she told the tale. She'd been listening to the people in the living room from the hall to the resident rooms. When every-

one went out front, she snuck in to get Sam's Winchester from the floor where she'd heard Bear drop it. Then she dashed through the kitchen, out the back door to the patio, and circled around toward the front porch. She saw a woman and two men load Sam and Will into the truck.

"The woman said to take then to the operating room. At a place called Bio something. Then she left with Bear to go to the funeral parlor. Lily, she said ... she said she was going to cremate him."

Bear!

We waited in fear, alternately peering out the car window. No sign of Vinny.

"We have to get moving," Chrissie said, sounding close to losing it again.

I rolled down the window and shrieked for Vinny.

"Yes, Miss Lily?"

"Yikes!" My heart did a couple shuffle steps. The Italian stallion was right next to the car. Never heard or saw him coming. "Don't creep up on me like that."

Then I noticed he was carrying the corpse over his shoulder like it weighed no more than a sack of potatoes. And the dead guy was plenty chubby.

"What's he doing?" Chrissie asked in a whisper as Vinny disappeared toward the back of the car.

We heard a slight creaking sound. "I think he's opening the trunk."

Thunk!

The Caddy bounced on its springs. The trunk lid shut. Vinny opened the car door and slid my walker inside the passenger compartment in front of us. "Here is walker, Signora Lily."

"Just great. I don't need it now."

"But now there is no room for it in the trunk."

"Lay rubber for the funeral parlor, Vinny," I said while I placed a call to Keegan.

As he slid into the driver's seat, started the big car and tore up the drive, Chrissie asked, "Why'd you put the corpse in the trunk, Mr. Vinny?"

"In my business, we no sell body parts. We dispose of whole bodies. Now nobody ever know you shoot the fat man. Nobody ask you awkward questions about three shots. Nobody ever find the fat man."

-Lily Gilbert, Accessory After the Fact and Assistant to PI Bear Jacobs

---

Jessica was cold from the waist down and hot from the waist up. The water, not much over fifty degrees, cooled the kayak's fiberglass skin and the neoprene skirt around the hatch. But above the kayak, the sun blazed. She'd peeled down to a tank top under her life vest, but was still sweating from the exertion of paddling in the currents of Puget Sound. Ben said she was in great shape from wrangling all those horses and old folks. But this kayaking was something else again. New muscles were making themselves known.

Yesterday, hauling the horse trailer behind Ben's SUV, they'd crossed to Whidbey Island on the Clinton ferry. They'd driven up the island's spine, visiting charming towns and tourist sites, until they reached a B & B near Possession Point. It was in a secluded location where several bridle trails crossed. One of Jessica's boarders had told her about it, saying they even had pasturage and stalls for people who brought their own horses.

In the morning, they'd put Latin Dancer to the test. It was the first trail ride since the harrowing attack on the colt all those months ago. It still made Jessica's stomach lurch when she thought about it.

Dancer had been a beauty, likely to be as great a champion as his sire, Latin Lover. But a pack of feral dogs swept out of the forestland in the Cascade foothills and ambushed the colt. Their slashing teeth destroyed his looks and worse, his spirit. He'd lost the *brio* needed for the show ring. Latin Dancer was damaged goods. He'd never have a history of wins or earn top stud fees now. The loss of that income had been crippling to Jessica's dreams and plans. But the colt's pain had been even more so.

Ben Stassen saved the day. He bought Dancer as well as Jessica's commitment to train the colt as a trail horse. Ben paid all the vet bills as Dancer mended, bills that Jessica could never have covered.

She'd worked for months to dispel the young animal's fears and prepare him for the sure-footed, level-headed commitment he needed to maneuver through woods and over narrow rock ridges. She'd chosen a mild-mannered mount for herself, thinking the steady gelding would reassure Dancer. She was a better rider than Ben and wished they could switch, but Dancer was his horse and it was time the two of them faced this music together.

A colt, even a sweet tempered one, can be hundreds of pounds of willful, non-compliant silliness. Dancer was no exception. He took Ben for a jaunty four-step down the forested trail, expending his energy with juvenile prancing and sidestepping. He shook his head and fought the reins. The flutter of a plastic Kmart bag caught on a tree branch spooked him into a wild leap forward. If the gelding hadn't blocked his way, Dancer might have carried Ben back to the mainland at a dead gallop.

When they made it back to the B and B, it was a toss whether Ben or Dancer was more drained. But Jessica was thrilled. As she ran her hands over the scars on the colt's neck, she gushed, "Did you notice he didn't stumble? Not even once? What a star!"

Ben wasn't quite as enthused. "Guess I didn't notice. I was too busy hanging on."

"Even with all that nonsense, he is one sure-footed fellow. He wasn't scared of the trail or that wolves were going to attack. Just in high spirits. He did great. You both did. You'll be a super team. All it takes is practice now."

After cooling and pasturing the animals, they'd rented the kayak and paddled along the shore, watching orcas blowing in the distance and two bald eagles fishing from a dead tree snag. The waters were tricky here, and Jessica was glad Ben was an experienced kayaker. He might not be the world's best horseman, but he excelled at this paddling stuff.

They'd pulled into a tiny inlet with a narrow rim of pebbly beach. A two-little-trees-on-two-big-rocks islet sheltered them from the open water, and the cliff behind them rose to towering heights, a perfect place for a lover's leap.

"Let's hope nobody goes plunging past us," Jessica said staring up the cliff face until it was lost in a topknot of hemlock and spruce.

"Won't happen. It's against local ordinance to commit suicide on a sunny day," Ben assured her.

"Pretty hard to convict the person who does it," she answered, smiling at him as he spread out a blanket then set down the picnic lunch the B&B had packed for them.

Ben was a big guy who needed a regular schedule of workouts to keep from looking like a linebacker gone to seed. Jessica knew he was sensitive about his hairline which was allowing a bit more forehead to show than used to. But the rich dark hair, with its touch of mahogany in the sun, still had not a speck of gray. From experience, she knew the complete six-pack could still be counted on his abs.

Jessica found his shoulders and arms especially inviting, capable of surrounding her in a mantle of safety unlike any she had ever known. Ed, the man whose impetuous decision to drive the icy mountains had left her a widow, had been rangy and slender, a sexual explorer who pushed her into frontiers she'd never explored before. Their lovemaking had been frantic and punctuated with repeated orgasms for them both.

Ben was not such a pioneer, but took his time with every bit and morsel of her landscape. He'd bring her to a peak then back off, not allowing her release until she thought she'd die if she didn't come just this second. But then he'd show her that they still had distance to travel together until they finally arrived at the same time, exhausted and fulfilled.

Ed was wildfire. Ben was a long slow burn.

"What're you thinking about?" Ben stretched his strong body out on the blanket.

She realized she was standing over him, staring. And that her body temp below the belt was becoming just as warm as above it. "I'm thinking about this." She began her strip by lifting the tank top from breasts already tight with anticipation.

Sometime later, they both sat nude, wolfing down the sandwiches, fruit and chicken they'd found in the picnic basket. They drank from a bottle of the island's wine, passing it back and forth; the B&B had forgotten glasses. When they finished their meal, Jessica sat between Ben's legs and leaned back against his chest. They watched the pleasure boats and ferry out in the Sound, protected from full view by their little islet.

"Wonder what's going on at home," Jessica said lazily, not really caring very much.

Ben snickered. "Oh, probably Aurora has just arrived and started arroz con pollo for dinner, ordering everyone out of the kitchen."

"Frankie is reading aloud the next chapter of *Riders of the Purple Sage*. Eunice is beading a bracelet while she listens. Lily is listening too, but she's tapping away at her computer. Bear is probably in Sam's trailer where they think I don't know they smoke cigars now and then."

Ben held her close and kissed the top of her head. "I got a call from a Seattle rehab two days ago. Recognized the name on caller ID. But I didn't take the call."

Jessica understood his meaning. His daughter Rachael had tried to reach him, and he had not responded. It was his way of telling Jessica that he was trying to loosen the tie. She decided that the Latin's Ranch gang shouldn't be with them here on this beach either. She changed the subject to how much she loved the way his hair curled behind his ears when it was a little too long like now. And how his shave only lasted until three before the five o'clock shadow began to show.

For this sunny afternoon, on this lovely island, she began to believe. She'd been so worried that gratitude to this man obligated her to him. That one day she would see it as a trap, and she would resent him forever. But today she was sure her love for him was as pure and simple as his was for her.

Who could have imagined she'd be this happy ever again?

✦ ✦ ✦

The drug kept Bear in suspended animation. It was not unpleasant although he was vaguely aware he should be upset. Angry, maybe even terrified. He just couldn't remember why.

He knew he was in a car. At first it had been okay, but now it felt confined and dangerous. Like the big cardboard box he played with as a kid, shutting himself inside before he saw the giant spider in there with him. He'd been scared and cried for help. He considered crying now, but his mother wouldn't come running to save him this time.

The car transported him out of the sun into the dark. He knew that. It happened fast like the earth really whizzing around on its axis. The heat on his cheek where it was mashed against the window turned cool.

No, wait. Not night. A cave or something. Indoors. An oily odor. Doors slamming. Echoing. A garage!

He came to enough to open his eyes just a slit. He was alone, cramped in the front seat of the ugliest green car he'd ever seen. That kid's car. Will.

Where's Will? And who else ... the Redhead.

Bear's mouth was dry. He realized it was gaping wide open and his own spit was drying on his chin. He closed his yap and unstuck his cheek from the car window, then opened his eyes full wide. His vision cleared. The drug was wearing off.

The big man sat up straight and tried to stretch out his legs but there was no room to do it. He took inventory, and nothing seemed broken. Just stiff as hell and aching. He looked around and recognized where he was. The little car was inside the funeral parlor's garage where he and Lily had parked Sitting Bull. That was the night they'd broken in.

This is a different night, right?

The door to the embalming area was open. Bear worked hard on the puzzle with his fuzzy brain, and finally figured out that the she-devil must have gone inside. Will was gone. Sam was, too. He had to get free if anyone was to free them. He had to get his shit together.

Does the bear shit in the funeral parlor? No, this is serious. Fight the drug. Danger.

He tried to open the car door but it was locked. Bear patted around the inside of the door for a while until he found the lock release and pushed it. He felt too weak to stand, and the world began to spin. Like a carousel, round and round. He whimpered.

Where's my cane?

Finally the carnival ride stopped. Bear gave his head a tentative shake, trying to disperse the last of the drug. He leaned forward and cupped his left leg with his enormous hands and lifted it out of the car. Then he turned sideways on the seat until he could drag his other leg out. By grabbing the seat back and the door frame, he pushed himself up. When he stood, the carousel ride began again. He had no strength to take a step. In even parts fury and despair, he roared, "Where's my cane? Bring me my fucking cane!"

"My goodness, such language," said the Redhead, hip switching her way out of the embalming room. His head cleared at the sight of her, as if focusing through a spyglass on the enemy. Red crossed to the car, opened the trunk then came up to Bear where he clung to the car window for support. He smelled her musky scent even before she got near enough to pat his cheek. He made a grab for his cane but she took a step back.

Before she released it to him, she removed the H&K snub nose from her jacket pocket and held it on him. "Now let's get one thing straight. You need the cane. I get that. So I won't tie you. But the second you step out of line you're dead."

The exertion of walking helped dispel the last of the fog from Bear's mind. By the time he *kachunked* through the cold embalming room, down the short hall and into the warm crematory, he was exhausted, gulping for air. Red didn't need to direct him; he'd taken this route once before.

The cremation trolley was in front of the oven like it had been the night he found the bodies there. This time it was empty.

"Sit there," Red said giving Bear a nudge toward the trolley. Tamping down his pain, he managed to lift himself, a butt muscle at a time, and shove back onto the metal surface.

"Good boy," Millicent Chesterton said.

The woman was used to giving orders, and Bear had every intention of taking them until he had his chance. She had to be closer to him.

Closer.

But she moved away to the oven and tapped its stainless steel door. "Cal taught me how to prep the oven. He'll be here soon to help me use it."

"Pretty sure I know on whom," Bear muttered.

"Oh, yes. We'll pop you in and watch you bake like the Pillsbury doughboy. You can't save yourself, but maybe you can avoid a lot of suffering. Tell me what I want to know, and I'll give you another hypo before you burn. Then you won't feel a thing."

Millicent took a quick peek inside the chamber, all the while holding the snub nose on Bear. "Just making sure no other guests are inside." Then she turned back to him. "Now while we wait for Cal, tell me who else knows about us."

"Hell, lady, I don't even know who us is." He blinked with as much innocence as he could project. He was proud of his deadpan.

"Give it up, Bear. You know I'm a nurse. And Orlo's widow. Now who else can connect me to the murder of my dearly beloved?"

Bear thought about his cell phone, still back at Latin's Ranch. He had no chance of recording this confession. "Far as I can tell, nobody else knows."

"What about that old broad at the hospital with you and dear Mr. Hart?"

Lily!

"She was at the hospital, sure, talking to friends, not to us. And she wasn't at the ranch today. She was miles away. So she can't connect Red to Millicent."

Millicent's smile was cold. "Neither can the cops. The officer who saw me at the hospital? She sent a young guy to interview me here. Neither saw me at both places."

"They're not stupid. They'll figure it out. They're closing in." He added, "I've told them about the seniors missing from their homes. Things will go better for you if you let me go now."

Millicent dropped the smile. "Oh, you think you're clever, Bear. But if you're so clever how come I'm the one standing here holding the gun?"

Bear had to admit she had a point. He knew his best chance to save his own hide, as well as Sam and Will, was to keep her talking. "What I don't understand is why you killed your husband. Wasn't he part of your scheme?"

"Orlo had a tiny brain. Couldn't think outside the casket. He only wanted to run a funeral parlor. I finally convinced him we could make a bunch more on bodies we were supposed to cremate. We'd just sell them instead of burn them. It was so easy. All we had to do was file the proper permit with the county, throw out the metal tag that identifies the body, and give the family seven pounds of ordinary ash. Don't you love living in a state where Mount St. Helens blows her top now and then?"

Bear refused to respond to Red's sorry joke. "And Orlo went along with this?" he asked.

"I convinced him we weren't hurting anybody. I mean, the families didn't know. And I can be very persuasive."

Bear had no doubt of that. "Then you just needed a buyer for the bodies."

She snorted and checked the oven. While they'd been talking, she'd closed the chamber door with the push of a button, silencing the natural gas flames which whooshed inside like a jet engine.

Red said, "If you're already in the cremation business, finding a pipe line for distribution of human organs is a piece of cake. I started a company called BioTetics to sound scientific and all. Clinics that aren't too choosy about background checks came to us. They need organs too badly to ask questions."

"But that wasn't enough for you. Demand grew bigger than supply." Bear was having no trouble keeping her talking. Like most criminals, Millicent seemed eager to tell him how brilliant she was.

"Not enough by half after that asshole from Driscoll Manor came to dinner one night. Russ and Orlo were buds. He talked about senior citizens with the money to pay anything just to keep them going a little longer. I already knew there was a huge black market for human organs. Some of that's big, organized crime at work. I didn't want to play in that sandbox. Too dangerous. But bodies of oldsters for even older oldsters? That's a fresh idea. Room for new players to get started. And to grow."

"Opportunity was knocking."

If she got his sarcasm, Red ignored it. "After Russ left that night, I told Orlo all we had to do was identify a group that nobody would miss until the trail had gone cold. They had to be healthy enough for a successful harvest without being primary targets for the black market looking for younger bodies. I could set up the surgeries to harvest the good bits, and we had the means to dispose of the remains." She indicated the oven.

"But he didn't agree?"

Keep her talking.

"The nadless jerk was too scared. Said absolutely not."

"But you did it anyway."

"I did it anyway. And what could he do about it? He'd already stepped across the legal line himself, so he had to go along. He called it blackmail. I called it smart business. I set up Carefree Occasions on my own. Got lists of deaths in the area, and approached the widows and widowers, knowing they were likely alone. Placed a brochure in nursing homes where caregivers could pick it up. The attached application they filled out told me for sure if they lived alone and were worth our time. It grew from there."

"So you went after easy kills."

"Well sure. That was a nice side benefit. Our victims weren't young toughs. I could take them with only a couple guys to help. Cal, who's an idiot but trusts me. And Luke. My son."

Luke Carmichael was her son? That was a surprise to Bear.

"But you must have guessed a lot of this," Red said.

If telling her his part of the story kept him on the outside of that oven door, Bear's best move was to talk. "I figured Carefree Occasions was the tie to the people disappearing. We'd found your brochure in too many places. Senior centers, nursing homes, a geriatric clinic. So I set up the appointment using Sam Hart's information."

"You're not as dumb as you look."

"But you're no surgeon. How did you pull off the surgeries?"

"Easy. I know all types from hospitals around Washington. I met a doc who lost his license because he's a boozer. Needs the cash. And another who paid his college loans by selling drugs. Now that he's out of prison who else is going to hire him? I attend as surgical nurse, Cal assists, the organs are passed on, the patient dies, and the leftovers are cremated. Everyone keeps quiet, because nobody can speak without incriminating themselves."

"Orlo had to die because he found the bodies in the crematory that night just before we broke into the funeral home."

"Bingo. I knew he'd go to the cops sooner or later so I shot him, but had to finish him off at the hospital. Cal waited for you to leave the crematory that night then he disposed of the bodies and got out before the cops arrived. That old lady was with you then, too, wasn't she? That Lily?"

"Can't imagine who you mean."

"Doesn't matter. She's dead by now anyway." She looked at the digital control panel for the cremation oven. "It's ready. All we need now is Cal."

✦ ✦ ✦

Lily and Chrissie willed the Caddy to go faster even though Vinny was already gunning it. They blew like a high wind toward Chesterton Funeral Parlor, hanging on as they squealed around curves. During the wild ride, Lily placed a panicky call on Chrissie's phone.

When Lily told Keegan that Sam and Will had been taken to BioTetics, the detective sounded soothing, as if Lily was a crazy old bat who should be humored like a child. "Now, Miss Lily. You know we've checked that location before. It just looked like an empty office in a small business park. Nothing much more than a mail drop."

It pissed Lily off. "You've never really believed in old people being slaughtered, but if you don't hurry, you'll have more than enough proof. Sam is about to be carved like a Christmas goose."

"So is Will!" Chrissie shrieked loud enough for Keegan to hear. "And he's really young." Over the phone Lily heard the siren in Keegan's car begin to blare. The detective, not sounding as placid now, said, "Okay. We're on our way."

Next Lily told Keegan that Bear was being held at the funeral parlor.

"Held?"

"By the redhead nurse that murdered Orlo Chesterton. She took him at gunpoint from Latin's Ranch."

"What?" Keegan now sounded as distressed as Lily.

"Chrissie saw them."

The aide nodded as if Keegan could see. Her pale skin was deadlier white than usual.

Keegan said, "I'll send a team there, too."

"I'm almost there now."

"Don't you dare go into that building or I will arrest you for interference!" Keegan actually yelled at her. Lily could hear Galligan in the background saying something about old farts who refused to behave like they're supposed to.

"Yeah. You bet." Lily hung up and hung on as Vinny squealed to a stop in the alley behind the funeral parlor. He burst out of the car and tried to lift the garage door but it was locked.

"Don't all you mobsters have lock picks?" Lily screamed out her window at him.

"I have a faster thing," he said as he got back in, reversed the big Cadillac into the driveway across the alley. "Check seat belts. Lean back." Next he floored it. The big car leaped forward like it had been goosed. It tore across the alley and smacked into the garage door full force. Shards of wood and glass blew in all directions. The car did not stop until it dug its way into the garage like a Sherman tank on speed.

Lily and Chrissie sat stunned, mouths agape.

Vinny brought the Caddy to a halt next to Will's green toad. "She is armored car, my Black Beauty," he explained with obvious pride. He leaped out as the last of the door bits rained down all around, and he ran for the embalming room door.

Chrissie got out, handed Lily her walker and they followed Vinny at a far slower pace. As she watched him disappear into whatever evil awaited him, Lily thought that for a very bad man, Vinny had a very good side.

✦ ✦ ✦

As Bear sat on the trolley listening to Red tell him how clever she was, he was hurting. The metal surface was hard on old muscle and bone. He leaned forward and put part of his weight on his quad cane to relieve his back and loosen his leg muscles.

The cane was the only thing he owned that had any value. He'd custom designed it for himself. It was just right for his height and strong enough to support a man his size. He'd have none of the little bird-like appliances the rest of the gang could use, those made of tubular metal instead of good sturdy chestnut.

Red must have noticed his concentration on the cane. "Don't even think it. I won't be getting close enough for you to hit me with that thing." She laughed. "Besides, you're not that fast."

Maybe she's right. Maybe I'm not so fast anymore. But I'm still strong.

He began to twist the cane's handle a quarter turn to the right, but was interrupted by a thunderous crash from the direction of the garage. Red looked startled and turned toward the door. In one motion, Bear removed the cane's handle and pushed off the trolley, seizing this as the only opportunity that was coming his way.

He plunged the dagger into Millicent Chesterton's back, slicing between ribs, nicking a lung and piercing her heart. She probably didn't even know it when he used his full weight to propel the weapon home, nearly crashing down with her as she fell. The cops would consider it a very lucky strike, to kill someone with one stab of a knife. They would certainly call it self- defense and be done with it.

But Bear knew the real truth. He'd meant to kill the one who'd killed so many. He stared at her body. Red curls of hair, red curls of blood. Such a loss that those green eyes would never make a man shiver again. Bear wondered if he might still be feeling some of the drug.

He was leaning heavily on the trolley when Vinny burst into the crematory. The Italian's eyes sliced from Bear to the oven door to the woman on the floor with a knife hilt in her back. After eyeballing the scene, Vinny took Bear's arms and steadied them so the big man could stand tall.

"Is a fine thing you do, Mr. Bear. You are now a made man," Vinny said with respect. Then he leaned to pick up Bear's cane where it had dropped. "The handle is missing."

"No, it isn't." They both looked down at Millicent Chesterton again. The knife hilt protruding from her back was the cane handle. Bear's custom made cane had enough weight to bludgeon, sure. But it held a deadlier secret buried inside. The long dagger had been more or less a joke to Bear. Something old world, something Sherlockian. He'd never really thought he'd use such a thing.

Slowy, Chrissie and Lily entered the crematory, too. They stopped short, and for a frozen moment all of them looked at the body on the crematory floor.

Finally Bear said, "Wonder how long it will be before Cupcake gives my knife back to me."

Lily looked up from the corpse and around this sterile room with its grim purpose. She finally glanced at Bear. "Once Keegan gives it back, I may take it away for good."

Bear smiled at her lovely old face. She smiled back and patted his hand. Then Lily said to Vinny, "You need to disappear before the cops get here. They'll have too many questions for a man with a corpse in the trunk."

Vinny nodded. As he turned to go he stopped and looked at Chrissie, Lily and Bear. He bowed slightly then said, "Signore Frankie's old mob? They not so tough as his new gang."

CHAPTER TWENTY

Case Notes
April 14, 9 p.m.
It was pretty much all over but the shouting after the showdown at the funeral parlor, but I'll try to tie up all the loose ends what with these being 'official' case notes and all.
After the cops released us, an officer drove Bear, Chrissie and me back to Latin's Ranch where we all awaited word about Will and Sam. When Keegan called, she said she and Galligan had sped down to the south side of town to the BioTetics office. When they broke in, they found Luke and a couple of has-been doctors in what looked like a hospital operating room. They were waiting for Millicent Chesterton to arrive. Sam and Will, her intended patients, were hogtied in an attached room, each with a good sized goose egg or two. In time, the crime team would gather enough fingerprints in that room to know that Candi Kenilworth, Bronek Pokorski, and at least one other missing woman had spent time there. That woman was Louise Barker. Charlie could fully grieve for his missing wife.
They took the doctors and Luke Carmichael into custody. His real name was Chesterton, like Orlo and Millicent. Looks like he won't be carrying on the family business any time soon. Speaking of Millicent, a final bit of irony. She had an organ donor card in her wallet, so she'll be sharing with strangers herself.
None of us ever mentioned Vinny's part in the whole affair. As far as the authorities know, Frankie just has one large, threatening-look-

ing aide who likes to wear sunglasses and dark suits. Vinny drove the Caddy out of the garage taking the body of Cal the janitor along with him, vanishing just before the sheriff's department arrived. So Chrissie didn't have to go through a grilling about whether three shots could be considered self defense. If anyone at all asks "Where's Cal?" I don't know a soul who will answer.

Oh, Deputy Detective Keegan has her doubts, of course. She knows that Chrissie and I didn't hitchhike to the funeral parlor. And black automotive paint was found on broken boards from the garage door, but they'd have to find the car to match it. It's probably just as well that cars don't have DNA. Neither Chrissie nor I had anything to say. If we keep our mouths shut, what's Keegan going to do with a fragile oldster and her loyal aide anyway? Despite Eunice's fears, I really don't think the lady cop owns waterboards.

When Bear and I got home that afternoon, Eunice, Charlie and Frankie were there. Vinny had picked them up as usual at the senior center and delivered them to Latin's Ranch. We had a while with just the five of us before Jessica got home. Aurora was in the kitchen, Rick was just coming on shift, and Chrissie had gone to meet Will.

It was important to Bear that we residents had a chance to talk before anyone else interrupted. So we gathered in the living room. Eunice and Frankie sat on the sofa, holding hands. Charlie parked his wheelchair next to Bear who had chosen the big wing back chair he favored. While he waited for us to assemble, he hummed "I've Got a Lovely Bunch of Coconuts."

Once we settled, he began to talk. "I was a private investigator for a lot of years, mostly for law firms. I hunted down my share of villains and the evidence to convict them. I'm sure I put colleagues in danger before but not often, and I had the physical ability back then to get them out of it."

He stopped for long enough that I thought he was done. Then he continued. "One thing I never did back then was set myself up as judge and jury. This was the first time for that. I could have wounded Millicent Chesterton. But a good enough defense attorney might have gotten her off. I've seen it happen before. She might have said that Orlo was behind most of the scheming and forced her to go along. A woman like that could have hung the right jury. I thought it was better that she didn't get that chance."

The rest of us looked at each other, surprised at this candor. Finally, we all nodded in silent agreement. "The world's better off, Bear," Charlie said. "My wife doesn't deserve that the mastermind goes free."

Bear gave him a nod. "We no doubt saved lives of other seniors. And we've brought to light an issue that needs serious consideration. That's to the good. But I've endangered some of you in one way or another. That's up to me to live with."

"None of us were forced, Bear. Neither was Sam nor Will," I said. "We wanted to stop the craziness."

"I'm inclined to think if I had it to do again, I'd do it again. At this point in my life, I like the idea of helping out. Even if it means cutting a few corners that I might not have done as a younger man. Keegan says she welcomes the help. Galligan might take longer to convince. But I wondered whether you might ever want to do something like this again."

He shouldn't have worried about it. We all agreed. Bear has shown us a way of feeling useful again. If in our old age we can help make the lives around us better, it gives us reason to go on. If a few unpleasant people pay the price along the way, well, we all will live with it. We're just too old to quibble over a little thing like due process when it comes to the body snatchers of the world.

Charlie had something to add. "Louise is gone for good. Maybe being a better man all along would have made her proud of me. Time I started working on it."

From now on, the Latin's Ranch gang will follow Bear wherever he might lead us. And if I'm going to continue as Bear's number one assistant, I think I need to do something for myself. I'm pretty good with a walker now – don't need the wheelchair as much as I used to. Even though a passing infection could level me again, I'm making progress. And I still have that brochure I picked up at It's Swell to Be Well.

Receptionist Suzie didn't want to make an appointment for me with Dr. Flannery, but she finally did when I promised not to show up with Bear. That works for me because I don't want him to know what I'm up to until I have an answer one way or another.

I'm going to investigate whether a spring chicken like me can get a prosthetic limb. Who knows? Maybe I can stand on my own two feet again one day, even if one of them is metal and plastic. Maybe I can win a footrace with a hooligan. But that's for another story.

Now let's see. What else? Oh, yes. When Jessica and Ben came home from Whidbey Island earlier in the day, nobody else was here yet. Jess just figured we were still at the senior center, but that didn't explain where Folly was. She called for him again and again, inside the house and out. When she got to the barn, she heard that big work-horse of Ben's let out a whinny. She looked in the manger where Folly often sleeps, but he wasn't there. Instead, she heard a whimper along with a meow. She looked down. At Gina Lola's front feet, Furball had curled himself next to Folly. Knowing that the cat chooses terminal patients to comfort, Jess panicked.

But Folly was alive, jaws locked on a piece of torn material the way a dachshund will often hang on tight. Jess had no way of knowing at the moment that it was the one piece of physical evidence that Luke had been at Latin's Ranch. That could be important since Luke is the only one who's left to go to court. And also since a video on Bear's phone had never been shot. Sam hit the wrong button and got no more than a still picture of the front door.

Anyhoo, Ben called Doc McGrath while Jess bundled up the dog, applied a cold compress to the swelling, and then they hustled off to meet at the vet's office. That must have been happening about the same time Vinny brought all of us home. It was still early so Doc was sober enough to x-ray, fuss, push and bandage. He said the dislocated shoulder and cracked ulna should heal good as new in time. In the meantime, Furball seems to be allowing Folly to spend time in his dog bed again.

Tonight, we had a big dinner to commemorate the case of Charlie's missing wife. It wasn't a Sicilian night, but everyone was here around an informal table nonetheless. Aurora set out all the fixings for tacos, and she even made sopapillas for dessert. Most of us had at least one beer or better yet, some of the wonderful South American wine my daughter Sylvia brought along.

Will was here looking happy to be seated next to Chrissie. Much to her own surprise, she was a heroine. Based on the fact that she's damn near glowing, I swear he's helping that girl discover her self-worth. He's out of work, of course, because the funeral parlor is closed. For now he's lending Sam a hand with all the chores around here. Sam will be okay, the docs say, but he is having serious headaches after the double whammy he got from Luke. It'll take some time.

There aren't many surprises to report. Well, I guess I was surprised at the way Vinny looked at Sylvia and maybe even more surprised at the way she looked back at him. And I suppose Aurora, Eunice and I made far too much over that boy toy, Clay Galligan.

Jessica and Keegan seemed to chat a lot. Might be a friendship brewing there. I'm not sure that Bear would be too pleased if his landlady and his cop get to be friendly; they might team up against him someday.

Keegan told Jessica in front of everyone how much assistance we had been. Maybe that will help Jessica accept that we all need freedom, regardless of our age. I have a hunch there will be more mysteries to solve in the days ahead.

The one big surprise of the evening was an honest to goodness gobsmacker. I was constructing my second taco when in walked Ben's daughter, Rachael.

"Dad?" she said, and we all looked up. Conversation stopped. We were as still as a family of 'possums playing dead.

"Rachael?" Ben said.

Okay, so now they had that established.

"I tried to reach you last weekend," Rachael said.

"I ... I ..." Ben sputtered.

"I wanted to tell you I'm pregnant," Rachael announced, as if that hadn't been obvious when her belly entered the room ahead of the rest of her.

"You ... you're ..." Ben said, getting closer to a whole sentence.
"I have nowhere else to go."
Ben set down his taco. He turned pale. He cleared his throat. Then he looked at Jessica. "My daughter's pregnant with nowhere else to go."
Jessica looked at him for no small amount of time. Finally she quit biting her lip and nodded the least bit, just once. She turned to all of us. We looked at each other, then back to her, and we all nodded.
Jessica smiled at Ben. "We have an extra room."
Latin's Ranch is having a baby.

- Lily Gilbert, Delighted Assistant to PI Bear Jacobs

THE END

Author's Acknowledgments

For statistics on the number of missing seniors as well as other factual content in *Bear in Mind*, I am indebted to many experts, librarians and websites.

For critiques that range from sweet to pit bull in temperament, I am sincerely grateful to my friends Jan Schamberg and Mindy Mailman, my sister Donna Whichello, and to readers of my blog who were cheerleaders when I was flagging.

I am indebted to Bear, Lily, Eunice and Charlie who simply refused to disappear after I finished writing *Fun House Chronicles*. If it is the story of how they got together, then *Bear in Mind* is the story of their friendship and mission in the days to come. It is the first in the Bear Jacobs mystery series.

About the Author

Linda B. Myers won her first creative contest in the sixth grade for her *Clean Up Fix Up Paint Up* poster. After a Chicago marketing career, she traded in her snow boots for rain boots and moved to the Pacific Northwest with her Maltese Dotty. You can visit with Linda on her blog at www.lindabmyers.com

Look for more 'mysteries with bite' in the Bear Jacobs series:

Hard to Bear

Bear Claus

Bear at Sea

Check out Linda's other novels:

Lessons of Evil

A Time of Secrets

The Slightly Altered History of Cascadia

Fun House Chronicles*

*Many of the characters in *Bear in Mind* made their first appearance in *Fun House Chronicles*.

On the following pages, please enjoy this excerpt from

Hard to Bear

The Second Book in the Bear Jacobs Series

EXCERPT:
Hard to Bear

PROLOGUE

Pain.

As Solana Capella came to, she groaned, her head pounding like a jack-hammer.

What happened to my head? Ouch, my arm. Where ...?

Her eyes fluttered open and slowly focused on the feral eyes of a swamp monster staring back. Pain was joined by its old friend, fear.

But wait. Not a swamp thing.

The hollow-cheeked face wasn't really green. It was smeared with camouflage muck. The stranger was pushed up against her and seemed to be spreading the same green and brown ooze on her face.

Panic.

She yelped and began biting and scratching at Camo Man's hands. She inhaled the breath she needed for a championship scream, but his enormous hand clamped down over her mouth and pinched her nose, shutting down the air passages. She fought, but he tightened the grip. "Shhh," he hissed low as a whisper. "They're coming. You must be very still. Do you understand?"

They're coming? Oh, God.

Now she remembered. She tried to control her fear of this new captor. She did her best to nod and, failing at that, blinked her eyes rapidly. Maybe he'd take that as, "Yes, I understand." He may hurt her, but at least he wasn't one of them.

Any old port in the storm, right?

She felt a hysterical bubble of laughter behind the hand over her mouth as it eased up, letting air rush into her lungs. He glowered a warning at her, then slithered down prone, pressing hard against her. That shoved her backside up to a damp cold wall of earth. The kind with spiders and centipedes and worms. She shivered, pressing back against him in hopes of moving her ass off the wall.

Solana was afraid she would suffocate as her face squashed into his slender chest. But some deep instinct of a small cornered animal told her to be ever so quiet, to freeze in place. Playing dead, she took inventory. From the little she could see pressed against him, it appeared they were in a shallow, low cave. Roots from a million plants laced through the dirt and clay, holding its walls in place. It smelled of mold and rotten vegetation, overcoming even the fetid odor of filthy clothes and man sweat crushed against her nose. She could hear the sound of rushing water, and through the mouth of the cave, she was aware of only deep grey light. It must be nearly dark.

The pain reasserted itself. They had not marked her body. The scrapes, bruises and sprained wrist were from her wild flight. The real ache was buried deep within, raw and torn, from the rape. She shuddered against this stranger who now held her fate in his control.

Fear had been her companion since she'd been taken. It rose and fell like swells on the ocean. Now it was ebbing, as she accepted that Camo Man was helping her hide from them. When she felt his muscles tense, hers followed in lock step. Then she heard the sounds he was hearing.

Movement in the underbrush above. More than one hunter. Footsteps overhead, coming to a halt. Shuffling feet. Men swearing.

Flashlight beams crisscrossed the grayness in front of the cavern's opening. Then she heard in a voice she knew, "It's too dark. We'll miss her again. She'll be easier to track in the morning. Killing this bitch will be more fun than most."

They left. It was still. A minute, five, maybe a year. Then the man next to her moved back just enough for her to see his face. "They call me Ghost," he said. "You knocked yourself out trying to run under a tree limb. I brought you here. But we have to move on."

She considered his ragged military jacket as well as the face paint. "Are you a soldier?" she whispered.

"Was. Can you walk?"

She nodded, although she was unsure how far she could go. Her stolen sandals were no more than shreds now, one sole flapping loose against the bottom of her foot. She'd run so far, so fast that vine maple whips and blackberry thorns had cut her feet and her legs. The cowboy shirt she'd taken was so big it had caught on snags, and now shreds flapped like home made fringe. Same with the basketball shorts. But she was a fighter, and she would not give up. Her sister's life depended on it.

Ghost turned and slid on his butt out of the cave. "Follow," he said and she did, mimicking his action. As she slid out and down, he caught her just as her feet entered the freezing water of a fast moving creek. She gasped.

"We'll walk in the creek for a while. No tracks to follow. No detectable odors unless they bring dogs tomorrow." Ghost headed upstream.

Solana looked back at the cave but could not see the mouth. It was hidden in the dusk behind the grasses on the bank. Her instinct was to go back there and hide forever. But she told herself it would not be so hard to see in the daylight. She had to swallow her exhaustion and fear.

Her baggy shorts rode so low on her hips that they dragged in the water. Holding them up with one hand, she followed Ghost. He seemed to sense where he was as the darkness became absolute, the journey only lit in patches where pale blue moonlight soaked through the forest canopy. He grabbed her uninjured wrist to lead her, and in time the freezing water dulled the pain in her feet. It seemed like a thousand miles until he stopped and pointed up the bank.

"There," he said. The massive root system of an ancient Sitka spruce looked like clutching fingers in the moonlight. The tree must have crashed to earth many decades before. Now other trees were growing from the nurse log which was at least twelve feet across near the base. The massive old roots swept out into an impenetrable arch of tendrils that intertwined with boulders rising above the muddy bank.

Ghost left the creek and pulled her up the bank to the far side of the roots where they jammed against a casket-sized chunk of volcanic rock. "Kneel here and crawl forward."

She did as she was told. On her knees she could see that there was room for her to shimmy between two tangled roots. She crawled through and found herself in a hollowed out cavern inside the fallen tree.

Ghost followed her in. He reached for a flashlight tucked inside the entrance and turned it on. "This is one of my hidey holes," he said to her. "Nobody knows it. We're safe. For now."

Solana watched him open the padlock of a battered foot locker with a key that hung on the chain with his dog tags. He lifted the lid of the locker and handed the flashlight to her. "You can leave it on for a little bit."

While he removed fur pelts from the locker and spread them over the bottom of the cavern, Solana flashed the light around her. She could see the space was a circle with maybe an eight foot diameter. "How did you do this?" She asked. "It's awesome."

"Burned it. Like some tribes hollowed out trees to make canoes." Next he rummaged out several strips of jerky. "Venison," he said, handing some of the dark, smoky slices to her. "Eat then sleep. We'll leave at daylight."

Solana took two of the pelts and crawled under them. If he meant her any harm, there was little she could do about it. She tried to chew the tough meat, but she was so tired. Too tired. The last thing she remembered was Ghost pulling out a satellite phone and calling somebody named Vinny. They made plans to meet. Solana was asleep before she heard where or when.

CHAPTER ONE

Case Notes
September 16, 2 p.m.
Society places certain expectations on Italians like Frankie Sapienza. Maybe his family puts horse heads in each others' beds. Maybe they use car trunks as portable caskets. A person can be forgiven for thoughts like these if you've seen enough movies.
The rest of us residents at Latin's Ranch Adult Family Home are fascinated with the Sicilian octogenarian. After all, gossip is our numero uno group activity. We like to speculate that he's a don of the highest order. But, alas, Frankie pretty much keeps his trap shut no matter how much the rest of us bump our gums. Oh, he's a smoothy all right, with a fine line of patter when it serves his purpose. But about his past he reveals zip, zilch, nada. And we don't push it, not as long as Frankie's goomba Vinny Tononi hangs around looking threatening as a hawk in a henhouse.
Maybe my roommate Eunice Taylor could make some inroads now that she's what Frankie calls his little dove, which is apparently somewhere between first date and betrothed. But she doesn't ask him awkward questions. She likes him and the gifts he bestows, but she isn't actually interested in sleeping with any fishes. Eunice is smart that way.
Anyhoo, imagine my surprise when Frankie up and asked Bear Jacobs to handle a private investigation. That's right. The could-be capo, who should have a lot of young hot shots on his payroll, chose a cane wielding, overweight, grouch of a has-been shamus to trust. I

take it as a show of respect for Bear's brain. Bear takes it as nothing less than his due.

Of course, when he elicited Bear's help, the secretive Sicilian didn't mention that the rest of us would soon be hiding a terrified young woman. Or that murderers might climb right over us to get to her.

- Lily Gilbert, Curious Assistant to PI Bear Jacobs

Lily Gilbert shut down her laptop, sat up and swung her leg over the side of the bed. Ever since she had become the eWatson to retired private investigator Bear Jacobs she'd kept her version of case notes. They weren't official files, of course, in the sense of admissible court documents. There were no "pursuant tos" or "time of the incidents." But they were the kind of notes that appealed to Lily, and if Bear needed something else, he could go find another assistant who worked for goose eggs. He could do that right after he pounded sand.

She fluffed up her cloud of light gray hair, pinched a little more pink into her cheeks, and hopped down from the bed on her one remaining foot. With the help of her walker she traveled out to the Latin's Ranch kitchen in search of a cup of tea. Lily actually knew that Bear was grateful for her case notes and even more so for her help. But everyone had been a little edgy since Frankie had consulted with Bear. What the hell was up?

Bear Jacobs, Lily Gilbert, Eunice Taylor and Charlie Barker had all come to the adult family home together, after departing a nursing home. Frankie Sapienza was the only resident who had arrived from points unknown. Latin's Ranch was a lot smaller, friendlier, and homier than a nursing home. And usually safer, too, from things like communicable illness.

But safer from gangland warfare? Well, that wasn't the kind of thing most care facilities worried about. It hadn't been an issue at Latin's Ranch either until Bear gathered the rest of the residents together to tell them what Frankie wanted him to do.

"He's honorable by crook standards," Bear had begun. "His family made their living in the traditional rackets of gambling, protection and prostitution."

Eunice's feathers ruffled. "A friendly card game or two, maybe helping a few storekeepers out with security, but prostitutes? Not my Frankie." Her lips compressed into a tight little pout as she crossed her arms over her kaftan-covered chest. With that orange spiky hair she looked like an irritated pin cushion.

Bear rolled his beady black eyes. "Right. Not that. What was I thinking?" He crossed his own arms over a chest covered in an ancient flannel shirt that must have been an XXL.

Lily the Peacemaker quickly intervened. "Keep going, Bear. I'm sure there's more you want to tell us."

"Okay, but only if you're interested," Bear grumped.

Lily knew the big man could pout every bit as well as Eunice. Based on his mass, Alvin Jacobs might have been a retired lumberjack instead of a sleuth. He was in his seventies with silvertip hair and beard surrounding his massive head. Size and hair together provided his nickname. But Lily knew that *Bear* described his personality, too. He could fool you into thinking he was a big ambling dope, slow and easy to underestimate. You'd be wrong. Bear was steely sharp. It was never wise to underestimate him.

"We're all interested, Bear," Charlie said, glancing up from the hand of solitaire spread on the living room game table. He was tall enough that his voice should be in the basso profundo range, but instead, it was sort of a squeak. "Really. Tell us."

"Okay. As I was saying, the Sapienza family made its nut in traditional cri- , um, pursuits. Frankie has his standards." He tipped a metaphorical hat to Eunice.

She brightened and returned the nod vigorously, moussed spikes bobbing with her. "Thank you, Bear. Of course he does."

"He says he never condoned things like street drugs or kiddie porn or the slave trade. All the seamy shit that newer gangs are into. To an old Italian like Frankie, *newer* gangs mean Latin or Asian or Russian." Bear paused, momentarily pushing out his lower lip before saying, "And, to be honest, I've never heard about anything like that in Frankie's past."

Bear should know, Lily thought. He'd had a long career as a private investigator before bad health ended it. If the cops had dirt on Frankie Sapienza, he'd have heard about it. As far as she could tell, Bear's noggin was a bulging filing cabinet of all his past adventures.

"He's heard rumors of a business one of those gangs has started. Innocent people dying in a bizarre way. In Frankie's system of ethics, it's bound to bring the wrong kind of attention to mob activity, and that's bad. He wants it stopped. He doesn't want organized crime under a spotlight. I imagine none of the families really want one going rogue."

"Why did Frankie come to you with this, Bear?" Lily asked.

"You think I'm not capable?"

"Oh, quit it." Lily took just so much guff from her old friend. "You know I mean instead of going to one of his own people."

"He wants to know exactly what's happening, and which gang is behind it. He can hardly go to the cops. And someone in his own family would be recognized by the others." Bear leaned forward in his easy chair and looked from one to the next. "I'm telling you about it because you all have a decision to make."

Our ears cocked like bird dogs sighting quail.

"A frightened girl was found out in the woods by one of Vinny's pals. She's involved in this somehow. Thugs were chasing her and are still trying to hunt her down. She needs a place to hide until I can hear her story and work this all out. A place nobody would guess."

"A place like Latin's Ranch?" Charlie piped up.

Bear nodded. "You guys willing to hide her here? Could be dangerous."

Invite murderers into our little safety zone just to help a girl we don't know?

Even as she thought it, Lily said, "Of course."

"Of course," said Charlie still slapping red cards on black.

"Of course," said Eunice, giving Bear a why-would-you-even-ask shrug.

Bear nodded at his little band of operatives. "Good thing we all see eye to eye. Because she'll be here tomorrow."

"But Bear, you need to ask Jessica about this first," Lily cautioned. Jessica Winslow was the owner and caretaker of Latin's Ranch as well as Lily's closest friend. Jessica believed the seniors in her care needed a certain amount of freedom and control over their own lives, that being old didn't make them a bunch of big babies. But would she allow them to put each other in danger?

Fat chance.

"No, Lily," Bear said. "We'll get the girl here first, then *you'll* tell Jessica."

"Me?"

"Sure. That's what BFFs are for."

CHAPTER TWO

Case Notes
September 16, 4 p.m.
The girl arrives tomorrow. Frankie told Bear she was found in the woods by a former special ops buddy of his bodyguard, Vinny Tononi. Just being that goomba's pal makes him one spooky dude in my book. It really ups the stakes when you know the guy's name. It's Ghost. Yeah, normal people walk around with a name like that. Ghost.
After a lunch of our cook's homemade enchiladas – with the best kick ass salsa in todo el mundo – Bear and I figured out what to do with the girl when she arrives. First, we considered the layout of Latin's Ranch. It's a rambling affair that was a farmhouse at the beginning of its life. After Jessica decided to take us in, the upstairs was expanded and a wing added, a porch was built across the front and a patio across the back. A lot of it was done with my daughter Sylvia's money. More about her later. She's on my list of worries, too.
Anyhoo, Jessica lives here along with the five of us residents, plus Ben Stassen's daughter, Rachael, and her baby. Ben is Jessica's hunka hunka but he's not a live-in, at least not yet. We also house a fat cat, a dog with a limp and two canaries. The staff includes three aides, Aurora the cook, and a youngster who swing-shifts as Aurora's kitchen slave and housekeeper.
It's a full house. There's certainly no room to hide another person. Outdoors, there are the sheds, riding ring, and horse barn. Fertile

pastures are surrounded by woods, a mix of deciduous trees, cedar and fir typical of the Pacific Northwest. It's all owned by Jessica who splits her time between caring for us and caring for horses. She boards them for other people, gives riding lessons, and raises a breed called Paso Finos. The Latin's Ranch name came from her stallion, Latin Lover.

"There's only one place on this property that Jessica doesn't feel free to go uninvited," I said to Bear. There was little chance Jess would agree to this plan, and until we sprang it on her, we needed a place to hide the girl even from her.

Bear was ahead of me. "Sam's trailer."

Sam Hart is Jessica's barn manager and handyman. He lives in an old Airstream between our house and the barn. "Bingo. But we can hardly put a girl in there until we get Sam out."

"I imagine he would notice a thing like that."

We sat on the patio in the sun. The days are still long enough for a breezy warm afternoon. It makes me think of my garden, the one that was sold along with my house when I went into the nursing home. I loved that garden, even the autumn chores that coaxed it into glorious bloom the following springs. But I've come to love Latin's Ranch about as much. In some ways maybe even more. Proof that there's at least some gold in the golden years.

"We could talk Sam into taking a vacation. Frankie would probably pay for one."

I was pretty sure Bear knew that was hopeless when he said it. "He wouldn't leave the horses with no notice to Jessica." Sam loves those hay burners almost as much as she does. If horses can have bodyguards, they have one in Sam.

We sat and rocked and thought and rocked. Bear hummed Come Fly with Me. *He always hums old standards while he thinks.*

"I've got it," Bear said. "The dogs."

It took me a sec before I caught on. "Yes, of course!"

Other than Folly, the cocker/dachshund mix that Jessica calls her cockadock, pooches are canis non-gratis around the ranch these days. A pack of feral dogs had attacked her colt, Latin Dancer. They had severely damaged him in the flesh and in the spirit. He would never make a show horse or command a stud fee as high as his sire. It was a heartbreaking loss to Jessica's emotions and financial plans, even though her lover, Ben Stassen, bought the colt. Jess trained Dancer for him, and Ben now uses him as a trail horse.

The night it happened, Sam shot one of the dogs, a Rottweiler. It was tearing off a piece of the colt's hide at the time. The rest of the pack took off unmolested. Nobody knows for sure if they were wild marauders or local dogs banded together for sport. Either way Animal Control hasn't been able to catch them, and that's a big worry for stock owners. Now, just lately, Sam has heard them again, howling in the night. They may be coming back around. His rifle sits next to his trailer door, loaded and ready.

"I think he'd move to the tack room in the barn to be closer to the horses," Bear said. "Leave the trailer for a few days. That's all it should take."

"He'll do it if you ask. But if Jessica probes for more of an explanation, he'll never lie to her," I said. And then I just had to add, "I won't either. I made a promise."

"Yeah, I know what you mean. After we get the girl here so Jessica can see it's really okay, we'll tell her."

"You mean the she-followed-me-home-can-I-keep-her defense?"

"Sure. Jessica would never turn down an animal in need. And old farts like you and me prove she's a marshmallow when it comes to people in need, too."

- Lily Gilbert, Needy Assistant to PI Bear Jacobs

The residents were in the living room, staring through the big front window at the long driveway. Lily figured they looked like meerkats with mobility equipment. Bear had asked Frankie to have the girl delivered in the afternoon because Jessica would be away at a Paso Fino show with her stallion, Latin Lover.

Lily agreed. "The timing is serendipitous."

"It's what?" asked Charlie. "Isn't Serendipitous that group from the sixties?"

"That was the Serendipity Singers, Charlie." Eunice focused a pair of mother-of-pearl opera glasses on the road which was barely visible at the end of the drive.

"Whatever. Nice young people. Those boys had short hair and ties. The girls wore skirts and curled their hair."

"Well, here comes Serendipitous now," Lily said, always eagle-eyed. They rushed outside as fast as a wheelchair, two walkers and a quad cane could rush. Only Eunice sailed along under her own power, even helping Frankie move forward.

It was the first time any of them had ever seen Vinny Tononi's Cadillac look anything but sleek as a black panther. Now its hood was littered with twigs stuck in every crevice. Small fir branches clung to its mirrors, wipers and grill. The polish was scratched, and when Lily touched the hood, it felt sticky with tree sap. At least the car smelled fresh as a cedar chest.

Vinny Tononi was a hulking big guy who preferred dark glasses and darker suits. Lily maintained that if you really listened, you could hear his weaponry clank as he walked. With no more than a nod at the five oldsters and a baleful glance at the front of his car, he opened the Caddy's back door.

A waif stepped out and faced them. Little, fragile, with eyes that rivaled those old Keane paintings.

Lily thought she was one of the sweetest looking girls she'd ever seen. Seventeen or eighteen, maybe. Her slight build might make her look younger than she was, but the wounded look in her eyes aged her. Her brown hair hung straight to her shoulders as though it had been washed but not styled. She wore a new pair of jeans that were rolled at the ankle, and her blouse had fold marks. Even her athletic shoes were bright with newness. A bandage around her left wrist looked clean and newly applied.

As Vinny unloaded shopping bags from Fred Meyer, Lily moved forward. "Hello, my dear. We're so glad you are here. My name is Lily."

"This is Solana," Vinny said, handing the shopping bags to the girl and going back to his stricken car. "She is for your care now."

"This is Eunice, Charlie, Frankie and Bear. Once you're settled, Bear will want to speak with you. He's a private investigator. And a good one. Whatever is going on, he will fix it." Lily gave the girl an encouraging smile but received no such gesture in reply.

Bear bowed slightly, a nod of the head but not of the body. "We'll find the bastards, miss."

The girl eyed the old PI then seemed to back away from someone his size. Lily thought a frightened child might find his gruff manner intimidating.

"Please," whispered the girl looking back at Lily. "Can I talk with you instead?"

"Well, but ..."

"That will work fine, Miss Capella. You tell Lily and Eunice your story," said Bear. "In the meantime, Vinny will take me to meet Ghost."

"Why didn't he come here?" Charlie asked.

Vinny, who'd been mourning over the hood of his car, said, "Ghost almost never talks with people. And even *more* almost never, he does not leave the woods."

✦ ✦ ✦

Solana Capella didn't know whether to be charmed or scared shitless by these geriatric weirdoes. She was sitting next to Lily in an old trailer's tiny banquette, watching Eunice search from one cabinet to the next. "Lily believes in the restorative powers of tea. I myself believe the same about whisky. Ah! Here we go. Apparently, Sam Hart believes in both." Eunice assembled the ingredients, along with the honey and lemon she'd already found.

Lily looked at Solana and smiled before she spoke. "Sam vacated the premises earlier today before you arrived. Set up a cot for himself in the barn's tack room. We're sure that will be okay with Jessica, our caregiver."

Solana noticed Eunice roll her eyes.

What's that about? Maybe I won't be staying here after all.

Lily looked calmer and smarter than the other one, maybe because she wasn't tinkling with jewelry and adrift on a sea of perfume. Too bad she only had the one leg. Solana wondered what it would be like, not being able to run.

Fucking scary, that's what.

She herself would be dead if she hadn't been able to race like a gazelle. Both old women were kind enough at least. Of course, Solana's experience with geezers was limited, but she knew they usually weren't scary. Maybe she'd be safe here until she could get to her sister. Surely the bastards wouldn't think to look for her in this place.

"You'll be snug as a bug until Bear can figure all this out," said Eunice as she fussed with the drinks. "You're just a child, but this much whiskey won't hurt you a bit. Warm you right up." She set the beverages down in front of them. One teacup had lost its handle and the others were mismatched mugs from Reggie's Tavern and the Black Sheep Diner. "The pickings are sparse in Sam's dinnerware department." Eunice seated herself on the other side of the table.

Meanwhile, Lily had booted up a laptop and looked ready to take notes, bony fingers poised above the keys. "Take your time now. And tell me what happened. But first, I guess we should call the authorities. Will you do that, Eunice?"

Eunice looked like a little kid told to go to her room. "I want to hear – "

"No," said Solana, sharply. "Nobody calls the authorities. It's too dangerous for Rosie."

It was the first thing she'd said since they came into the trailer. Lily and Eunice both stared at her. Solana looked from Lily's old face to Eunice's older one, making her decision. She needed to talk with somebody, and these two dinosaurs were all she had. Maybe it would be okay even if they were old. They didn't smell bad or anything, and a couple kids she knew actually liked their grams. She'd never met her own.

At least these two wrinklies are women. I'm sick of men. She thought about the ones she'd met outside, Frankie and Charlie and Bear. *Bear, right. How can that toothless old grizzly figure this out if I can't?*

She looked into Lily's clear eyes and saw the intelligence there. Slowly, awkwardly, she began to speak. "I don't trust the authorities for good reason. You know about homeless camps in the woods, don't you?"

"I know what I've read," Lily answered. "As the economy keeps tanking, many families reach the end of the line. They're living rough." She began to tap notes into the computer.

Solana nodded. "We lived with a family like that, my little sister Rosie and I. She's just fifteen. They were good people. Let us stay with them as long as they could pay the fee out at the county park." Solana glanced around Sam's comfortable but utilitarian mobile home. "This place is a palace compared to theirs."

"Sam's loaning it to you for as long as you need to hide."

Solana cringed with a shiver of fear. "Sam. He won't ... come for me, will he?"

"Sam?" Eunice and Lily asked looking surprised. "Sam would never hurt you," they continued in unison.

"He's a very good man," Eunice's earrings tinkled to punctuate her emphatic nod.

"I haven't met many good men," Solana said. "It's not been easy keeping Rosie away from pimps and sex slavers."

"No, I'm sure it hasn't," Lily concurred. Solana saw a warm shade of scarlet work its way up the old woman's neck and into her cheeks. "This country went to war against slavery over a hundred years ago. Now it's back, just in a different form. It's an outrage."

The old girl took a deep breath while her sidekick Eunice said, "The men you meet here have nothing but your safety in mind."

The men I've met here so far are too old to have anything else in mind.

Solana, slightly ashamed of that thought, continued. "The family we stayed with fed us and let us sleep in their pickup in return for cooking and cleaning. But the park kicked them out once they stayed the maximum amount of days. When they hit the road, they left Rosie and me behind. So we had to join eight other families living in the forest not far from the park. It's safer for us to band together. And when you stay near a park, it's not such a long walk to get to clean water."

"But ... but that's horrible for two young women," Eunice gasped.

"These camps are today's answer to the hobo jungles of the Depression," Lily said, one old hand leaving the keyboard to pat the hand of her friend. "Only instead of men on their own, these are families."

"Isn't it dangerous?" Eunice asked Solana.

"Duh," Solana said, instantly ashamed of her snotty tone. The old lady was probably just naïve, that's all. Most were. She softened her voice. "We only have tents and tarps, so we're pretty vulnerable to everything. Including each other. The camp managers, they're real careful about who they let stay."

"Can't you get help? Are you totally out of resources?" Lily asked.

"Where are your parents?" Eunice said at the same time.

Solana tightened her jaw to control her emotion. She'd learned tears rarely helped anything. But it had been such a long time since anyone had seemed to give a rat's ass about her. And now these old ladies acted really distressed. "For most people in the camp, public aid is long gone. Rosie won't go to children's services because she wants to stay with me. I'm her only family since we both had to get away from mom's boyfriend. I get some food stamps. And we go into town to look for work when we have the bus money. But that's a fuck-, um, joke. Even if we find jobs, nobody will rent to us without a deposit, and nobody at the camp has enough for that. So we're stuck."

"How long have you been there?" Eunice asked.

"Mmm. Maybe two months? The camp isn't supposed to be there, but unless someone complains, it's easier for rangers not to roust us. Or cops for that matter."

"Can you tell us about your kidnapping?" Lily asked, keyboarding away once again.

"The bastards are like invaders or something. Last time, they swept through screaming and knocking heads. This time it was a sneak attack. Either way, they take people away with them."

"You mean it's happened *before*?" Eunice took a big slug of her spiked tea.

"Twice that I know of. To an older guy and a boy about my age. But this is the first time they showed any interest in me." Solana's control abandoned her, and she began to weep. "What if they come for Rosie before I get back? And what will they do to her if I talk to the cops? I can't do that. And you can't either."

Lily leaned toward her. At first Solana stiffened, but then she allowed the old arms to close around her. They stayed that way for a long time, the girl expelling her fear and misery into the woman's circle of comfort.

Finally, Solana could continue. When she began again, the tale she told was like a horror story. Not just scary but brutal. Sick. It wasn't long before they all needed more whiskey, this time without the tea.

✦ ✦ ✦

Bear wasn't surprised when his roommate chose not to go with him to interview Ghost. Charlie had perpetual sores on his nuts from sitting in a wheelchair all day. The home care nurse who paid particular attention to that delicate situation was scheduled to visit Latin's Ranch late that afternoon. Charlie wouldn't miss the appointment for any amount of wealth or wishes.

Vinny drove the Caddy away from town and east toward Washington's Cascade Mountains. He left the highway on a two lane paved road that plunged into national forest land. It narrowed even more when Vinny maneuvered the huge vehicle onto a dirt track, punching a tunnel through cedar and fir. Bear presumed this had been a logging road many years ago. As branches slapped against the car, he understood why Vinny's prized possession was covered with twigs and pitch. He must have driven this way before when he picked up the girl, Solana.

Bear, in the backseat, listened when Vinny placed a call. "We are near," Bear heard him say. The dirt track petered out on the edge of a small meadow where there was just enough room for Vinny to turn the hulk around between volcanic boulders and enormous stumps from fallen giants.

"You okay, Mr. Bear? We wait here."

Bear rolled down his window after Vinny shut off the Cadillac's powerful engine. It was impossibly quiet, as though every living forest thing knew humans as threatening interlopers. A breeze produced the only rustle through the leaves. Then, one brave bird began to sing again. Others joined until they crescendoed in a merry racket. Bear never paid much attention to such things himself, but he knew Lily could have identified each singer, along with the wildflower remains that dotted the meadow. Now in September, the Indian paint brush, lupine and glacier lilies were brown or gone altogether, replaced by wild daisies. The breeze blew a chill through Bear's window. For a while he hummed *Autumn Leaves.*

Minutes passed without a word from Vinny. Finally, Bear said, "Time for you to tell me just who this Ghost is, don't you think? Now that I've joined the Sapienza family as Frankie's personal PI?"

Vinny turned sideways in the driver's seat and glanced back at his passenger. Bear could see the sharp planes of his chiseled face and the hawk nose. "You are not a member of the *famiglia, Signore* Bear. A friend, yes. Like Ghost. He es specialist, resource we trust. Same with you. But *famiglia*? No."

Well, that settles that. Always the bridesmaid, never the bride.

Bear snorted to himself, glad not to be part of this tight knit mob. Fine by him. He still valued his rickety old carcass, and it would stay a damn sight safer out of the direct line of fire.

Vinny glanced at Bear again with eyes cold and grey as stone. Then he stared off into the woods. "Was year 1991. Ghost and me, we do, ah, special ops in Iraq. What they call counter-terrorism. *Capiche*? He move with such stealth, unseen as a ghost. Got his name that way."

"Good name. Ghost," Bear said. He'd been rather fond of his own nickname ever since a crazy old crock at the nursing home had thought he *was* one. He was a lot fatter and meaner back then. Now he liked to think of himself as merely big, as well as pleasant.

Vinny squared his jaw and continued to face down the past. "We placed an explosive in enemy camp late one night. We could not know they had prisoners. Families. Families we were there to save. That night, they died by our hand.

"We left, silent as we came. But not Ghost. He stay behind. Frozen, you see, numb with guilt. The terrorists, they caught him. It went bad for him until our team got him back. Very bad. They ship him home and patch him together. But he still sees bodies of children who died that night. He keeps to himself now, wild in these woods for ten years. More. I bring him supplies time to time. We each have satellite phone. He has solar battery packs."

Bear rumbled a disgusted sigh deep in his throat. So many war stories with damaged veterans who do what their country asks. He shook his head and looked back out his window.

A wild man, in the green and brown of a woodland camo jacket, was staring in.

END OF EXCERPT

Hard to Bear, the second book in the Bear Jacobs series, is available at amazon.com

Visit with Linda B. Myers at

www.lindabmyers.com
www.facebook.com/lindabmyers.author
myerslindab@gmail.com
www.amazon.com/author/lindabmyers